I0824626

Rabbit,
Fox,
Tar

Catapult New York

Rabbit, Fox, Tar

A Novel

P.C. Verrone

RABBIT, FOX, TAR

This is a work of fiction. All the characters, organizations, and events portrayed in this novel are either products of the author's imagination or used fictitiously.

Grateful acknowledgment for reprinting materials is made to the following: Spillers, Hortense J. "Mama's Baby, Papa's Maybe: An American Grammar Book." *diacritics* 17:2 (1987), 64. © 1987 Cornell University. Reprinted with permission of Johns Hopkins University Press.

ISBN: 978-1-64622-317-6

Library of Congress Control Number: 2026930052

Jacket design by Emily Mahon
Jacket linocut © Osborne Samuel Ltd, London / Bridgeman Images, birch bark © Zoonar GmbH / Alamy
Book design by Laura Berry

Catapult
New York, NY
books.catapult.co

Printed in the United States of America

10 9 8 7 6 5 4 3 2 1

For the two who made me out of love

I am a marked woman, but not everybody knows my name. [. . .] My country needs me, and if I were not here, I would have to be invented.

—Hortense Spillers, "Mama's Baby, Papa's Maybe: An American Grammar Book"

"Did the fox eat the rabbit?" asked the little boy to whom the story had been told.

"Dat's all de fur de tale goes," replied the old man. "He mout, an den agin he moutent."

—Joel Chandler Harris, "The Wonderful Tar-Baby"

Rabbit,
Fox,
Tar

Original Hill

•

The streets of Original Hill were alive with talk of the old man's niece. The Bushes, the Reeds, the Woods, the Iveses, the Burdocks, the Thornes, and the Branches each had their own theories. These conjectures were batted around over girls' night margaritas, during game night commercial breaks, and between over-the-shoulder glances at the grocery store.

It was Mrs. Bush that first spotted the niece in the second-story window of the house at 1 Orchard Street, though she had assumed the girl was a new maid or maybe a nurse. Strange, as the old man had seemed healthy enough the last time that she'd seen him. Then, the Reeds' little boy spied her picking flowers in the Foxes' yard and tossing them into a small wicker basket, a large yellow hat on her head. Mrs. Reed was sure that her son was mistaken, as it was unheard of for any hands other than Mrs. Fox's own to touch her garden. Days later, Mr. Burdock noticed Mrs. Fox shouldering an extra bag of groceries from her car and offered to help her carry them. She told him that she could manage as she propped her front door open, and Mr. Burdock caught a glimpse of the girl within, wearing what looked to him like a billowing nightgown buttoned up to her neck. Mrs. Fox shut the door before he could say anything more. Despite these brief sightings, serious speculation only really started once the niece began to sit on the Foxes' garden wall.

The house on Orchard Street stood at the peak of Original Hill, overlooking the sprawl of the city and its other suburbs from a respectable distance. On clear days, the neighborhood's residents could see the Mississippi winding its way along the edge of downtown and the fields of wheat and sugar beets beyond the city's edge. Orchard Street was the aorta of the neighborhood, traveling down from the Fox residence past smaller but still splendid homes and through a quaint commercial square that they called "the Village," which included a bank, a supermarket, a salon, a French café, a pricey Italian restaurant, a seasonal ice cream parlor, Burdock's hardware store, and Bush's convenience store. While the residents would have been happy for Orchard Street to stop there, it continued on, transforming into the Orchard Street Bridge and sailing across the I-94 highway. Municipal maps incorporated a few blocks past the I-94 into Original Hill, but the neighborhood itself drew its line at the bridge.

To call Original Hill a place alone would have done it a disservice, for Original Hill was a dream. It was—its residents assumed—the only dream. This assumption was corroborated by occasional features in lifestyle magazines and real estate websites, boasting that Original's quality of life was as high as its average income. Perhaps its only demerit was its lack of diversity, though residents attested that it was easy enough to drive downtown and enjoy the city's variety of ethnic foods and cultural arts.

The neighborhood's name alone was like a conjuring. To say you were from Original Hill, or were looking for some place *like* that, would instantly conjure the image of spacious porches, pristine lawns, and quiet, well-paved roads. It was modern comfort without the over-digitization or trend chasing that soured modern living, the last holdout of a kind of life that every sensible person hoped would return sooner than later. It existed almost as much as a dream in the minds of its people as it did in concrete and wood and grass and tar north of the I-94.

It is possible that this is what allowed the old man's niece to step into Original Hill from some equally phantasmic place. She took some time to fully solidify in the neighborhood, appearing only as a flicker in windows and doorways, which the residents may have been able to ignore had the girl not insisted on being seen.

On their usual evening walk down Orchard Street, Mr. and Mrs. Ives were confronted by a figure perched on the Foxes' brick garden wall. She wore an enormous pale yellow sun hat, from which two thick braids descended just past her shoulders, and a blush-and-canary sundress that billowed past her knees, stopping just short of two bare feet. Mrs. Ives thought the dress looked almost obscene the way it hung off her skinny figure. Its sleeves sagged around the girl's elbows, and two bright white gloves met them at the edge of her forearms. Her wide eyes, full lips, and faultless skin reminded Mrs. Ives of a model she had seen on a magazine cover.

The girl had been staring into the nothingness of the road ahead of her before shifting her attention to the Iveses. She offered neither a wave nor a nod, just the intensity of those moony eyes. Mr. Ives offered a "Good evening," to which the girl only smiled. Brilliantly white teeth, Mr. Ives would later recall. Like milk teeth, Mrs. Ives would agree. Then, the girl extended her bare foot out to them and wiggled her toes. The couple hurried past, trying not to stare.

The neighborhood spent the better part of a week speculating why she was there. Some wondered if her appearance might be related to those protests—some kind of occupation or demonstration. But after numerous afternoons observing the figure swinging her bare feet from atop the brick wall, it became clear that she was just . . . sitting. This display of leisure convinced everyone that she couldn't possibly be in the Foxes' employ. But what was she looking at? Or waiting for? Why was she wearing such an old-fashioned sundress, and white elbow-length opera gloves, and no shoes? The Foxes themselves did not weigh in until a week later, when Mrs. Fox entered Bush's convenience store asking for strawberry candies.

In all the decades that Mr. Bush had catered to Mrs. Fox, he had never known her to have the taste for strawberry candies. He told her as much as he rang her up. Mrs. Fox replied, "They're for my niece. She's visiting."

"She a brother's or a sister's girl?"

"Eugene's brother's," she said, before thanking Mr. Bush and departing.

A new round of rumors erupted. Those who wanted to believe Mrs. Fox insisted that it was possible the girl could be related through adoption. Or perhaps it was the brother who was adopted, as no one could recall having ever met a sibling of Fox's in all the years that they'd lived there. Dr. Wood pointed out that despite the girl's incredibly dark complexion, it was still possible for her to be a blood relative, depending on her mother. But very few neighbors entertained this.

Those who chose to be incredulous harped on the fact that Mrs. Fox had clarified it was her *husband* who had brought the young, undeniably beautiful "niece" into the house. These parties would be swiftly reminded that this was Eugene Fox they were talking about, not some gossip-mill lecher.

Regardless of their bias for or against Mrs. Fox, they all continued to watch the house on Orchard. Behind window shades and between fence posts, they kept their eyes on the young woman, who continued to sit on the garden wall wearing her enormous sun hat and opera gloves. She never wore any shoes, never said a word, and rarely smiled. She simply gazed out into the world. They began to suspect that maybe she really was waiting for something or someone to come along after all. How curious it is that, when that somebody did come, no one person saw it all at once.

It was Ms. Branch who noticed Lucius Foote walking toward Orchard on that temperate June afternoon. Unlike most, Lucius Foote was a walker. You never caught him shuffling into a car or engrossed in his phone. During the warmer months, he would often drop by a group brunching outside the café and fold himself into their conversation with ease. The Iveses regularly bumped into him on their evening strolls and insisted the jovial bachelor join them for a few blocks. The Bushes were delighted whenever he visited their store and chatted for the better part of an hour while helping Mr. Bush restock the shelves. Even when the temperature dropped, Mrs. Thorne might catch him in his coat and scarf admiring a window display with that genuine smile. Busy as he was as their city councilman, he always made time to be their neighbor.

Had it not been for how quickly Lucius passed by, Ms. Branch might have flagged him down, pulled him into a conversation, even offered to drive him so that he would not have to pass by 1 Orchard Street. But by the time she realized who it was in that gray blazer, he had already rounded the corner.

When Mrs. Thorne looked up from the carrots she had been peeling in the sink, Lucius was approaching the girl on the wall. Through her kitchen window, she watched Lucius nod to the girl and move his lips—"Good evening" or maybe "How's it going." The girl, as usual, did nothing, did not even slow the momentum of her ticktocking leg.

Dr. Wood, stepping outside to collect a package, had not seen Lucius greet the girl but did see him stop just a few feet past her. She caught the queer expression on the young man's face. Both Dr. Wood and Mrs. Thorne later commiserated over sharing the strong urge to avert their eyes as Lucius turned back around to the girl.

So it was Mr. Reed, clearing leaves out of his gutter, who saw Lucius lean against the wall, right beside the girl, who kept her face forward, never acknowledging his presence.

When Mrs. Thorne glanced back at the scene, the man's closeness to the young woman made her drop a carrot. As she gathered herself, she noticed the irritation in Lucius's face.

No, not irritation, Dr. Wood would later insist. More like curiosity. Intrigue, maybe.

Everyone agreed that the girl treated the man as if he were not right there beside her. But as Ms. Branch drove down Orchard on her way home from Bush's store, she noticed that Lucius's lips were moving. In the flash that she saw of him before speeding past, she corroborated Lucius's physical stance as being casual, familiar. That was always how he was, though. Easy, relaxed, with everyone.

Yes, *but*, Dr. Wood would go on to say, there was excitement behind his eyes.

Lucius spoke for some time, every now and then pausing and waiting for the girl to respond. And what did she do? Nothing, Mr. Reed would say. Didn't even look at him.

Until she did, Dr. Wood would remind Mr. Reed.

Yes, and when she did, when the girl finally turned her head toward Lucius Foote, it looked like he was nearly knocked back onto the sidewalk.

And so, then did they strike up a conversation? Not at all. Her large hat obscured her face from Mrs. Thorne and Mr. Reed, but Dr. Wood could confirm that the girl's lips remained shut tight.

Lucius, on the other hand, kept talking.

Sounds like Lucius, alright.

Could talk to anyone.

You remember when he talked down those protesters that set up in the Village?

A great guy.

A nice boy.

One of the good ones.

And then the girl kicked him.

Well, perhaps *kicked* is too strong, Mrs. Thorne would admit after hearing other accounts of the interaction. Mr. Reed believed that he saw the girl tap him with her toe, and Dr. Wood insisted that her riotous leg had merely grazed him. But they all agreed that they saw Lucius Foote holding the girl's naked heel in his hand. This display was so suddenly intimate that all three neighbors blinked at the same time. During that blink, Lucius Foote vanished.

Mr. Reed grabbed his ladder to keep from losing balance and Mrs. Thorne nicked herself with the peeler. Not even Dr. Wood, with her largely unobstructed view, could tell where he had gone. All that was left was the girl on the wall, once again swinging her leg and staring at nothing. After a moment, all the observers returned to their activities, though each felt a new chill, as if someone had cracked a window.

Birch & Oak

I am listening to the world's palaver when he touches me. The sun warms my bare legs, and a breeze tickles the hairs on the back of my neck. I dig my fingernails into the garrulous grit of the wall, pressing as hard I can. I make a wish to be more in the world, and then he is there beside me. My One and Only. His skin meets my skin, but then it is as if the world resets its pieces, and I cannot sit on the garden wall any longer.

Lucky

•

For days now, Lucky Foote had not been able to think of anyone but that girl on the wall. He had crossed her path a week ago, and yet he could recall her face vividly as if it had only been an hour.

At the time, he'd had the birchbark on his mind. For years he'd tried to chase away the memory of the birchbark, but those black and white slashes were imprinted behind his eyelids. He could still smell the mulching leaves and hear his heartbeat thudding against his eardrums as those hands gripped his body. Even now, Lucky's mind threatened to return there, but he redirected his thoughts to the image of that girl as he stepped off the city bus.

He checked the time on his phone. Auntie Riri was expecting him at six thirty, and he would only just make it if he headed that way now. Even so, he walked in the opposite direction, up Orchard Street.

It wasn't every day you saw a sister chilling on the streets of lily-white Original Hill, especially not in that getup. With the hat blocking her face and the old-timey dress covering up everything above her knees, Lucky might not have realized she was also Black were it not for her bare leg swinging to and fro. She hadn't said much—really anything—to his attempts at initiating conversation. He was just about to get on with his walk and leave the girl be when she turned and looked at him with those mother-of-pearl-button eyes. Then she had let him catch her naked foot in his hand.

Since then, whenever his mind wandered, he kept reaching for that foot—its slender arch and impossible softness. Every morning, he awoke with a fading vision of those nacreous eyes, and each night he dozed off picturing that light-yellow fabric against her ebony skin. Strange that in his dreams, she never undressed, never contorted herself into ecstatic poses beneath his body. She only ever sat on that wall, hard and real, looking at him or not, as if daring him to come closer. When he dared, the moment his skin made contact with her thigh or shoulder, he would wake in his bed, beads of sweat blooming on his chest. In dreams, he could not even touch that perfect foot.

So he had returned to Old Man Fox's house again and again. Each time, he had found the garden wall empty, and there was no promise that she would be there this evening. Still, he couldn't help himself from taking the gamble.

Lucky slapped on his red-carpet smile and waved or winked or howdied as he passed his neighbors. His voters, his base, and at times, his eyes and ears on the ground. They would be the ones to decide if he was reelected to city council, and ultimately, they would catapult him to loftier seats.

Not that he had any gnawing political ambitions. He wanted Original Hill, the dream of it, and he was just about there. Politics was just a way to fluff his pillow and stay comfortable for a good, long time. He spent his days sewing himself so tightly into the fabric of this community that when he finally stopped renting Stu Hoffman's townhouse and purchased his own home in Original, it would be merely a formality.

Had he not been Lucky Foote, he likely wouldn't have been able to pull it off. A Black bachelor not quite thirty-three from a place like Briar Heights? Please. But then, he *was* Lucky Foote, so despite his Blackness, he walked freely among these white PTA moms and their Pillsbury Doughboy husbands. He could loiter by their houses, wave to their neighborhood watch, and chat with their wives at their picket fences without the slightest reservation. This was his gift—a kind of trickster charm that allowed him to convince his neighbors that *they* had allowed *him* to lay his bindle down here.

Maybe that was why he was so fixated on this girl. No smile, no nod, no recognition of any kind. He'd stumbled into some game, but she seemed to hold all the cards. He was burning for a chance to play again.

But arriving at the wall, he found it empty once more. He froze on the sidewalk, glaring at the bricks, willing her to reappear. In his peripheral vision, he saw movement in one of the windows. A hopeful flutter in his chest sank like a cannonball when he realized it was likely the house's owner. Not wanting to draw Old Man Fox out,

Lucky turned and made his way back down Orchard Street. As he left the empty wall behind, he felt a gnawing sensation in his stomach. He chalked it up to hunger, now that he would be at least twenty minutes late for dinner.

Really, Lucky knew it was something else. He wasn't used to being denied.

Lucky because he was, in most ways that mattered. Bernie Orson had given him the name when they were boys in Briar Heights, after they jumped the fence to clip roses off of Old Man Farmer's rosebush. Back then, he had been known as Junior. Junior to whom? A man that he hardly knew, who had left him nothing but his own name and an old vest with mother-of-pearl buttons. It was a name that fit him like a sandpaper suit.

Wanting to impress some of the girls in their homeroom, he and Bernie knew better than to settle for the puny rosebuds that poked through the fence, routinely snapped off by passersby. The real boon lay just over Farmer's six-foot-high fence. As their lithe brown bodies tumbled into the yellowed grass along the side of Farmer's house, they saw the bush's splendorous bounty. Assured of their safety, these roses had minimized their thorns and yawned their petals out wide.

Trouble was, Old Man Farmer had seen them jump his fence. As soon as Junior plucked the first bloom, the old codger appeared like a burst of fire and brimstone. Bernie, who was still by the fence, easily scrambled back up and over. But Farmer wrapped his wrinkled hand around Junior's arm before the boy could make a break for it. Despite his age, Farmer's grip was strong, and his hooded yellow eyes bore down onto Junior. "Boy," Farmer spat, "what the hell are you doing on my property?"

But rather than whimper or grovel, the boy smiled. This was enough to disarm the old man, giving Junior time to think up a bullshit excuse. "But, sir, don't you remember? You asked me to come by and prune these larger roses, to keep them from crowding one another. Otherwise, these little buds won't be able to bloom."

Farmer was no fool, but his memory was not what it used to be. Whether or not Farmer truly believed the young man, something in Junior's puckish smile and earnestness struck a chord in him. He felt it was best to embolden this young man to do some honest work and keep him from sitting at home watching the boob tube or playing shooting games. When Junior met back up with Bernie, he had not only a fistful of blooming roses but also a dollar for the pruning he'd done. Bernie just stared at him, mouth agape. Finally, he said, "You must be the luckiest bastard in the world. Lucky Foote."

When Bernie rechristened him as Lucky Foote, he flung himself into the name, becoming it absolutely. By the time he arrived in Original Hill, he'd been Lucky for nearly two decades. He had escaped from Briar Heights long ago, using his gift to keep himself cozy as he bounced from one city to the next. He knew Original Hill would be a challenge, but if he could get in here, he would be set for life. He found his way to Stu Hoffman, who hired him as a trainee on his community development campaign within minutes of their first meeting. "You've got that spark," Hoffman told him. It also so happened that the tenant who rented Hoffman's townhouse had suffered a nervous breakdown, so he offered the recently vacated place to Lucky. Within an hour of his arrival, Lucky was employed and housed in the most affluent neighborhood in the city.

When Lucky received a name tag on his first day on the job, he was surprised to see the name Lucius Foote. "Lucky's a little informal, I think," Stu told him. Rather than correcting the man's misunderstanding, Lucky tried the new name on for size and found he didn't mind it. It sounded silver and powerful in his mouth and, though he preferred Lucky, it was suited to his new environment.

This third christening became necessary in his campaign for city councilmember. Stu Hoffman would often remind him that folks don't want their politicians to be lucky; they want them to earn their accolades. What his campaign manager didn't understand was that luck *was* earned, or at least practiced.

The trick was to convince the mark that they wanted exactly what would make Lucky most comfortable. Didn't they want their children to grow up in a neighborhood that supported diversity? Didn't they want the neighborhood to feel youthful—hip, even? Didn't they want to seem like forward-thinking people? Well, a young Black representative would certainly project that. Lucky's gift shaved off all the negative connotations associated with these labels and allowed Original Hill to embrace him. Sure, he could depend on serendipity for some part of his success—Hoffman's townhouse being available, Old Man Fox retiring from city council at the right time, even these recent protests adding extra pressure on the neighborhood to project an image of racial acceptance. But the rest of his "luck" was his own meticulous design.

Which wasn't to say that Lucky's position wasn't precarious. If he didn't behave just so, then the veils he had placed over his neighbors' eyes might slip. If he ever lost the gift, if for a moment he neglected its maintenance, then he was sure he would find himself run out of town or at the wrong end of a shotgun. He might even find himself back in Briar Heights, though Lucky would prefer death to that.

As Lucky approached the Orchard Street Bridge, his muscles tensed. He took out his lighter and lit a cigarette. No matter how many times he crossed it, he couldn't help but feel anxious. It wasn't that this particular road was dangerous, though it was in a near constant state of disrepair. Maintaining the bridge had been a recurring nuisance since he was elected, requiring continual construction to fill in never-ending potholes, cracked asphalt, and fractured concrete. But there was something else, something that made his breath hitch whenever he walked along the bridge. He couldn't shake the feeling that some bogeyman might reach out of one of those cracks and grab him.

This time, however, his memory of the girl proved to be an engrossing distraction. He thought of her blacker-the-berry complexion, her luminous eyes, and her foot, soft and uncalloused, suspended in his palm like a peach. He gently pressed his thumb into the meat of her heel and worried that some sticky-sweet juice might flow if he pushed too hard.

Perhaps she had only been a visitor and had since

returned from wherever she'd come from, he reasoned. But that thought alone sent a pang through his chest so severe, he dared not dwell on it.

Breaking out of his reverie, he realized that he had already made it across the bridge. He stamped out the cigarette and hurried on to Auntie Riri's.

Auntie Riri's home was cloistered in a cul-de-sac that Original Hill had overlooked. Pocketed along the edge of the highway in the shadow of the Orchard Street Bridge, the shotgun house was surrounded by a handful of others like it. The noise and ugliness of the highway had protected these properties from developers, a blind spot further cemented by years of neglect. Each house sat crumbling away bit by bit, taking its own sweet time. Auntie Riri's was the only one still occupied. It was as if the rest of the neighborhood were waiting for the weeds to grow tall enough to swallow up these few remaining houses, and her stubborn presence was preventing the block from succumbing to its final ruin.

Auntie Riri was rubbing her wrists when she answered the door. She offered an "It's about time you showed up" before turning on her heel and marching back into the kitchen. Lucky followed her, grunting as the stench of stale cigarettes assaulted his senses. Auntie Riri swore she steered clear of those "sin sticks," but the house's smell and her chronic cough spoke for themselves. Lucky entered the cramped kitchen, where the smoky odor mingled with the scents of chicken, citrus, garlic, celery, paprika, and coriander. Auntie Riri returned to the immense bubbling pot on the stove and resumed scooping dumplings from a ceramic bowl into the broth.

"Food'll be ready in fifteen minutes," she said.

"And I thought you'd said I was running late," Lucky hummed, fingering the floral drapes that bordered the small kitchen window.

"You are," she shot back. "Just because food isn't on the table doesn't mean that six o'clock isn't six o'clock. What kept you?"

That dark leg swinging below the summery hem flashed across Lucky's mind.

He looked back at the woman bent over the stove, tucking some silver hairs beneath her headwrap. A caramel-colored shawl was draped around her diminutive frame, hanging all the way down to her bare feet and swaying as her whole body participated in the exacting motion of scraping spoonfuls of dough along the side of the bowl and laying them on top of the chicken soup.

"Got any new jobs for me?" Lucky asked.

"The sink's making noises again. And I think there might be a leak in the bathroom."

"I'll take a look," Lucky said, kneeling to open the cupboards beneath the kitchen sink before Auntie Riri waved him away.

"After dinner. You sit," she insisted.

Lucky took a seat at the kitchen table and kicked his feet up onto another chair just to give Auntie Riri the opportunity to tell him to get his shoes the hell off her furniture. Sitting in Auntie Riri's kitchen brought back all the best memories of aunties—blood or otherwise—who had doted on and needled him, bickering and gossiping and laughing until tears wet the collars of their housedresses. Auntie Riri would have fit right in at Briar Heights. She possessed that same deep-down knowing thing that the women of Lucky's childhood had, which in Original Hill was as rare as the melanin in this kitchen.

This house was the only place in Original where he didn't have to shield himself with his gift. Since he had first met Auntie Riri through Hoffman's community development campaign, he'd made a point of visiting her whenever he could. He would like to see her in a nicer place, but she refused to leave the house that she had been born in, despite it falling apart around her. So he let her cook for him and fret about him, and he fixed up things around the house and kept her company, even if for just an hour every week.

Auntie Riri suddenly cried out. The metal spoon clattered on the linoleum floor. Lucky went to her as the woman cradled her wrist in her arm. "Damn arthritis," she hissed.

"Let me finish," Lucky offered.

Auntie huffed, massaging her wrist. "There's only really two more scoops." Lucky laid them among the other dumplings, the first of which were already puffing up and crowding the head of the broth.

"Put a lid on that pot." Auntie Riri's chair groaned and tipped onto its half-inch-shorter leg as she settled into it. "And fetch my Vicks, would you, baby?"

He sat in the chair by her side, unscrewing the lid to the tub. The minty smell sliced up his nostrils.

"You working overtime, now?" Auntie asked.

"Sure, Auntie."

"*Sure, Auntie.* Well, something kept you."

"I was just checking in on somebody on the way."

As the VapoRub hit the heat of her skin, Auntie Riri started to cough, which devolved into a fit of chest-rattling heaves. Lucky tensed, ready to jump up for some water or to smack the eighty-something-year-old on the back, if necessary, but the fit ran itself through, as it usually did.

"When's the last time you visited the doctor, Auntie?"

"Honey, my lung's been like this since they built the I-94."

"I know, but it sounds like it's getting worse—"

"Nothing worse about it," she snapped. Her eyes narrowed at Lucky. "Back in the Sankofa days, there used to be a whole two blocks of houses where that highway is. Nice, too. Pretty, I mean."

"You've told me, Auntie—"

"And a commercial street that we called Main Street. Had a market, a butcher, a tailor, salon, pool house. A toy store my uncle used to work at. Used to be colored folks in Cadillacs who'd drive down Main Street, and sometimes they'd hand us kids candies from the windows. There was a church, too. Not on Main, but a block down, on . . . Was it Iglehart?"

"Yeah, I know, Auntie—" Lucky sighed. Once she was on Sankofa, there was little he could do to stop her.

"Highway pushed everybody out. City offered to buy folks' houses a week—*a week*—before the wrecking balls arrived, and for next to nothing. These were respectable people too, and nice houses. Didn't mean a thing to white folks. This was just land they needed for their cars."

Auntie Riri shook her head. "They split Sankofa in two like Solomon's baby. Most folks just up and left. Those who wouldn't go got torn out of their houses when the wrecking balls showed up on their doorstep. Women, children. Thrown out onto the street. And they knocked those houses down *first*."

This story was nothing new to Lucky. He'd had mere minutes to enjoy his election to city council before the "Justice for Sankofa" protesters reached out to him. Every way they told it was biblical—the elysian splendor of Sankofa, a settlement that grew from a few families of free Black folks into a thriving Black town; the I-94 coming down on Sankofa like a hammer on an anvil; the exodus of the displaced to other corners of the city or farther afield, neighbor torn from neighbor by the highway, which cut itself down the community's flesh from neck to navel. The city offered little aid and no remorse to these residents, and so Sankofa disintegrated.

Lucky couldn't help but laugh at the suggestion that help from the city would have been better than these folks finding their own way. He'd grown up in another city's rotted promise of a progressive housing project. All that creating Briar Heights had really done was pin its people down, cut their sightlines, and made them so prideful that anyone who even considered leaving was denounced as a traitor. The idea that Sankofa's residents would have gotten a better deal in 1956 showed Lucky how little these protesters knew.

Of course, Justice for Sankofa wasn't asking for housing seventy years later. They demanded reparations. Though as far as Lucky knew, none of the dozen or so organizers that established the fledgling group were even descendants of Sankofa's displaced residents. Most came from other pockets of the city's Black community with all manner of inquiries that they really should have been asking their own representatives.

But Lucky understood why they came to him. They wanted a slice of the pie from the city's wealthiest sector, and they thought a Black man would give it to them. After all, he had used the threat of the protesters' presence to sweeten his appeal as a candidate. The people of Original were happy to hide behind a Black man if he could make these protesters disappear. He was able to appease Justice for Sankofa without promising much of anything, persuading them to continue working with city council. Although these protesters reminded him of everything he had run from in Briar Heights, he would need these folks' support as much as Original Hill's if he ever ran for a citywide office.

Auntie Riri was the only person left in the city who had lived in Sankofa, so these protesters paraded the poor woman out at every opportunity. Lucky was forced to sit through multiple hearings in which they pushed her to recount the decades-old injustice against her neighborhood. It was a complete waste of time, but at least it kept them off the streets of Original. Now, Lucky found himself listening to the same script yet again.

"Only a handful of us were still here to see them pour the tar," Auntie Riri said. "Middle of July, they laid down the stuff. On top of the wood and glass, pieces of old houses and shops and whatever else was there. The noise kept us up, day and night. And that *smell*."

Auntie Riri pressed her eyes shut. "Worse than the noise was that smell. They mixed the tar not two feet from my backyard there. It filled up the air, and you couldn't escape it. It was worse than Hell. So bad, one girl's baby died."

Lucky perked up. "Somebody died?" It was rare that any new information was added to this rehashing.

"That was the story," she said slowly, squeezing her eyes tighter as if searching her memory. "Air was too polluted, and the poor thing wasn't two weeks old when the tar came. When the neighbors learned about the baby, it'd been dead days. And that foolish girl . . ."

"You never told me somebody died."

Auntie Riri's eyes flew open. "Tar got in my lungs, too, and God is my witness, it never left."

"And that's how you lost of your sense of smell, too?"

Auntie Riri capped the VapoRub. "No, baby. That came later." She wobbled as she stood and went to put the Vicks back in its cabinet. Lucky hummed, leaning back in his chair. A searing pain gripped his left hand, and he shot up out of his seat. He turned toward the rusting gray coils of the offender. "Jesus! That radiator's hot!"

The ache in his knuckles was joined by a sharp pain on the side of his head, compliments of Auntie Riri's spoon. "Do *not* misuse the Lord's name in this house."

"This thing's still overheated? I thought I fixed it—"

"Leave it," the woman demanded, pouring cold water onto a dish towel. "Sit." He did, scooting his chair away from the hissing radiator and pressing the towel onto the back of his hand.

"Auntie, are you sure you're alright here? I mean, we might be able to find you a better place—"

"My granddaddy built this house," she said simply. "Everybody else might've left Sankofa, but not me. Besides, now that young people are starting to pay attention, I've got to stay to tell the story. This is a new day for Sankofa."

Lucky winced. This was how badly those protesters had poisoned her mind. They'd given her a sense of righteousness to stay in this long-dead place. It was the same stupid pride that he knew kept his own people trapped in Briar Heights. They had synthesized a damning distrust for the rest of the world. Lucky alone seemed to balk at Briar Heights' rejection of any other way of living, and he was the only person he knew who had ever escaped his old neighborhood.

He would never forgive those Sankofa protesters for forcing Auntie Riri into the past again and again. And for what? Some handouts that Lucky had managed to earn for himself? But they had been working Auntie Riri much longer than Lucky had known her, so there was no convincing her that exhuming Sankofa was a lost cause.

Auntie Riri shuffled over to the stove, tasted some broth out of the pot, nodded, and began to ladle the soup into two bowls. "Who were you checking up on?"

"What?" Lucky asked.

"You said you were checking up on somebody before you got here."

"It's nobody," Lucky said.

Without missing a beat, she said, "You've got to stop running around with these silly little girls."

"Sure, Auntie."

"You're too old to be fooling around. Get yourself a real woman."

"Yes, ma'am," Lucky hummed. There it was. That deep-down knowing.

But Lucky liked that his women weren't serious. What was the point of chasing something he already knew he could catch? Of course, as a public figure, he had to at least feign a desire for that All-American wife-and-kids schtick. He had been able to avoid questions of his romantic relationships during his first run for office, but the upcoming election had brought a spotlight to his personal life.

What had Mr. Thorne told him the night of his election, a few beers too far with his pasty fingers gripping Lucky's shoulder? "You want to stay in politics? Get yourself a good woman. Soon. Young buck like you, running around freewheeling? Makes the women nervous, you know? If not them, then their husbands."

He'd been right, of course—right in the way that drunk men tell truths to other men that they believe are equally as drunk. In the past year, Lucky had already begun to sense his gift starting to falter. He'd had numerous conversations with country club ladies who alluded to their nephews and brothers who had just married their dream girls. Worse, some of these white women had offered to make him a cup of coffee if he ever wanted to drop by while their husbands were away. Nothing would have strangled his gift faster.

And then, there was always the birchbark.

For many reasons, he needed a woman to keep his gift intact, and not like the ones he usually went with. Auntie Riri placed the bowl of soup before him, and Lucky stared down through the steam at the broth, pale and summery. As his spoon cut through the soup, that dark leg swung across his mind once more.

Gina

•

The girl arrived a few days after the disappearance of that terrible odor. Gina Fox had first detected it on her husband Eugene's clothing. She surmised that the smell must have come from the tar he used to redo the roof but could find no remnants of the dark, sticky substance on the old button-up, overalls, undershirt, or underwear left for her in the laundry room. She didn't understand how the fumes could cling so strongly without any residue. No matter how many cycles she put his clothes through, no matter what concoction of detergents and pantry items she poured onto them, no matter that she scrubbed her knuckles pink, she could not rid them of the stench.

It clung to Eugene as well. His attempts to shower it away were futile. Gina implored him to sleep on the couch so that the smell would not be transferred to their mattress, but then it began to seep into the rest of the house.

It smelled like char. It smelled like a coal mine and a forest fire and something else, something that Gina imagined the bowels of the earth might belch up. It was so rank she lost much of her appetite. Even her dreams seemed perfumed by the stench. She suggested that Eugene stop the roof work, but he insisted he had everything under control.

The odor forced Gina to regularly flee the house, seeking refuge in the most trivial errands. She attended the neighborhood book club she had been neglecting and took Mrs. Thorne and Ms. Branch up on their invitations to afternoon tennis at the club. Even the exhausting ordeal of keeping up with their gossip was preferable to the smell.

Every moment she spent away, she worried for the house. She adored that house at 1 Orchard Street, with its wonderfully shingled, rust-colored exterior and immense bay windows framed by the wraparound porch and brilliant white columns that led up to those proud gables. Gina couldn't stand to think of its oaken walls, hardwood floors, and her carefully curated furnishings and decor corrupted by this stench.

Not to mention the garden that she had poured her soul into! Back in Queens, she had only been allowed a few potted herbs on the fire escape, which her mother was constantly picking at to season the Sunday sauce. But in Original Hill, her green thumb flourished, coaxing tomato vines up trellises, cultivating communities of peonies, and plucking ripe, rosy turnips out of warm dirt. A few days after the odor had arrived, Gina noticed daylilies starting to wilt, and the squash seemed hesitant to grow. It was as if the smell was siphoning the life out of her earth.

Still, Eugene asserted that he had everything under

control. He had been so stubborn since his retirement, and his resolve seemed to her not only illogical but self-destructive. Gina considered suggesting he stay in a hotel, but the humiliation of asking him to sleep on the couch in the parlor had been overwhelming enough. But after a week passed without improvement, she informed her husband that if the smell persisted, she was going to have him looked at by a medical professional.

Then, the next morning, the odor was gone. There wasn't one lingering note of it in the air. It was as if it had never been there. When Gina made her way down to the parlor, she detected only the light scents of floor wax and the begonias from her garden.

Eugene was already up and had made them both coffee. When she entered the kitchen, he locked eyes with her and said, "I told you I had it under control."

Maybe it was the need to prove that she did, in fact, trust her husband of thirty-four years that made Gina so receptive when, a week later, she came downstairs to find Eugene sitting at the kitchen table with the beautiful midnight-dark young woman in an oversize frock. Gina froze in the doorway, unable to move until she met the girl's large, lovely eyes.

She was proud of the fact that her first impulse had been to feed the skinny young thing. Gina considered herself distinct from the usual Original Hill set—those quick to meet any difference with suspicion and wicked theories—and was glad that when tested, she proved her intuition right. Still, she was perplexed when Eugene introduced this stranger as his niece, not because of her color—Gina had grown up alongside families that contained a variety of shades, though perhaps never *this* dark—but because she had never met her brother-in-law.

By the end of breakfast, the girl had eaten three bowls of cereal in milk and an entire grapefruit doused in sugar. All through the meal, Gina snuck glances at her husband, who simply watched the girl with a grim expression. He had neither manifested any familial warmth toward her nor did he appear mistrustful. The girl was so full by the end that she nearly dozed off at the table, and Eugene had to guide her up to the guest room.

By the time he returned to the kitchen, Gina had prepared two cups of coffee, which granted the morning some sense of normalcy. She sat and waited for her husband to speak. His gray eyes gazed into the dark liquid in his mug. Finally, she ventured, "She's Isaac's, then?"

Eugene nodded. So, there it was. Though Gina had never met her husband's estranged brother, she had known of him for almost as long as she had known Eugene. As a naive bride-to-be, she had dreamed of perhaps reconciling the two, going as far as to put Isaac's name on a wedding invitation. But, when Eugene discovered her hopeful mischief, he had judiciously torn the envelope to shreds in front of her. After tossing it into a wastebasket, he turned to Gina with a look so severe, it had singed away the rosy veneer through which she had viewed him, leaving behind a hard reality that most brides were not introduced to until after the honeymoon.

Eugene took another sip of coffee and cleared his throat. "Isaac said he was going off somewhere—he didn't say where—and he couldn't take her with him."

"Isaac was here?" Gina bristled at the thought that

this phantom brother had been right here, on her doorstep, and she had just missed him.

Eugene nodded. "He wants me to look after her."

"For how long?"

"I don't know."

"When was the last time you spoke to him?"

Eugene shook his head. "It's been decades. Probably before she was born."

"And you didn't know—"

"I had no idea he had a kid."

"Why does she need taking care of? She can't be younger than twenty."

"She just needs a place to stay," Eugene said.

"And there isn't someone else? What about her mother?"

"Mother?" Eugene frowned, as if he had never considered that the young woman must have one. "I don't know."

"And where are her things?"

"I took them up to the guest room before you came down."

Gina nodded. She searched her husband's face for some other insight into this girl, Isaac, anything. He must also find the scenario strange. All these years, his brother had never shared news of a child? Why now, when the girl was already an adult? But Eugene had disappeared somewhere behind his eyes, no doubt trying to reassemble his world to accommodate this new relative.

"I've got some campaign work to do," he finally said. As he stood, he winced and gripped his shoulder.

"Are you alright, dear?" Gina asked.

"Fine," he grunted.

"I can call Dr. Wood—"

"Just sore, Gina," he insisted, trudging out of the room.

This girl, whatever her story, was clearly in need of comfort. So Gina prepared a chicken broccoli casserole, macaroni salad, green beans, and cornbread. When the girl emerged from her nap later that afternoon, Eugene guided her back to the kitchen where Gina waited, arms outstretched in a welcoming hug.

The girl immediately recoiled, eyes wide with fear. Gina retracted her arms, and the girl scurried past to the dinner table. Gina looked to Eugene for direction. His eyes only bored into her, as if she had committed some grave sin. "Do not touch her," he said. "She does not want to be touched."

Trying her best to fan away the awkwardness of the refused hug, Gina took her seat on the girl's right. Then, a thought occurred. "You know, your uncle never mentioned your name."

The girl blinked at Gina before opening her mouth and, in a voice like crackling embers, said, "Baby."

Gina suppressed a laugh. What a silly name to call an adult woman! "Baby," Gina said. The girl broke out into a vibrant smile and nodded enthusiastically. "That's beautiful, isn't it, Eugene?"

But her husband looked as if the casserole on his fork had gone rancid before his very eyes. He stood from the table abruptly and left the room, having taken only two bites of dinner. Gina sighed and smiled apologetically to

Baby. She could see that the girl was hurt by Eugene's coldness.

"Don't worry, dear. He's just been in a mood lately," Gina assured her.

If she was honest, Eugene had been in a mood for three years. Once upon a time, he had talked of his retirement from city council as a new chapter in life, one rife with possibility. No more haggling with the mayor or talking down protesters or campaigning. With him just a few years shy of seventy, and Gina nearly sixty herself, it seemed fitting that they sit back and enjoy the fruits of the community they had helped construct over the past thirty years.

But once it became clear that Lucius Foote was going to win Eugene's seat over his handpicked successor, Mr. Burdock, her husband's attitude soured. Foote was young—in Eugene's book, a bit of an upstart. He had just arrived in Original Hill and hadn't "done his time" yet. But this did not seem to deter many of their neighbors.

"Young blood," Mr. Thorne had insisted to Eugene the night before the election. "Folks want young blood now and, you know, Burdock's not ten years younger than us."

"Burdock's been a part of this community for fifteen years," Eugene asserted. "People know him. His kids went to school with theirs."

"Well, and that's just it. People want something new," Mr. Thorne said. "Besides, it's a better look for us, having someone like Lucius speaking for the neighborhood. Especially with these protests."

"Oh, they're nothing serious," Eugene scoffed.

"Still, you've got to consider the optics."

As much as Eugene had tried to convince their neighbors that Foote hadn't proven his roots yet—he didn't own property, and he had no wife or family—it was to no avail. Everybody liked Lucius Foote, and so he was elected.

Last March, Eugene announced his intention to run against Foote in the upcoming election. Gina did not discourage him, though she generally found politics quite silly and had been more than ready to leave it all in the past. She knew her husband, and a lack of support on her part would not deter him. The only argument she had was a gentle reminder that his health wasn't all it used to be and that an election campaign would strain his nerves. But in Eugene's eyes, this didn't compare to the distress he felt over the threat of Foote's reelection.

Original Hill's reaction to his announcement had been tepid. Many of their neighbors told him that they were happy to have him back in the game, but they also *liked* Foote. He hadn't done anything controversial or proven in any way that he was inadequate to be their city councilman. Sure, he acted the part of a bachelor—"I've stopped bothering to learn these girls' names. They're gone the next week," Mrs. Bush joked—but it wasn't as if he was disrespectful toward these women. Eugene seemed to be the only one who didn't find this charming, even enviable. In any case, Eugene didn't receive the wave of adoration from the neighborhood that he had expected.

Gina could have dismissed her husband picking this fight as postretirement restlessness if Foote had not begun to taunt Eugene. The walks by the house were, really, a step too far. They were so scheduled, so calculated, that

Gina knew down to the minute when she could look up and catch the flash of his gray jacket disappearing around the corner. Eugene all but planned his days around these sightings, planting himself in front of the bay window and refusing phone calls or meetings in the meantime. Foote not owning a car was hardly an excuse, as he could have avoided their block entirely. Gina suspected he continued to forego leasing a car *because* he preferred peacocking around the neighborhood in this manner.

After a few weeks of this, Eugene became more disturbed. He was up at all hours of the night. Gina noticed strange items disappearing from the house—an old broom from the cleaning closet, a large plastic bucket from the garage, a pair of gardening gloves. She was briefly encouraged when Eugene expressed an interest in repairing the roof, though he continued to keep strange hours, sleeping through the day and working at night. It was difficult for her to ascertain what progress he was making on the roof, and her intuition told her that this project was more a way to get his mind off the campaign than a necessary repair. But then the odor came and Eugene's stubbornness deepened, and Gina truly worried for her husband's mental health. Perhaps reentering politics had been more emotionally taxing than she had anticipated.

And now, in the midst of all this, the appearance of an unknown niece? It seemed to Gina like some cruel devil was playing on her husband's last nerve. But she couldn't very well ask the girl to leave, at least not so soon. As she watched Baby polish off the food from her plate, Gina breathed in a strange scent. She panicked, thinking that the odor had returned, but then registered it was a pleasant smell coming from Baby. Notes of ozone and atmosphere, like daybreak after a stormy night, wafted across the table to Gina and steadied her heartbeat.

Neither Gina nor Eugene had ever been interested in children of their own, and while Baby was certainly not a child, Gina worried that her caretaking instincts might leave something to be desired. But Baby proved to be incredibly easy. She was not particular about her food or sleeping arrangements. Though Gina offered to take her shopping, she was content wearing the vintage dresses that she had brought. She was quiet, often happy simply sharing space with Gina.

Gina was delighted to find that they shared a common interest in her garden. She would often spy Baby outside picking daisies and daffodils or just sitting on the garden wall. Some afternoons, Gina would be pleasantly surprised by a peck basket filled with flowers placed on the kitchen table. She had instructed Baby to stay away from the vegetable patch and berry bushes, which she had put too much time into to have tampered with. But soon, Gina began to fantasize about teaching the young woman how to care for the produce rather than avoid it. As lovely as the baskets of flowers were, imagine if the girl could help with the beans and tomatoes and squash in the fall.

Gina quickly learned that Baby adored sweets. Having been on some form of diet for the past twenty years, Gina reserved sugar exclusively for holidays—Christmas cookies, Thanksgiving pies, modest birthday cakes. She had entirely forgotten that one could bake at any time of year. She whipped up batches of molasses cookies, sweet potato pies, and candied chestnuts. Even the almond pastries that Gina had lost a taste for in her youth were given a renewed vibrance as Baby gorged on wedding cookies and lemon ricotta cake.

The reintroduction of sugary treats brought a sweetness to the air that Gina inhaled deep into her chest. At Sunday brunches or meetings at the club, her neighbors began to say that she looked like she was floating. Strangers stopped her in the grocery aisles to tell her how radiant she looked. Some guessed that a new skin regimen or hairdo had produced such an effect, but Gina would only smile, the sugar dancing in her lungs. By the time she arrived at Bush's store to purchase Baby some strawberry candies, Gina had become so enthralled by the sweet air that she pocketed a few for herself.

Even Eugene's mood seemed improved by the sweetness. His gruffness toward Baby softened, and he began to engage her in conversation at dinner, asking if she had met anyone while she was out in the front yard. Baby always shook her head, though Eugene continued to ask.

It wasn't until Gina overheard Mrs. Ives whispering to Mrs. Reed at the club one morning that she discovered the rest of the neighborhood found Baby's presence unsettling. "That girl's still perched on the garden wall," said Mrs. Ives.

"It's getting hot to be sitting outside like that," Mrs. Reed muttered. "I'm sure she'll stay inside if she doesn't want to get heat stroke or burn."

"I don't think those people burn. They're predisposed to the heat."

"God help us."

Gina grabbed her coffee and hurried to a table at the other end of the cafeteria. How could these two women possibly think so negatively of Baby? But then, she realized, they had never met her.

How could that be? Nearly a month had passed since Baby had arrived. Had Gina really never brought her around to the club or the café, or to any of the neighborhood socials?

As she meditated on this, Gina's gaze drifted to a painting hanging on the wall across from her. It was new—a recent commission, which Gina had read about in the club's bulletin. The title on the plaque read *Breaking Ground on Original Hill.* Stylistically, it reminded her of a Rockwell, though perhaps that was just the 1950s clothing. A trio of men in hard hats were depicted in the foreground, smiling at one another as one drove a large shovel into a plot of smooth, virgin soil, while another leaned casually against a jackhammer. In the background, two aproned women with gentle blond curls looked on admiringly. Behind them, cars rushed by on a distant highway, cutting through pastoral green hills. Beneath a handsome oak on one of these far-off hills, the artist had drawn the small silhouette of a figure—a woman, given her dress. Gina squinted to try and make out the little character, but she was too small.

Gina turned from the painting to the tables occupied by her whispering neighbors. Perhaps she hadn't brought Baby to any of Original Hill's social gatherings to shield her from the inane patter—someone's son getting into a "good school," someone's daughter "wearing *that* to a luncheon"—and those constantly shifting, judging stares. Gina knew as well as anyone how difficult it was for an outsider to get in here, and Baby was about as different as a person could be.

Gina took a sip of coffee and searched for the small figure beneath the painted oak but couldn't find her. Gina shook her head. She'd been breathing in so much sugar; she wasn't thinking properly.

When she returned home, Gina discovered the garden wall was empty. She found Baby in the kitchen, staring out the window at the front yard.

"Baby," Gina said. "Wouldn't you like to be outside? It's a nice day." Baby shook her head. "What's the matter?"

"I think I did something wrong. I think he wants me to leave." Baby's hangdog look nearly broke Gina's heart. She wanted to give the girl a comforting squeeze, but she knew even a gentle touch would only upset her more.

"You haven't done anything wrong," Gina assured her. "I'll talk to him."

Gina stormed up to Eugene's study, only to find him slouched in his desk chair like a discarded marionette, face pale and sickly. She smoothed out the righteous tone she had anticipated using with him, gilding it with careful sympathy. "Dear, did you tell Baby she couldn't go outside?"

"I saw it happen. Just now, through the window."

Gina glanced through the window in his office to the garden wall below. "What happened? Did something happen to Baby?"

Eugene's eyes would not meet hers. "Nothing happened. I don't know what was supposed to but . . . *something*. He just walked right on by."

"Dear, I don't understand—"

"It's not working. She shouldn't be here. I should never have— It's too damn strange. I don't know what's supposed to happen, but it isn't working—*she* isn't working."

Gina paused. Working? She was a guest; why would she need to work? That wasn't part of the arrangement. Unless Eugene meant that the *arrangement* wasn't working. She thought back to Mrs. Ives and Mrs. Reed's conversation. Eugene must have heard something similar. Gina hadn't even considered that Baby's sudden appearance might reflect negatively on them, particularly in the midst of Eugene's city council campaign.

Gina tucked her lips into an encouraging smile. "She's a lovely girl, Eugene. We've just got to introduce her to the neighborhood."

Eugene shook his head. "Gina, I don't think—"

She rested her hand on his. "It's my fault, really. Baby has been here since May, and I haven't even shown her around."

"No, she can't—" His reply was interrupted by a sudden, horrid cough from deep in his chest. Gina knelt by his side.

"Eugene! Are you okay?"

Just as swiftly as the cough had come on, Eugene snapped back to an upright position. "I'm fine," he muttered. His face was still pale, but Gina knew pushing him on his health would only stoke his stubbornness.

Gina straightened her own spine and stood. "Sweetheart, Baby is a young woman. You can't keep her from meeting the rest of Original. Even if you did, I think it would do more harm than good. The Midsummer Soiree's in two weeks. We can introduce her to everyone then. Once they meet her, they'll love her just as much as we do. Have faith." Gina watched her husband's head nod slowly, his eyeline shifting from her to the window. The muscles in his arms and shoulders seemed to be straining. She was tempted to ask if he was *sure* that he felt alright but knew he would just close up on her.

Instead, she said, "I'll tell Baby it's too hot to be outside today, and I'll get you some Alka-Seltzer, dear." Then she turned and left her husband alone in his study.

Lucky

•

This year's Midsummer Soiree at the country club was one of Lucky's most important political appearances. Hidden beneath the crush of elm and sugar maple, the club's sprawling complex housed a fitness center, a cafeteria, and several ballrooms. Behind its mid-century modern building stretched a pristinely manicured eighteen-hole golf course, completely obscured from public view by towering hedges. Membership was by invitation only, and while Lucky had been invited to the club's Holiday Parties, Fall Fundraisers, and past years' Midsummer Soirees, no one had ever suggested he join. One of the prerequisites, he had been told, was owning property in Original Hill. Renters need not apply.

So tonight was a rare occasion of access to this most exclusive neighborhood space. The club's regulars would be crucial donors and advocates for Lucky's reelection. They were also the most likely to hold a preference for Fox. If he could coax any of these folks to endorse him, it would move mountains for his campaign. But the club was also the least likely place for a beautiful Black girl to turn up.

It had been over two weeks since he had met her in front of the Foxes' house, and yet he could not shake her. He was suffering a vague discomfort all over his body, which clouded his mind and troubled his sleep. At first he assumed it was a persistent cold and that his preoccupation with this girl was the illness throwing his libido out of whack. Whenever his mind wandered to her, it conjured feverish fantasies of that gliding leg, those mother-of-pearl-button eyes, those gloved hands hovering above his naked torso. But when he willed them to touch him, he was bucked out of the daydream by a piercing stomach cramp.

Now, an abdominal ache accompanied the general discomfort, which no amount of food, exercise, or massage would remedy. He made detours past 1 Orchard Street, sometimes multiple times a day, hoping that seeing her again might right his body. But she refused to reappear for him.

Mr. Thorne greeted Lucky at the entrance to the club, grabbing him by the shoulder. "There's our fearless leader! Hope those protesters aren't giving you too much trouble downtown, buddy."

"Nothing I can't handle." Lucky smiled.

"That's what I like to hear." Mr. Thorne chuckled. "I mean, they are really getting out of hand. Some of the things they're saying about us? Like we're a bunch of, I don't know—"

Mrs. Thorne nodded beside her husband. "Exactly. No

doubt every neighborhood's got some skeletons in their past, but why dredge it up? It's painful for us, and it's got to be painful for them, too."

"Better to look forward," Lucky said.

"Hear that? What a guy!" Mr. Thorne laughed.

Mr. Thorne gave Lucky an enthusiastic handshake, which began a trend that led Lucky hand over hand around the chandelier-lit ballroom to the crystal punch bowl. With each new handshake, the neighbor's eyes would seem to refocus before they would exclaim, "Lucius! How're you doing, buddy?" As if, until they were directly confronted with his presence, he was only a shadow in their lives. Regardless, Lucky enthusiastically chatted with his constituents, subtly slipping in mentions of the initiatives he had successfully put forth and how necessary a second term would be to complete them. His eyes trailed over to the door each time it opened, but it was always just another familiar face from the neighborhood.

For a moment, he allowed himself to picture her stepping over the threshold and was rewarded with another cramp in his belly. He cursed under his breath and submerged two shrimp in a vase of tangy cocktail sauce. Biting into them, he locked eyes with a Black kid with a greasy mustache and zit-spotted sideburns in the caterer's uniform. Lucky's instinct was to offer a nod or "sup," but he stopped himself. Seeing this hesitation, the kid smirked and turned away.

Swallowing his shrimp, Lucky caught the tail end of the sentence "—girl's stopped sitting on that wall, thank goodness." Lucky traced the voice to Mrs. Ives, who was huddled beside Mrs. Reed.

"I haven't seen her at all, either," Mrs. Reed whispered.

"Oh, she's still *there.* I saw her through the window on one of our walks."

"I don't think I've had the opportunity to say hello." Lucky chuckled while sidling up beside them with his red-carpet smile. Both women broke into broad grins and gripped his hand. Before they could begin fussing over him, as women like them often would, Lucky interjected, "I hope I'm not interrupting something?"

"Oh, no." Mrs. Reed giggled, blushing. "We were just talking about—" Her eyes darted to Mrs. Ives.

Mrs. Ives squared her jaw and looked defiantly at Lucky. "We were talking about that young woman who used to spend all day sitting outside the Foxes' house."

"Do you know her?" Mrs. Reed quickly followed up, grabbing Lucky's bicep. Mrs. Ives leaned in expectantly too.

Lucky widened his smile. "We met in passing, I think. I didn't catch her name."

"Well, I don't know her name," Mrs. Ives huffed. "Just that she's his niece."

"Niece? Whose niece?" Lucky asked. But both Mrs. Reed's and Mrs. Ives's gaze had shifted beyond Lucky. He whirled around, and there she was, staring him down from the other end of the party.

She was no longer wearing the canary-and-blush ensemble but instead a cream prairie dress with indigo vines swirling into blooming flowers across its skirt. The ruched neck was buttoned just below her chin, while the long sleeves were tucked into those same white opera gloves, which took on an opalescent shine under the chandeliers. It was bizarre seeing the youngest woman in the room wearing the most conservative fit. Her large-brimmed hat had been replaced by a pale pink headband, which framed two uneven braids. Her face was bare—no lipstick accentuating her soft mouth or mascara elongating her lashes. Lucky didn't know a single woman who would have considered herself presentable like this, particularly at a party thrown by white people. Yet he couldn't shake an almost painful urge to be near her.

The other partygoers' conversations appeared to continue on undisturbed, though anyone paying close attention would have noted how the men's cadence had momentarily slowed, how the women's eyes kept sliding in the girl's direction, how Mrs. Burdock kept flipping her hair over her shoulder to sneak glimpses, how Mr. Bush had spilled beer on Mrs. Bush's dress without her noticing.

Lucky had barely noticed Old Man Fox and his wife enter the room until they were all assembled near the door, the Foxes flanking the girl, forming a triad despite none of them touching one another. The Foxes seemed aware of all the eyes aimed in their direction. Their smiles were unnaturally tight, their hellos saccharine.

So, she was *Fox's* niece? Lucky quickly cycled through denial, confusion, and apprehension before the cramp in his stomach twisted, making rational thought impossible. Those eyes he had dreamed of nightly once more dared him to come closer.

Lucky felt the entire room watching as he strode up to the girl and extended his hand. "How do you do, Miss? Lucius Foote, but friends call me Lucky."

The dimple between her brows deepened as she seemed to aim all her concentration on him. He grasped her petite gloved hand, feeling its delicacy as he shook it. His entire body relaxed as the cramp vanished.

"Lucius Foote," a deep voice thrummed from beside her.

Lucky had never troubled himself to learn exactly why Old Man Fox had it out for him. He couldn't imagine that it was especially personal, as they had only ever exchanged neutral pleasantries. True, they were vying for the same seat, but that did not justify the ire with which Fox spoke about him behind his back. Once more in his presence, Lucky took the man in.

Fox stood with the discipline of a man attempting to appear younger than he was. His slick silver-blond widow's peak rebelled against his receding hairline and combined with his strong nose and penetrating eyes to give him the appearance of a large austere bird. Lucky shook the man's hand, noting the effortless strength in his grip. The old guy kept himself in good shape.

Lucky flashed his red-carpet smile. "Eugene Fox. What a pleasure."

Old Man Fox's stern expression seemed to waver for a moment. "I'd like you to meet my niece, Baby," he said.

"We've met before," Lucky said, winking to Baby. She responded with a knowing smirk, throwing a bit of mischief back at Lucky before Fox glanced down at her.

"Oh? I didn't realize you made your way over to our part of the neighborhood." Fox scowled.

"Oh, sure. You know, I'm surprised we don't run into one another more often," Lucky hummed, slipping his hand against the small of Baby's back. He gently guided her a step closer to him, asking, "May I get the lady a drink?"

Fox furrowed his brow and studied Lucky for what seemed like ages. Lucky could still feel the other guests' eyes burning the back of his head. Finally, the older man conceded. "That's very kind of you, Foote."

Lucky sensed a shift in the room as he led Baby toward the bar. Now that he had broken the seal, others eagerly approached the young woman. Each came with questions, to which she offered shallow answers. Who was she? Fox's niece. Where from? An awfully boring place, not nearly as nice as here. Every compliment of her hair or her dress or the fineness of her gloves was met with silent ambivalence. Then, another guest would push forward, impatient to make their introduction, forcing the ousted party to join the others in whispering and glancing back at her. Baby left them all insecure and wanting.

Ms. Branch was the last to shake Baby's hand, though she directed her comments solely to Lucky. "It's so good to see you, Lucius! It's been so long. I didn't realize you two were . . ."

"Oh, we're just getting to know one another." Lucky smiled.

"Well, you make a handsome pair." Ms. Branch chuckled before turning to Baby. "And this must be your first time at the club! Don't you just love it? It's so nice to have a place where the community can come together."

"Well, some of us still need the invitation . . ." Lucky hummed.

"Of course! Those silly rules. I can't believe they haven't made an exception for *you*, Lucius." Ms. Branch giggled. Her gaze shifted back onto Baby. "Of course, it's good that we've got *some* standards. Though, I guess we always have, even in the old days before the club."

"Now, Ms. Branch, you're much too young to remember 'the old days.'"

"Of course, I'm not speaking from *experience*." She swatted at him playfully. "Mama and I only moved here ten years ago. But we learned from people like Eugene Fox. It's good to know how things used to be, you know. Gives you a sense of pride in the neighborhood."

Ms. Branch leaned in, grabbing Lucky's forearm. "And isn't there something kind of romantic about the old days? Those women in their heels and pearls, whipping off the apron, serving a homecooked meal? Of course, I wouldn't trade places. I am glad we can just hire the food so *I* can enjoy myself—"

Ms. Branch caught herself as Baby bent over sharply to press her ear against the woman's stomach. Then, just as abruptly, Baby straightened back up and eyed Ms. Branch suspiciously. Ms. Branch was so flustered that she excused herself and darted away.

"Loud," was the only explanation Baby offered.

Lucky burst out laughing. "Why don't we get some fresh air?" he suggested.

Guiding them toward the exit, Lucky could still sense the partygoers' focus on the two of them, but it held something new, something electric. In the neighborhood's eyes, Baby fit with him. As the Foxes' niece, she was incongruous, but on Lucky's arm, she shone.

Immediately upon stepping outside, Baby kicked off her heels and pressed her toes into the crisp grass. The moon danced across Baby's cheekbones and lips, making them appear slick as oil as she stared out across the vast lawn of the golf course, tilting her head as if listening for some sound carried on the late-June breeze.

"You know, I came back to see you," Lucky said. "So, where've you been?"

"Inside," Baby said.

"Right, okay." Lucky smirked. "You're living with the Foxes? You're the old man's niece?"

She nodded, not taking her eyes from the lawn. Lucky decided to try a different tactic. "You really don't say much, do you?" Baby cut her eyes back at him. He was on the right track. "Nah, nah. I mean, I'm trying to get to know you, girl. Where you're from, what's your deal. I told you I came to see you, and you're giving me crumbs—"

Then, Baby was pressing her gloved fingers against his lips. His stomach twisted painfully, but the pain eased into a strange kind of pleasure. Baby held her hand there for the longest moment, and from the look in her eyes, Lucky could tell that she felt a similar sensation.

Smooth as honey, Baby floated over to the hedges at the lawn's perimeter, following it to a latched gate. She glanced back to Lucky, the light from the party glinting in her pupils. Then she took off through the gate into the night, quiet as a thief.

"Hold up!" Lucky called, lurching forward. The rapid slap of her bare feet against the asphalt echoed off the roofs of the neighbor's houses as she sped toward Orchard Street. Lucky's throat burned as he pulled hoarse breaths into his lungs. He hadn't run like this since he was a kid.

Then, as suddenly as she had started, Baby hooked her arm onto a young oak tree and pressed her cheek against it. Lucky stopped a few yards away, slapping his palms on his thighs to catch his breath. They were across the street from the Foxes' house, back on the block that he had returned to time and again looking for her.

Despite the protest of his sore lungs, Lucky began to laugh. He straightened up and smoothed his jacket. "Girl, you are crazy."

Baby placed her gloved hand in his and brought him to a thick root that had broken through the sidewalk—a woody hump punctuated by a few gnarled tendrils reaching toward another oak tree at the end of the block. Baby slowly pressed Lucky's hand against it. He waited, assuming that something was supposed to happen. But all he could feel was the bark of the tree.

After a minute, Baby stood and the two of them made their way down Orchard Street. At first, they were quiet as they strolled shoulder to shoulder.

"It was getting hard for me to stay in that party," she finally said.

"Sure," Lucky chuckled. "So, how long are you going to be in Original?"

"As long as I can be."

"You don't miss home?" he asked. She stayed silent, her eyes on the street. "Where'd you come from, anyway?"

"Nowhere."

Lucky smirked. "And what's it like, this Nowhere, U.S.A.?"

"Dark. Hot. Noisy. Nobody to talk to, really. Even if you wanted to, there's this roar that never goes away, like rushing water, but hard and angry. And this smell, like burning."

"Sounds like hell."

"Not Hell," Baby said. "But it was a wrong place. I shouldn't have been there. I'm glad my father took me out of there."

"And brought you here?"

"First, I was in a room for a long time," Baby recalled. "I couldn't leave. My father wouldn't let me. He said it was to protect me, but I think he was . . . Afraid. Confused. I hated being shut up like that."

"That sounds . . . terrible," Lucky whispered.

"That's why I like to be outside."

"But your father . . . That's not the kind of thing anyone should do to a person."

"It was better than the other place. The dark, loud, hot place."

"Okay, yeah, but, Baby, that sounds borderline . . . I mean, have you told anybody else that?"

"What about you? Where did you come from?"

Lucky looked down at her, slapping on his red-carpet grin. "Why? You gonna call and ask for references?"

She frowned. "I'd just like to know is all."

"I grew up about as far away from here as you could get. Wasn't really my speed either."

"Do you ever go back?"

Lucky scoffed. "That place is dead to me, and I am dead to it."

Baby's mother-of-pearl-button eyes finally focused on Lucky. "Then you understand."

Lucky nodded. "Still, I can't imagine living in the Fox house."

"I love them," Baby said, simply.

A breeze blew up the street, and Baby shivered. Lucky slipped off his blazer and threw it around her shoulders. She offered no look of recognition or gratitude. "You aren't cold walking around with no shoes on?" Lucky asked. She did not answer, instead kneading the lapels of his coat.

He imagined she had come from somewhere rural, with dirt roads and acres upon acres of nothing. Maybe a factory town, loud and industrial but where it wouldn't be unusual to walk around barefoot. She seemed fascinated by the paved road. Lucky could see her eyes darting just ahead of their feet, as if she were reading some incredibly interesting book.

He liked her quiet company. Politically, he could use quiet. If the party at the club was any indication, the two of them could certainly win a crowd over. She might need a little styling, a little warming up, but Lucky could see that beneath her quiet was a drive not unlike his own. He looked down at the girl in his jacket. The discomfort in his abdomen was no longer a sharp stab but something more akin to the weightless feeling of a roller-coaster drop.

"You know, staying here's not an easy thing for folks like us. But if we play our cards right, I think we can make it work. Is that what you want?"

"More than anything," she said. Then, she slowly slipped her hand out of her glove and took his hand in hers. A chill shot through him like a morning shower, seeming to open him wholly to her touch. Yet, the longer he held her hand, the more he felt as if a buffer was preventing them from really touching.

They walked like this until they reached the bridge. Once Baby came to the edge of the sidewalk, she would not budge. "It's okay, we've got the go," Lucky reassured her. The I-94 was silent, not a car in sight, and the walk signal shed an uneasy glow onto the placid road. Yet Baby glared at the highway ahead of them until the red hand appeared.

Lucky exhaled into half of a laugh. "And here I thought you wanted to sneak away from those old white folks—"

The divot between her eyes deepened. "I can't," she sighed.

"What? Got a curfew or something?" he asked with a chuckle. The night had hardly begun, and he hadn't felt this good in weeks. But the total sincerity in Baby's eyes told Lucky their little jaunt was over. He had a sneaking suspicion that somewhere in their game, he had made a wrong play. Hopefully it was nothing he couldn't come back from.

Making their way back up Orchard, Lucky heard Baby gasp. There, a few feet ahead, something lay in the shadows. As Lucky took a few steps forward, the light shifted to reveal a dead rabbit in the middle of the road, bisected by some vehicle. Threads of its soft gray fur and shredded pink innards trailed away from the body.

It was only roadkill, but Baby's mother-of-pearl-button eyes were wide with revulsion. Lucky wrapped his arms around her shoulders, allowing her to submit to his chest, burying her face entirely in his shirt. Still, she didn't feel quite there, like he was holding a billow of steam rather than a woman.

"Come on, Baby," Lucky hummed. "Baby, Baby."

She looked up at him, clasped her bare hand around his, and urged him back in the direction of the country club. As they slipped back through the gate, a furious Eugene Fox came charging toward them.

"What the hell was that?" he shouted. "You cannot just disappear without warning! And why aren't you wearing any shoes?!"

Lucky's eyes flicked between Old Man Fox's red face and the group of onlookers huddled by the door. Being berated by Fox was an extremely bad look, especially after he had disappeared with this girl. Of course, the truth was innocent enough—Baby had run off and Lucky had pursued her—but how would that reflect on her? The smart thing to do would be to play the concerned citizen, but he couldn't bring his lips to say a word against her.

Lucky grinned and prepared to put his charm to work when Mrs. Fox came running across the lawn. She stopped a few feet from them, eyes fixed on Lucky's hand. Her fingers covered her lips as she gasped, "Eugene!"

"What the hell is the matter, Gina?" Fox demanded.

"He— He's touching her," she finally whispered. "They're holding hands."

Fox turned back to Lucky and Baby, taking them in as if for the first time.

Then, Fox smiled. Lucky wasn't sure he had ever really seen a smile crack the old man's face. Fox clapped Lucky on the back, leading him and Baby past his unsettled wife and back into the party. By the time Lucky left the club that evening, after wishing everyone goodnight and pulling Baby aside to tell her that he would like to see her again, Fox had not stopped smiling.

Before my One and Only touched me, I wondered how I might know him. I sat on the garden wall and imagined whether we might have a love affair like the two oak trees across the street. Was it fate that had paired these two lovertrees? Was it simply cruel circumstance that planted them so close yet separated them by so many feet of sidewalk? Or had these young oaks heard one another's voices in the soil when they were only seedlings? Had they twisted their new growth toward that lovely sound until destiny gave way and planted them on the same block? How would I know which voice to bend my boughs toward? When I found the right sound, how could I close the space between us?

In the end, it was not difficult at all. I knew him because he touched me. I made my wish, and there he was beside me.

I try to show my One and Only my lovertrees, but he does not seem interested. He does not listen to the sweet nothings they share. He does not even seem aware of all the voices covering that dead rabbit in the road—horrible, putrid voices. He is more interested in the darkloudhot place.

Gina

•

"Do not touch her," Eugene repeated to his wife that night in bed. But Gina could not banish the image of Baby's hand trapped in Lucius Foote's. In the moment, she had felt compelled to wrench the girl away from his grasp, if only to press her own hand to Baby's palm.

"He was holding her hand without the glove," Gina argued. "Baby seemed perfectly fine with that."

"Do not touch her skin," Eugene said firmly.

"I just don't understand why—"

But he turned from her before she could finish. He had said very little since they had returned from the Midsummer Soiree, neglecting to even wish Baby goodnight before marching up to bed. As Eugene began to snore, Gina rolled over and concentrated on the rumbling hill of her husband.

It was unusual for Gina to believe that Eugene was keeping something from her. Even if he wasn't the most communicative man, she could always intuit the cause of her husband's dissatisfaction. Over thirty-four years of marriage, her intuition had afforded Gina a tranquility envied by many of her neighbors, though none would admit it outright. She knew better than any wife when to indulge her husband's ego and when to push against it. She evaded unnecessary spats with only minor sacrifices. In a feat that bordered on telepathy, her intuition had even helped her deduce Eugene's favorite birthday dessert without his input. Though it occasionally ran counter to her intellectual assessments of situations, the pride she felt in having developed such a sharp intuition eclipsed all doubt.

Even before she officially met Eugene, she understood him. Sitting on a bench outside her Wall Street office building and unwrapping the sandwich that her mother had packed for her, she studied the man who wore burgundy suits and worked on the twenty-first floor as he purchased and ate a hot dog for lunch. Like a tarot reader examining her cards, she kept stock of everything she could glean through mere observation: He was a transplant, and while he enjoyed New York, he was already becoming exhausted by the constant pound-and-grind of the city. Wherever he had come from—escaped from, more like—was a place with fields for miles, with beautiful houses that sprouted from perfectly squared-off lawns, like the ones she had seen in *Better Homes & Gardens.* He was very good at his job, but he was in it for the perks rather than a genuine interest in finance. She could see that he was a bit haunted, but she would have to draw closer to learn his ghost's name. She could tell that he was not married, nor had he ever been, which given that he was well into his thirties led her to believe that he was either a scoundrel, a romantic, or possessed some blockage in his heart that needed clearing.

When her intuition told her that the time had come for an introduction, she asked to join the man for lunch, and these mysteries were addressed swiftly. The place he had escaped from was called Original Hill, a lovely neighborhood on the edge of a corn-fed Midwestern city. The ghost was hardly a phantom at all, only a delinquent brother named Isaac. He was too analytical to be romantic and, though he had a devilish sense of humor, he was no scoundrel. He treated her with the utmost respect and offered to accompany her home after work. So, then, there must be a blockage.

The source of Eugene's emotional blockage proved difficult to diagnose, even as their friendship shifted into courtship and then wavered on the precipice of engagement. Of course, his decisive, pragmatic, and discreet way was what attracted Gina to him. She had no interest in men who were soft and pliable. But she couldn't shake the feeling that some other secret whispered beneath the surface, something that Eugene would prefer to keep locked away forever if he could.

Perhaps that was why she had rashly addressed a wedding invitation to Isaac Fox. She would never forget the look Eugene gave her after he eviscerated the unmailed letter—the sort of look that might have made a weaker woman shrivel up like a sunburned flower. She could have pushed if she wanted—rewritten and sent the invitation—but then, why have a wedding if she was just going to reduce the marriage to rubble? So, she concluded, sometimes, it was enough to know the name of a thing and leave it at that. She knew of Isaac Fox and need not pick at the wound. How else would it heal?

Though now, lying beside her husband, Gina considered that if she *had* pushed to learn more about Isaac, then perhaps they would have known of Baby sooner. But then, if she were the kind of woman who needled her husband for answers, their marriage would have been much different.

Her mother had taken a wicked joy in pressing her father, which had led to the explosive brawls that had punctuated her childhood. She had watched plates shatter beside her mother's head and seen yellowish-purple welts decorate her father's back. The violence seemed to rub off on the Morettis' sons, who were frequently brought home by police for starting fights with Irish and Polish boys, which in turn ignited new bouts between her parents.

Early on, Gina became accustomed to abandoning the twin bed that she shared with her nona when her parents' shouting in the next room made sleep impossible. She would sneak out onto the fire escape and tend to her basil and thyme. If she cared for them enough, she imagined they might grow higher than the Empire State Building and take her up to a castle in the clouds, all her own. It would be nothing like the two-bedroom that her family of eight shared, no leaky faucets or screaming matches or Mrs. Hubbard next door muttering, "Those people should be put in a zoo." No, Gina's castle would have twice as many rooms as the Plaza and a big iron gate that she would lock shut if her parents or brothers ever tried to get in.

As a girl, Gina had placed equal blame on her parents for the fights. But as she aged into adolescence, she saw how effortlessly she could disarm her father's temper when her mother could not. Giuseppe Moretti was a consistent man who loved baseball and Sinatra and disliked being interrogated on his habits or his opinions on frivolous matters. Through quiet observation and gut instinct, Gina could reliably pinpoint the perfect adjustment, gesture, or sympathetic words to appease him.

As Gina honed her intuition, she became increasingly annoyed with her mother's insistence on crudely demanding answers from her father, pushing him past his limits and provoking new fights. She came to resent her mother for what she chalked up to neglect—an unwillingness to open her eyes to her own husband's obvious ways. Gina swore that, when she had a home of her own, it would be nothing like that crowded apartment with shouts that tumbled out onto the filthy streets.

Eugene was hardly Giuseppe Moretti, but still, Gina attributed the peace of her marriage to her own refusal to replicate her mother's willful neglect. And her intuition, of course. Though not even that could have tipped her off to Baby's arrival into their life.

A sudden cough brought Gina out of her thoughts and back to the man lying beside her. The hacking went on for long enough that Gina reached over to pat her husband on the back, and her touch settled Eugene back into a steady snore. Listening to his breath, Gina's intuition teased that there was more to Baby's sudden appearance than Eugene was letting on. Perhaps her husband was not as transparent as she believed.

After the Midsummer Soiree, Lucius Foote began to show up at the Foxes' door asking after Baby. The pair would walk to local restaurants or the movies or around the neighborhood. Gina caught the flush in Baby's cheeks when Foote dropped her off and forced herself to swallow down the hurt of seeing the young woman so delighted by someone else's company. Fortunately, their jaunts never strayed beyond Original Hill.

Then, one day, Foote showed up in a shiny sports car, and the small consolation Gina took in the pair staying close by vanished. As he drove Baby to other parts of the city, Gina couldn't help but feel that Foote only wanted to be out from under the neighborhood's watchful eyes.

She tried not to let her suspicion of Foote show too blatantly. It really wasn't his fault, Gina had to remind herself. She would feel this apprehension toward any man who took an interest in Baby, for the girl's protection. Besides, she could do worse than Lucius Foote. He was genteel, respectful, sharp, and he seemed to make Baby happy.

Even so, Gina began to suggest that Baby accompany her to lunches and various errands. She sought out excursions that appealed to both their interests: "There's a flower show this weekend just off the I-94." "Oh, Baby, I think you'd love this movie, and it's right by that ice cream parlor." More than a few times, upon their return to the house on Orchard Street, Eugene would inform them that Foote had come to call on Baby while they were out. This news never sent Baby tumbling to the floor like a lovesick teenager. In fact, Gina noted, she didn't seem fazed by missing Foote at all.

"I do hope that he's being a gentleman," Gina said

over breakfast at the café one morning. The place was bustling with diners, but Gina was so focused on Baby that the two of them might as well have been in her own private room. Baby only nodded vaguely. "Your father *did* tell you about—you know, intimacy?"

"Gina!" Baby smirked, hiding her face with a forkful of blueberry crepes.

"Well, you're two young people and I just want to make sure you're using protection—and I don't just mean the usual kind." Gina could feel her own cheeks growing red. But she had already begun, so she barreled on. "Please don't take this the wrong way, but since I've known him, Foote seems to have a different woman on his arm at every chance. I just want to make sure that if you think of this relationship as serious, he's got the same idea."

"Thank you, Gina," Baby said. "But Father told me everything I need to know."

"Well, sometimes men don't have the kind of intuition a young woman needs."

"Don't worry, Gina!" Baby leaned forward and the light caught her smile at an angle that made her look like a 1950s movie starlet.

Gina's mouth felt dry, so she sipped her coffee. "Well, I'd certainly like to know what exactly your father would say now that there's a real *somebody* in the picture." Something flashed in Baby's eyes, prompting Gina to ask, "Have you told your father about Foote?"

Baby looked down at her crepes. "Oh, no. I mean, I haven't told him very much."

"But a little? You've let him know you're alright here? You have his phone number?"

Baby shook her head.

"No phone? Email, then?" Gina asked. Baby was just as tight-lipped about Isaac Fox as Eugene. This was the first time she had hinted at any contact with her father. Gina couldn't help herself from pressing. "You do have *some* way of getting in touch with him, in emergencies for instance?"

Baby shifted uncomfortably in her seat. "Father is very . . . private."

"Did something happen to your father? Is that why you had to come here?"

"I don't know," Baby muttered. "I— He— He doesn't tell me much, even though I know there's something—"

Baby sniffed and buried her face in the sleeve of her glove. Gina was struck by an intense desire to grab the girl's shoulders and pull her into a tight embrace, press her pale cheek against Baby's skin and feel the thick curls of Baby's hair against her eyelashes. She wanted to squeeze her until all the pain and all the secrets came pouring out. But, she reminded herself, that was impossible.

"And what about your gloves?" Gina cleared her throat. "Did your father give you those?" Baby hid her hands under the table and looked away from Gina. Gina murmured, "Is he the one who told you that no one could touch you?"

"I can't touch anyone."

"That's what your father said?" Gina ventured, but Baby said nothing. "But you touch Lucius Foote."

A small, secret smirk grew on Baby's face. "That's different."

"Why?"

"I'd like to use the restroom," Baby said, standing.

Gina nodded. She had pressed too much. Anytime she came close to learning about Baby's upbringing, the girl became evasive. When Gina asked where Baby had grown up, she always answered, "The road." When asked about her mother, she said, "All I can remember is her voice." When asked why she had come to Original Hill, she laughed and said, "I didn't have much choice. My father picked me up and made me come."

Gina had told her own share of these half-truths in order to blend seamlessly into Original Hill. She never revealed to her neighbors any details of her cramped childhood apartment, or even what borough she had come from. She flattened the lyrical bounce in her cadence and was attentive to adding an *uh* to the ends of *mozzarella* and *ricotta*. She marveled along with her neighbors at how women and—and even young girls!—could possibly risk taking public transit alone downtown, despite having ridden buses and trains for her entire youth. No one in Original even knew that her maiden name was Moretti.

Even so, it took nearly a decade for the women at the club to stop referring to her as "the New Yorker." It took pruning and grafting and sticking it out through hard winters for Gina to grip her roots into this soil, and as curious as she was, she did not want to exacerbate Baby's process.

As Baby wove through the tables toward the restroom, Gina noticed how all the other diners seemed to adjust their seats in anticipation of her. Some shifted far out of Baby's way, while others moved so that Baby had to brush up against the seat. Introducing Baby at the club had alleviated some people's trepidation, but still, none of their neighbors offered Baby the greetings or small talk necessary for polite coexistence. But neither did they avoid her. Instead, their actions—like the adjusting of chairs—seemed contradictory. It was impossible to judge what they really thought of the girl and whether her presence made them more or less inclined to vote for Eugene come November. Although this ambiguity mildly concerned Gina, what dominated her thoughts was that secret smirk that Baby had kept on her mouth even as she'd walked away.

When Gina and Baby returned to the house on Orchard Street, Eugene once again informed Baby that Foote had dropped by to see her. Baby nodded and drifted off to the garden.

"You have to stop whisking Baby away," Eugene grunted.

"Oh, Eugene. It's just a little girl time."

"Do you really think she'd rather spend time with you than with the young man who's been showing up at her door almost every day?"

Gina refused to feel wounded by this comment. "She's her own person, Eugene. She can do as she wishes."

A condescending expression crossed her husband's face, only to then fade into general disgruntlement. "I don't want you getting too close to her."

"Eugene, that's ridiculous—"

"Are you calling me ridiculous?" Eugene barked.

Gina snapped her head back to him. She'd let this discussion go too far and it was teetering on the verge of an argument. She made some quick adjustments in her posture and tone, projecting a calm rationality that would hopefully dispel the charge building in the air.

"Why don't we have Lucius Foote over for dinner?" Gina suggested. "That way Baby won't have to choose how she spends her time."

"He won't come to dinner here. I'm his political opponent."

"He's been driving here almost every day for Baby. It's not a secret that they go out together. And I'd like to get to know the man better."

"I don't need to have dinner with that man. I already know everything I need to."

"Eugene, we are this young woman's guardians. I'm sure that her father would want us to at least have a meal with this man." Eugene scoffed. Gina glanced down at her husband's hands, which were gripping the back of a chair like it was the only thing keeping him standing. "Dear, are you feeling alright?"

"What?" Eugene grunted.

"I said—"

"*Fine,*" he interrupted. "Invite Foote to dinner. But I'm telling you, he won't agree to it."

Foote agreed to dinner at seven o'clock the next evening. That morning, Gina vacuumed the ornate Oriental rugs in the living room and the parlor twice over. She dusted the leaves, ivy, cherubs, and songbirds carved into the trim and mantel. She polished the wooden banister of the staircase that led from the entry room to the second floor and then the attic. She massaged linseed oil into the dining room table and cleaned every mirror with old newspaper. She left Eugene's office untouched but paused by the door when she overheard a hacking cough within. She made a mental note to call Dr. Wood.

As Gina prepared dinner, Baby floated in and out of the kitchen with what Gina assumed must be nerves. The girl's secretive smirk endured, distracting Gina more and more until she finally sent Baby to her room to get ready.

Gina opened the door to Foote at seven exactly. "Thank you so much for inviting me," he said, all white teeth. Gina watched with satisfaction as his eyes passed over the rich oakwood walls lit by the warm glow of the Tiffany chandeliers. "You have a beautiful home, Mrs. Fox."

"Thank you. We've tried to preserve as much of the original architecture as we can."

"How old is the house?"

"Nineteen twenty-five, I believe?"

"Really? I didn't think this neighborhood was that old."

"I believe that, originally, this was some kind of a meeting hall. When Eugene bought it in 1995, it had been in disrepair for twenty, thirty years? We had planned to knock it down, but fortunately, they found that the bones were still good and there was all this beautiful woodwork underneath." Gina stroked a ledge that had been carved to resemble a curling oak leaf.

"Must've seen the neighborhood change quite a bit," Foote said.

Before Gina could reply, Baby appeared at the top of the staircase with Eugene by her side. Dressed in her usual style of a loose vintage summer dress, the young woman glimmered beneath the light of the chandelier. Her deep eyes fixed on Gina with an intensity that sucked the air from her chest.

Eugene descended a step ahead of Baby, extending his hand to Foote, who greeted him with a smile. "I was just telling your wife how grateful I am for the invitation."

Eugene's face was stern but pleasant. "The pleasure's all mine. Now, let's eat."

Gina had grown so used to seeing Foote walking past her windows that having him inside her home felt as if a stray animal had wandered in. Still, she had to give the young man credit for his charm. He complimented her cooking and conversed in a way that was at once casual and friendly but never slipped into presumption or impropriety. Yet she could sense the faintest sheen of phoniness about him. It wasn't all-consuming—he had an earnestness that seemed true—but it was enough to make her itch.

The only time he seemed to break character was when his eyes drifted over to Baby. His broad smile would waver, and Gina could see his dark eyes deepen into bottomless pools of desire. It relieved Gina to see Foote's humanity on display, just as much as it unnerved her to see Baby's eyes reflecting desire back at him.

If Eugene noticed these clandestine glances, he did not let on. Predictably, most of the discussion centered on city council. They were careful to avoid the subject of election campaigns, instead focusing on current initiatives and gossip.

"I hear you've got your hands full with these protesters from . . ." Eugene paused. "What's it called?"

"Justice for Sankofa. They come around now and then, but they're behaving." Foote nodded.

"They only sprung up toward the end of my time. Petition after petition telling us to put up some kind of monument or establish some kind of reparations fund for an old town that was demoed way back in the fifties! I hope nobody's started taking them seriously."

Foote drank his beer. "You don't think it would be beneficial for us to make some kind of statement? Could ease some of the tension."

"I think give them an inch, they'll take a mile."

"Couldn't agree more," Foote said before turning to Gina. "You said this house was built in 1925?" Gina nodded as Foote turned back to her husband. "That puts it smack-dab in the Sankofa era. You're living in a piece of pre–Original Hill history, Fox. Don't you think we should acknowledge that?"

Gina looked to her husband, who continued to eat as he spoke. "Don't get me wrong, I think it's important to know the neighborhood's history. But what these people don't understand is that this neighborhood only had Blacks in it for about sixty years. Before that, there were French fur-trappers here. Before that, American Indians. Sure, it's important to *know* all this, but to act like we have to erase the seventy-plus years this place has been Original Hill and revert back to some arbitrary name from once upon a time? Well, you see how that wouldn't make any sense."

"You think we should be more forward-thinking," Foote said.

"Exactly."

"And what if thinking forward means Original Hill changes into something else?"

Eugene's knife froze as he sawed into his meat. "You want to know something about Original's history? I was just a boy when my daddy moved us up from Arkansas. Back then the I-94 was brand-new, and Original Hill was a fledgling community of folks looking for work. Of course, I didn't appreciate it back then. I left, worked on Wall Street for nearly ten years before I came back. A young buck has to go his own way, sow his oats, sample some other pastures."

"I know exactly what you mean." Foote smiled.

Eugene frowned. "It took mature eyes to appreciate this place for what it is."

"Well, I think that's selling young people a little short, Fox. Just because somebody doesn't have the same mileage doesn't mean that they won't appreciate a place like Original."

"Oh, age has got nothing to do with it," Eugene said. "It's all about intention. These days when people think of Original Hill, all they care about are our big houses and our money. People moving in think they need doorbells with cameras and flashy cars to prove they belong here. When I was a boy, Original had none of that. We had drive, and we had ambition, and that's how we built this neighborhood. That was a time when everybody knew one another, so you knew who you could look out for. You knew who to trust."

"Oh, Eugene, Original still looks out for each other," Gina said.

"Not like they used to. But you're right, Foote. As times

change, so will Original. But it's important not to sell this neighborhood's soul."

"Well, I think the spirit of the neighborhood can adapt to what it needs to be—"

"No." Eugene's voice was hard. "I'm talking about the thing that lives at the heart of a place. The worst thing that can happen to someplace like Original Hill is to lose its soul. It's clung on so far, but it's getting harder as more people come here for the wrong reasons."

"And how do you keep that from happening?" It was Baby who spoke, staring at Eugene with intense interest.

A peculiar expression came over his face. "Well, I think that's the job of our elected representatives. That's what democracy's about: putting our souls in our own hands." His eyes shifted to Gina. "Do you remember that year when those rabbits kept getting into the garden?"

"Yes, dear." She distinctly recalled waking up each morning and looking through the kitchen window to find their round brown rumps and cottontails nestled among her radishes and daisies.

"Remember how everybody thought I was a monster for getting rid of them?"

"I don't think the Reeds' little boy has looked at you the same way since," Gina agreed, trying to get ahead of whatever was leading her husband down this road.

"Neighbors acted like I was some bunny-murdering psychopath. But I think rabbits are just as cute as everybody else, when they're in the park or living on somebody's farm. But they shouldn't be in our garden, should they? They'd ruin all your hard work—"

Eugene was cut off by a sudden coughing fit. He

lurched forward, his entire body shaking with each hack. Gina threw her napkin onto her plate and rushed over to him, but by the time she made it to the other side of the table, the fit had subsided. He took a large swig of beer, grunted an apology, and excused himself from the table. The dinner ended with a whimper. Foote thanked Gina for the meal before whisking Baby out the door for a drive.

As Gina filled the sink with soapy water, she glanced out the window to her garden. She remembered the little bunnies hopping around her produce, the mix of joy and anxiety it spurred in her. Eugene had spared her the gory details of how he had trapped them, but she had caught a glimpse of one contraption in the garage. It had looked archaic to her—wood and twine rather than something sleek and metal. For whatever reason, this made the sudden disappearance of the rabbits more disturbing.

Gina felt a sudden lightness about her, as if gravity were weakening. Leaving the dishes to soak, she floated from one room to the other, unable to dig her heels into the floor and turn back around. As she wandered, the sconces and wainscotting seemed unfamiliar to her. She pressed her hand against one of the oakwood walls and felt a warmth, as if the house itself were a body creating its own heat. The summer wind had picked up outside, but it seemed closer than that, like the wall was breathing. Her intuition kept drawing her mind back to the discussion at dinner.

Lucius Foote had clearly been trying to unsettle her, throwing the history of her own house back in her face. She had never considered that the house at 1 Orchard

Street technically predated Original, the highway, even the name "Orchard Street." What had its address been before, she wondered. But then, what did that matter to her?

All this talk about the neighborhood's soul hadn't helped, either. Not that this was a new concept. Any change to the neighborhood, from the renovation of the school to increasing HOA fees, became a fight for Original Hill's soul. This was the political talk that Gina nodded along to politely despite the absurd melodrama. But something in the conversation seemed to have rubbed off on her house.

What if the house worried that it had lost its soul? Oh, it hadn't, it hadn't, she wanted to reassure it. *You aren't like the rest of Original Hill,* she thought to the walls and the floorboards. *You're mine.* But the house seemed closed off from her comforting. She continued to move from room to room, looking for some sense of openness, until she found herself in the attic.

A cold gust swept past Gina, sending a shiver zipping up her spine. In Queens, an attic had only ever been an idea, one that always concealed terrors. Even now, it was the one part of her house that she avoided. But the small unfinished room before her felt more inert than menacing. Stacks of boxes were covered by schmutzy tarps. Gina pulled the cord of an ancient incandescent bulb. The orange glow did more to illuminate the dust in the air than dispel the shadows.

Gina walked around the perimeter of the room, lifting the edges of tarps, bracing herself for something to crawl out. She did everything she could to convince herself that these were all nerves, that there was nothing to be afraid of. But she quickly decided that there was nothing for her here.

As she turned back toward the door, her shin knocked against a large plastic bucket. Inside, she found dark curdled swatches that streaked the smooth white surface. Tar. Next to the bucket, half hidden under a tarp, was a thirty-two-ounce can of turpentine. She gingerly lifted the tarp, which revealed a gallon can covered in thick black drips and labeled *Pure Birch Pitch.* This certainly did not seem like the sort of tar meant for roofing. Laid on top was a pair of gardening gloves that had gone missing, completely ruined with black gunk.

As she pushed these tar-stained items aside, careful not to get any on herself, she uncovered a plate from her dining set. The layer of dust suggested that it had been left here for weeks, but there was still a smattering of desiccated crumbs across its surface. Maybe Eugene had made himself a sandwich and left the plate up here. But the streak of jam perplexed her, as Eugene only ate ham or turkey sandwiches. The only one who spread jam on toast was Gina—or, of course, Baby.

There was something else strange about this corner, now that Gina was studying it. The way the boxes had been gathered around, and the tarp had been crumpled, it looked as if someone had been trying to build a large nest. An aroma drifted up from the tarp, like the air after a heavy rain. She had smelled this scent before. On Baby.

She pried open the flap of one box and discovered folds of fabric. She lifted one up, allowing it to unfold into the shape of a blouse. Beneath it, she found a pleated skirt, khaki culottes, and sundresses all in the style of something

Gina's mother might have worn in her youth. They also, she realized, looked exactly like the dresses Baby wore.

As she unfolded another, a framed photograph came tumbling out of the fabric and slammed onto the floor, sending an echo throughout the dim room. Gina carefully lifted it up and was grateful to see that the glass had not shattered. Within the frame, a black-and-white photograph of a teenager with an enthusiastic smile, bright eyes, and Sandra Dee–blond waves grinned back at Gina. She recognized the debutante as Eugene's mother, Babette, who had died when he was very young. These must be her clothes, then. Gina put everything back into the box and left the attic, her intuition buzzing.

Gina was in the kitchen when she heard the front door click shut. "Baby, could you help me rinse these dishes?" Gina called.

"Oh, sure." Baby laughed, dancing into the kitchen. The young woman slipped off her gloves and began to scrape the sponge over the soapy china. As they stood side by side, only inches between them, Gina felt as if there were a third person in the room. The house itself seemed to have abandoned its soul-searching and refocused on Baby.

Gina eyed the vintage sundress the young woman was wearing. The colors seemed old and faded like a hand-me-down, and it didn't fit her well at all. Her eyes trailed up to Baby's face, where she once more found that secret smirk quietly lurking on her lips.

"Baby. Where did you get that dress?"

"Father gave it to me," she replied matter-of-factly.

"Really?" Gina mused. "Did Eugene ever give you any dresses?" Gina noticed the circular motions of Baby's sponge slowing.

"No."

"Never? Not even as a gift?"

"I— I don't think—"

"Have you been going into the attic, dear?"

"Attic?"

"Don't lie to me, Baby."

"I'm not lying—"

"I know that you've been in the attic, Baby, so why were you up there?" Gina shouted, turning to face Baby. The look of shock on the young woman's face thrilled her.

"I— I wasn't—" Baby stuttered.

"I said don't lie to me!" Gina roared, snatching Baby's wrist away from the plate.

A rush of clarity nearly knocked Gina back. She saw the fear and confusion in Baby's eyes. She realized how irrational she was being. The girl had answered her questions, and she had snapped at her. Soapy water ran down Baby's wrist to Gina's and slapped onto the floor.

Gina released Baby and took a step back. Her hand flew to her forehead, as if searching for some kind of fever to account for her actions.

"I'm sorry, Baby, I don't know what that was . . ." she began. and arrested one apology after another, her words failing her. Without knowing what else to do, Gina scooped the girl into her arms, pressing her cheek against Baby's. "I'm sorry, Baby," Gina moaned. "I'm so, so sorry."

Then she felt the girl delicately place her bare arms around Gina's neck. "It's okay," Baby whispered in Gina's ear. "It's okay."

It makes me happy to complete Father's prophesy, to discover my One and Only. But the moment I let go of my One and Only's hand, his touch fades back to craving. I want to crash my body into his again and again, to let him bury his fingers in the depths of my soil. I want him to stick. But instead, I feel like one of my lovertrees, locked in its concrete cell.

Then, she touches me.

It hurts, her tight and angry grip. But we try again. Her skin meets mine with tenderness. When we part, she kisses me Goodnight. The world resets its pieces, but I am still here.

I am so happy, I soak my cheeks in tears.

Lucky

•

Baby's gloved hand was clasped in Lucky's as they strode up to Stu Hoffman, who was waiting by the construction site downtown. "Hottest fucking day in July, and they've got us out here," Lucky's campaign manager said before gesturing over to a table of refreshments. "Get yourself something to eat, sweetheart. You look thin as a bird. And there's shade, too."

Baby kissed Lucky's cheek before drifting over to the table. Watching her walk away, the memory of her lips prickled on his skin.

"You look like shit. What the hell is going on with you?"

Lucky flashed the older man a smile. "What are you talking about?"

Stu kept his voice just above a whisper. "I'm talking about, you haven't been picking up my calls. I'm talking about, I've been hearing you haven't been picking up *anybody's* calls. Haven't been showing up to City Hall."

"I've been busy."

"Busy with what? What the fuck could you possibly be so busy with, because it sure as hell isn't anything I've set up to help you get reelected. Is this what I have to do, show up myself to get you to cart your ass to these things?"

"What *is* this thing, Stu?"

"The city's breaking ground on that family center *you* voted in favor of, remember? They want you to hold the shovel or something. Who gives a *fuck*. The point is, there's a photographer here ready to take a picture of you in a hard hat, just like there've been photographers at every other event I had you booked on, but you *didn't show*. Do you think this is how I want to spend my time?"

Stu pulled a cigarette from his back pocket. Lucky took out his lighter and lit it for him. "Stu, my constituents are in Original Hill. I've been spending my time there. If you were still around, you'd see—"

"I told you, I am done with Original, Lucius. Happy to rent out the property, and happy to help you out, but after twenty years there with those *people*—"

"Stu, you are the only person I know who has ever wanted to get *out* of Original."

Stu patted Lucky's cheek. "Maybe I'll come back once it's *your* Original Hill." He took a long drag and exhaled. "Listen, kid, you've got a spark. I know that. You know that. But it takes more than schmoozing to win an election against somebody like Fox. You can't just not show up to these obligations. And when you do show up, your face can't look like you haven't slept in days."

But Lucky *hadn't* slept in days. He glanced over to

Baby, who had drawn a small crowd around her. *Like moths to a streetlamp,* he thought. His stomach cramped, pleading him to grab her arm and take her away from them.

Stu followed Lucky's gaze and frowned. "Where's that dress I sent over for her? The red number?"

"She didn't like it," Lucky said. He was glad that the dress she had decided to wear was long enough that it hid her feet. He assumed she wasn't wearing any shoes.

Stu's frown deepened. "I'll put you in contact with a couple stylists. They might be able to work with her, even just set her up with some fittings, a hair salon—"

"Stu, I told you, she doesn't like to be touched."

"Well, you tell her that she *has* to be touched. That's part of being in the public eye—you belong to the public. They have the right to touch you."

"Does it look like anybody cares about what she's wearing?" Lucky laughed, nodding to the ever-growing throng of people surrounding Baby. Of course, Lucky understood Stu's concern. It was almost inconceivable how people were embracing a dark-skinned woman with natural—and not just natural, but barely styled—hair, who dressed in flimsy vintage sundresses. Yet, everywhere they went, people were fascinated by her. At dinners, the kitchen would offer her free dessert. On walks, she could hardly take five steps without being complimented. Original Hill, as taciturn as it may be, was steadily coming around to her.

Stu watched Baby smile to her crop of fans and nodded. "She does have a spark. Maybe better than yours, kid." He took another drag and chuckled through his teeth. "Never in a million years would I have thought you and Fox's niece . . . Then again, I never would have thought Fox's niece would look like *that.*" Stu shot Lucky a glance. "Have you talked to him?"

"We've had dinner."

"Pure carnivore, I bet. Any inside information?"

Lucky shook his head. "We tried not to talk shop, but you know Fox. He thinks he's trying to save Original's soul."

Stu scoffed. "From you?"

"From bunny rabbits."

Stu puffed on his cigarette. "Look, Lucius, don't get me wrong. I'm glad to see you've got something steady going on. But what's important right now is your image."

Lucky furrowed his brow. "Look at her! She's great for my image."

"Of course she's great! Who's saying she isn't great? It's *you* who's the problem," Stu said. "I don't want you getting distracted."

Lucky smirked. But the truth was, he had not realized how many campaign events he had missed, how many calls had gone unanswered. He couldn't even recall the last time he had driven down to City Hall.

When he thought back on the past few weeks, it was all Baby. When he wasn't with her, he longed to be, and when he was, he wanted to press himself against her, let her seep under his skin. Lucky suspected the intensity of his craving was a result of how slowly they were taking the relationship. They'd been seeing each other for a month, and he had hardly gone further than slipping his hands beneath her dress. Compared to his past situations, this pace was glacial.

Of course, he always tried to be a gentleman, but he usually wasn't concerned with keeping a woman around beyond one or two public appearances. With Baby, things had to be different. Not just because he saw real potential for them but because he couldn't give Fox any fodder against him.

It wasn't as if Baby was against taking things further. Her sensitivity to touch did not seem to extend to Lucky. If anything, she was enthusiastic at their brief moments of intimacy, when they were sitting in his car in the evening and his palm would graze her thigh or the base of her neck. During their last drive, she had grabbed his hand and pressed it against her collarbone, letting his fingers slip beneath the soft floral fabric of her dress.

And *he* had pulled away. Why? Because when his palm felt the hardness of her clavicle, he'd been hit by an overwhelming urge to shove both his arms inside her sternum.

He had no idea where that sudden, grotesque fantasy had come from. Baby inspired so many strange desires in him. He assured himself it was the anticipation and sexual frustration, exacerbated by the uncanny distance he felt whenever they touched. He could never fully recall the sensation of touching her. Even in the moment, Lucky felt outside of his body, looking down at their points of contact from afar. Was this part of the game she was playing, this inability to fully feel her?

A small part of him was grateful for the fact that he was so addicted to Baby's touch. He *needed* to want her, to not resist her. As all-encompassing as she was, it would be worse for his campaign—his *image*—if he stopped desiring her.

An electric jolt shot through Lucky's arm, and he looked over to see Baby's gloved hand stroking his. Her mother-of-pearl-button eyes were dulled. "I'm starting to get a little tired," she said.

"I'll see if we can go ahead and get started," Stu said, excusing himself.

"Why don't we sit?" Lucky suggested, guiding her over to a stone bench. Baby slumped down and laid her head on Lucky's shoulder. "Is the heat getting to you?" Lucky asked, wiping some sweat from his own forehead.

"I'd just like to get back home soon," Baby said, her voice small.

"Soon," Lucky promised, running his hand along her bare arm. Trips downtown seemed to tire Baby out. In fact, the farther he took her from Original Hill, the more lethargic and distant she became. She would doze off in the middle of movies or lay her head down at their table in the middle of dinner. Everything south of the I-94 was off-limits. Whenever they approached the Orchard Street Bridge, Baby would dig her nails into the seat and press herself back. Before he came close to crossing the highway, she would tell him that she felt physically ill, and could he pull over? But as soon as they returned to Original, she was energetic as ever.

Even with the weight of her head on his shoulder, Lucky felt a buffer between them. The cramp in his gut twisted, tempting him to tear off his jacket and shirt, to press her temple into the meat of his pectoral. Thankfully, Stu Hoffman came hustling up to them.

"Alright, they're ready to start. You okay, sweetheart?"

"Let's get her some water," Lucky said, helping Baby to her feet. They walked over to the foreman and line of city officials standing in front of the photographer. Baby seemed almost weightless in his arms, as if he were guiding a balloon. Stu handed them cups of water as someone placed a hard hat on both of their heads and offered Lucky a shovel. He flashed his red-carpet smile and spent a few minutes chatting with folks as the photographer took candids. Lucky's eyes kept drifting back to Baby, who seemed lost in thought. He asked Hoffman to get her two more cups of water before the photographer gathered them all into a group.

"Alright, let's do a few like this," the photographer announced. "One . . . two . . . three!"

The flash snapped and Baby quivered beside Lucky. "Stay still. It's almost done, okay?" Lucky whispered.

"One . . . two . . . three!" The second flash snapped. "Okay, now we want to get one of you actually breaking the ground."

"Just aim the shovel right there," the foreman told Lucky, pointing to a painted neon line in the dirt beneath their feet.

"Alright, everyone ready?" Lucky chuckled. He glanced once more to Baby, who fixated on the same spot in the dirt. Lucky lifted the shovel.

"One . . . two—"

"Who the hell are they?" one of the officials asked.

Down the street, a group of five or six protesters had appeared, holding signs and chanting. Most of them were Black. As they drew closer, Lucky could read *Justice for Sankofa* on the largest sign. He smirked, turned to the other officials, and said, "This'll just take a minute."

Stu intercepted as Lucky stepped away from the group. "You sure you don't just want to let the police deal with them?" An officer was already headed toward the approaching group.

Lucky shook his head. "I'll handle it."

Flashing his red-carpet smile, Lucky asked the cop to stand by before he approached the woman at the front of the modest protest. She was dressed in all black with long braids down the side of her head, a nose piercing, and a defiant scowl.

Lucky grinned. "Hey, Nia. How's it hanging?"

"Lower than yours, Luck," she scoffed.

"Now, Nia, what're you all doing here? We're nowhere near City Hall or Original."

"But it looks like we found its city councilmember. And about time," Nia spat. "We've been calling your office for weeks and you've been stonewalling us."

"I promise I haven't," Lucky said, gilding his tone with sincerity. "Truth be told, I've had some personal stuff going on. But I give you my word here and now that I will make time for you all in my calendar next week."

"What an honor."

"Please." Lucky smiled. "These people just want to get this done and get out of the heat. They can't do anything about Original Hill or Sankofa. Let's make things easy."

"Then let's talk now," Nia said.

"I would, but I'm not exactly alone." Lucky gestured to the crowd. He noticed Baby was still staring at the dirt.

"If you want us to keep quiet, we'll talk now," Nia said.

"Look, there's just one more photo, and then everybody else can go. I'll come to you right after we're done here. Okay?"

Nia conferred with the other protesters before nodding. Lucky smiled and strolled back toward the group, where Stu caught him and whispered, "We got some great photos of you talking them down. Shit's gold."

Lucky nodded, though his attention was trained on Baby. Her shoulders were slouched, and her arms hung at her sides, but her eyes had not moved from the spot on the ground. *She looks like she's melting,* Lucky thought. He had to get this over with quick. He took the shovel and lifted it as the photographer lifted her camera.

"One . . . two . . ."

On three, the camera flash snapped, and Lucky buried the shovel in the dirt. Something hard crashed into his side. It took him a moment to realize that Baby had fainted onto him.

By the time they made it back to Orchard Street, Baby was bright and chipper. There had been a small hullabaloo after she passed out, with people fanning her and running for water while Lucky carried her into his car. Baby came to as he started to drive, and though he asked if they should go to the hospital, she insisted he take her home. Now, she was looking out the window as if nothing had happened.

"You sure you're alright?" he asked.

Baby nodded. "I just can't be away from home too long."

"Is that why your father kept you inside—in that *room*?" Whenever Lucky thought of Baby's father, his blood boiled. She had not said much about the man since the Midsummer Soiree, but it was enough to sustain his disgust. Just imagining Baby shut up in some room like a prisoner, or a princess in a fairy-tale tower . . .

But rather than answer Lucky's question, Baby reached over and slid her finger beneath the collar of his shirt. His skin began to burn, and all thought of Baby's past fell away to an urgent desire to grab the woman in his arms. So, he did, pulling her to him and pressing his lips against hers. As their tongues teased each other, he sensed her fingers wrap around his hand and draw it beneath her dress. She squeezed his forearm between her thighs as his fingers disappeared inside her. He kept his lips pasted to her mouth and urged his hand deeper, but he still felt the separation. She was there, her body humming beneath his, but he could not feel her.

Ten minutes later, he was watching her walk from his car to the Foxes' house, past the garden wall, and through the front door. Lucky's entire body felt strangely numb. He could feel none of the lingering sensation of what he and Baby had just done. He beat his fist against the steering wheel. Why was this happening to him? He needed to know, needed to fill in the sensation that seemed to have been redacted from his memory. He was tempted to jump out of the car and run after her. But then, Lucky noticed movement out of the corner of his eye.

~

Mr. Reed was perched halfway on a ladder along the side of his house. He seemed to be deciding whether he was going up or down. It was much too hot and too late in the day to be doing roof work, yet he stayed put, only turning his head now and then to look across the street to the Foxes' house. Lucky shouted a hello to him, but the man seemed not to hear him.

Next door at the Thornes' house, Lucky noticed the curtains open, then close, then open again. He was concentrating so hard, he jumped when Mr. and Mrs. Ives walked by. Lucky waved at them through his window, but they did not look his way. Instead, they slowed to a snail's pace as they approached the Foxes'. Though they never fully stopped, Lucky watched their feet leave their heads behind as they craned to look through the windows until their spines forced them to move on. Once they turned the corner, Lucky put the car into gear and sped away toward the faded cul-de-sac on the other side of the Orchard Street Bridge.

"What's come over you?" were the first words Auntie Riri said when she answered the door. As he stepped into the house, he guarded his nostrils against the familiar but nevertheless jarring smoky odor. Then he saw that they weren't alone.

Nia was stationed at Auntie Riri's kitchen table, straddling a chair with her combat boots solidly on the floor. Some official-looking forms were laid out before her. She glared at him with a disdain that he knew was reserved especially for him, which he countered with his most brilliant red-carpet grin.

"You left us hanging, Luck."

"There were extenuating circumstances."

"How is she?"

"She's alright now. Just the heat," Lucky said, taking a seat at the table. "Where's the rest of your posse?"

"Work. Kids. Getting them to show up today was enough of an ask."

"Not everyone has poet hours, I guess."

Nia cut her eyes at him. "And where the hell have you been in all this time? 'Personal stuff'?"

"I swear, it is nothing personal to you or the rest of the Sankofa crew, okay?" Lucky glanced down at the forms. "I see you've got Auntie Riri working like always."

"We're prepping for our presentation to the new EDI coalition in City Hall. Right, Auntie?"

"Sure thing, baby," Auntie Riri said, taking a bunch of black bananas out of a paper bag.

Lucky grunted, just loud enough to elicit a look from Nia. "Something the matter?" she growled.

"Not at all." He smirked. "Just glad our EDI coalition's getting some use."

"Well, it's not like city council's been much help."

"I told you all the last time, you need to choose your battles. What you're proposing as 'reparations' for Sankofa is too much—"

"From Uncle Tom's lips—"

"Will you two stop bickering and somebody help me peel these bananas?" Auntie Riri snapped. Nia and Lucky both stood and Auntie Riri handed each a banana. "Plenty to get done once you stop your nonsense," she said, rubbing her wrists as she measured out the flour.

Lucky shot Nia a smile, which she pretended not to

see. He knew that her dislike toward him was only a principled aversion to all politicians, and he delighted in the few times he could get her to smirk or scoff, when he knew that even she couldn't resist his gift. But right now, he was too distracted to concentrate on that. His mind was still in front of that house at 1 Orchard Street.

Lucky moved to peek over Auntie Riri's shoulder as she mixed the mashed banana into the brown sugar and butter.

"Why're you crowding me?"

"Let me take some strain off your hands."

"She doesn't need your help," Nia warned.

"Well, I'm asking *her.*"

"Well, I'm *telling you*—"

"Oh, you two," Auntie Riri sighed.

"All in good fun, Auntie," Lucky crooned, kissing the older woman's temple.

Her wrinkled hand flew up to the spot where his lips had touched her. "What's gotten into you?" she demanded.

"What do you mean?"

"It's like part of you never walked through the door." She held his hand in her own. "Baby, is something the matter?"

Lucky chuckled, extricating himself. "What? No. I— I just met someone."

"She's pretty, too," Nia said. "I'm surprised a girl like that would suffer your ass."

"Where did you meet her?" Auntie Riri asked.

"She's the Foxes' niece."

Auntie Riri chuckled. "That old man? You find your dates in the strangest places, don't you?"

"Isn't Fox the guy that's running against you? *That's* his niece? I never would've guessed—" Nia tossed her peels in the trash. "She can't be from Original?"

"Of course not."

"Well, where's she from?" Auntie Riri asked.

"Middle of nowhere, I guess."

"You *guess*?" Nia frowned.

"She doesn't talk about it much," Lucky said.

"Maybe you just don't know how to talk to her."

"You don't think I know how to talk to my woman?"

"Most men don't." Nia smirked.

"It's got nothing to do with me. She's quiet."

"Well, are you giving her Lucky Foote the Golden Boy, or are you giving her something real?"

"And who says the Golden Boy isn't real?" Lucky smiled.

Nia shrugged. "I'm just saying she's probably giving you right back what you give her, which sounds like a whole lot of nothing."

"Look, I think she got out of a bad situation. That's why she doesn't talk about it. She moved in with the Foxes around the start of the summer—"

"And she somehow bumped into you. Poor girl," Nia said.

"This summer? She's been living with that man Fox since the start of summer?" Auntie Riri asked. She had stopped stirring the batter. Lucky nodded. "Is she a Black girl?"

Lucky chuckled. "Auntie, what does that—"

"As Black as you or me." Nia cut him off. "I mean, I only saw her from a distance. Luck didn't introduce—"

"Oh!" Auntie Riri gasped. Her eyes were focused beyond Lucky, as if his body had suddenly become transparent.

"Auntie, you okay?" Lucky asked. He caught something shift in Auntie Riri's eyes before she refocused on him. A dreamy, melancholic smile lifted the edges of the woman's lips.

"Would you bring her around sometime? I'd really like to meet her."

Lucky nodded. "Sure, Auntie. Whatever you like."

"Soon?"

"Yeah. Soon."

Returning to his townhouse that evening, Lucky couldn't shake that look in Auntie Riri's eyes. He seemed to have vanished from the old woman's field of view. He knocked his shoulder against the doorframe as he entered. The enduring throb comforted him.

Moving through the dark rooms of the townhouse, he considered what Nia had said. Condescending as she might have been, maybe she was right. Maybe Baby's quiet nature wasn't as genuine as Lucky had first thought. He was convinced that she had developed her own magnetic gift while being trapped in her own dead-end reality, just as he had done in Briar Heights. That was the only explanation for her gravitational pull, for the swift change in the neighborhood's regard toward her. But it also meant that everything he knew about her was pose and posture, hidden by her silences—just like everything that he'd given her was hidden behind his red-carpet smile.

So, that must be the game, then—the game they'd been playing ever since he first saw her on the garden wall. Was that why he couldn't feel her? Why every touch was ephemeral? It wasn't just that her touch was fleeting; she was denying him the sensation. She was teasing him. His gut twisted angrily, making him bite the inside of his cheek.

Passing the bathroom, he noticed a dark shadow dart by in the mirror. He froze before realizing that it was only his own reflection. Maybe Nia was right. Maybe the only way for him to win this game—to *really* feel her—was to offer her something real, something he had never offered another soul.

I have made up a game.

I started it after my Goodnight Kiss touched me and the world reset its pieces once more. Father had warned me so often to never, ever let my skin touch another's, so I imagined that something awful would happen to both of us. Maybe we would be pulled out of this world and thrust into the dark-loudhot place, like socks stuffed into a drawer. But nothing happened to me or her, except that she returned again and again. Her kisses are so gentle and warm, nothing like the exploration and dance of my One and Only's touch.

So I have made a game of slipping off my glove, now and then, to rub my hand against a wall, a window, a lampshade, an apple in the kitchen. I note how differently it all feels against the naked pads of my fingers before putting my glove back on. I know I am disobeying, but that is part of the fun. I have to be quick and clever so that no one sees me. I am getting very good at it.

I have been listening to the voices of things for so long, but now I feel them against my palm. It is as if I was never really in the world before, and now I am a part of it. Still, the voices do not speak with me directly. They find me peculiar.

Gina

•

She and Baby had a secret now. Every night, before Gina retired to her room, she gave Baby a goodnight kiss. It might have been a fleeting gesture, her lips pressed to the divot at the center of the girl's forehead for only a moment, but Gina found herself looking forward to this kiss from the moment she awoke each morning.

Every minute leading up to the goodnight kiss was tinged with a mild but relentless discomfort, as if she were walking in new shoes. It began when Foote arrived to whisk Baby away and grew increasingly more bothersome until Baby's return. Sometimes Gina would accompany Eugene on his campaign appearances and photo ops, playing her well-practiced part as the politician's wife. But even Eugene noticed her constant fidgeting and readjusting, and so he left her at home more and more often.

Alone in the house, her mind always wandered back to Baby. She would lose whole hours of the day sitting at the kitchen table just thinking about the young woman. If she wasn't careful, a memory of Baby's wonderful eyes or the heat of her forehead beneath her lips would cause Gina to burn a batch of cookies or leave the freezer open to spoil all the meat.

The only reliable way Gina found to avoid these greedy thoughts was to concentrate on the persistent strangeness of her house. Perplexing details had begun to reveal themselves after she discovered the bucket of tar and the box of dresses in the attic. The rooms, for instance, seemed too large for the furniture inside them. The swans depicted in the wallpaper all had their necks turned around and eggs balanced on their backs. The carved cherubs that decorated the trim around the fireplace had curls that were too tight and noses that were wide and flat. There were moments when, if she concentrated hard enough, she could almost hear what sounded like the hum of a conversation, miles away. But if she tried to focus in on the voices, she would exert herself into a throbbing headache. Most disturbing was the perpetual feeling that her house seemed to be watching her, or rather, looking past her, searching for something behind her back.

Was this some latent effect of that awful odor? Gina would sniff the air now and again, but she only caught the pleasant rot and earthiness of the coming fall. Still, she wasn't entirely convinced the odor hadn't seeped into her walls and was now leaching out some terrible toxin confounding her senses.

And why hadn't she smelled the odor on the plastic bucket or canister of pitch in the attic? Of course, it was very possible that the odor had simply faded over the past few months, but her intuition told her it was not that simple.

It was difficult to attribute her unmoored feelings to some subtle poison when everyone else in the house seemed to be doing extraordinarily well. All through August, Eugene's ratings ticked higher and higher. According to Mr. Thorne, he would overtake Foote long before election day. Gina picked up grumblings from the neighbors about missed calls to Foote's office, late arrivals to luncheons and his own speeches, and campaign promises that must have gone stale. However, they spoke of these as if they were unfortunate blunders rather than reflective of Foote's character. If Foote knew anything about this, he certainly did not hint at it when he picked up or dropped off Baby at the front door.

Rather, Gina began to notice an intensity in the man's eyes as he watched Baby step into the house, as if he were about to snatch her back and take her away. Gina made sure to shut and lock the front door after a terse farewell. She took to standing by the bay windows, waiting for Foote to drive away, which took longer and longer each day. One evening, Gina waited three whole hours, only realizing how much time had passed when Baby came to request her goodnight kiss. When she returned to her spot by the window, the car was gone.

But Foote was not the only one acting more oddly around Baby. Gina had been pleased, at first, when the neighbors finally began to approach the girl. Whenever Gina brought Baby to the club, the ladies would immediately strike up a conversation.

"You have such interesting hair."

"How do you keep your skin so smooth?"

"Oh, what gorgeous eyes!"

Mrs. Ives or Burdock or Bush would offer any number of compliments before reaching out to touch Baby's hair or cheek. With Eugene's warning ringing in her ears, Gina found herself constantly having to push her body in between Baby and her neighbors. Gina's mother would have told these women to "keep those mitts to yourself," but of course, she wanted Baby to make a good impression. She was just glad that she could intervene on the girl's behalf.

But there were other peculiar things. When Gina took Baby shopping for new clothes to replace Eugene's mother's, she had to reassure three separate clerks that had been silently following them that they did not need any assistance. And at the grocery store, whenever Gina stopped her cart, not a single other wheel would squeak until she continued on.

One afternoon, as she watched Baby browse the candies on display in Bush's store, Gina felt a presence by her side. She turned to see Ms. Branch staring at her. The woman shuffled over to Gina and, just above a whisper, asked, "How did she know?"

"I'm sorry?" Gina replied.

Ms. Branch's eyes darted over to Baby. "At the Midsummer Soiree. She . . . put her head by my stomach, and a week later I had my first morning sickness."

"I'm ready," Baby said cheerily, standing by Gina with a packet of strawberry candies.

"How did you know?" Ms. Branch groaned, grasping at Baby. Gina intervened, grabbing the woman's hand

and congratulating her on the wonderful news before hustling them over to Bush's counter to check out.

After this episode, Gina decided to mention the neighbors' behavior to Eugene. "They keep trying to touch her," she explained as her husband proofread a campaign speech in his study.

Eugene looked at her sternly. "You haven't let them, have you?"

"Of course not," she scoffed. "But I don't know about when she's out with Foote—"

"He won't let anybody else touch her."

"Well, I certainly hope you're right," Gina said incredulously, though somehow, she knew that he was.

"Maybe you shouldn't take her out on errands anymore," Eugene suggested.

Gina nodded, though she felt a lump the size of a golf ball lodge in her throat. Baby's company seemed the only remedy to her constant discomfort, and Foote was already keeping her away more than Gina could bear. Baby was coming home later and later, with more secret smiles stowed away, reserved just for him. Gina already had trouble sleeping at night, her mind overrun with images of the two of them together. She couldn't imagine what would happen if the only time that she saw Baby was when they shared their secret goodnight kiss.

Gina jumped at the sound of Eugene clearing his throat. It sounded unnatural, more like gravel rolling in a tin can than anything human. "Dear, that cough—" Gina ventured.

"Oh, I'm fine. It's just getting to be that time of year."

"But you've had it for months. Don't you think you

should see . . ." But Eugene had turned his chair away from Gina, his concentration back on his work.

Leaving Eugene to his speech, Gina decided to peek into Baby's room. She found the young woman seated at the vanity, combing her hair. Baby's gaze shifted to Gina's reflection beside hers in the mirror. She smiled.

"Going out tonight?" Gina asked, drifting into the room.

"No. I told Lucky I didn't feel like going out," Baby hummed.

Gina watched her comb her thick head of hair. "Wouldn't you like to go to the salon sometime? They could do something nice with it. Straighten it, or give it some curl like mine—"

"I can't have anybody touch my hair," Baby said, simply, beginning to twist her hair into plaits.

"Of course." Gina nodded. "Does Lucius like it that way?"

"He likes whatever I do."

That secret smirk reappeared on Baby's lips in the mirror, held for so long that Gina feared it might burn itself into the glass permanently. She said, "Do you like the way that he touches you?"

The comment wiped the smirk from Baby's lips. She turned around and looked directly at Gina, one completed plait hanging over her shoulder and the other half done. Her eyes were filled with wonder, and she spoke in a hoarse whisper. "Sometimes. I'm still deciding, I think. I've wanted to touch somebody for such a long time, and I just haven't been able to."

"Why?"

"My father told me that I'm only supposed to touch one person, my One and Only. He told me horrible things would happen if I touched other people."

"I see." Gina nodded. "But maybe he meant touching them in a certain way, you know, or in certain places?"

Baby had begun to study her fingers. "Maybe."

"You've touched me and nothing horrible has happened, right?" Gina offered.

"Yes, I know. And, really, you don't know how happy that makes me." Baby grinned. "But I can't be careless, or else I might have to go back to that place, where I was before."

"You mean with your father?"

Baby's smile faded. "I don't want to go back there."

"You never have to go," Gina said, kneeling beside Baby and pressing her hand against the girl's cheek. Static seemed to tickle her palms. "You never have to leave this place, ever. Do you understand, dear?"

"But my father—"

"You may be his daughter, but you're still an adult human being. You're free to make your own decisions."

"But I love him."

"Lucky?"

"My father."

Gina exhaled. "Of course you do."

"I don't want to disappoint him. He's put so much into me."

Gina nodded. "That's what fathers do. That's how they love you. But you're still your own person, Baby. And if it's what you want, I can personally ensure you stay here. Just have faith."

Baby lifted her naked hand and placed it against Gina's own cheek. Gina could hear the blood rushing in her ears. "Gina, you care for me so much."

It was strange. She knew that Baby's hand was touching her skin—she could see it in her periphery—but it felt as if the palm were floating just beside it. There was a distance still to be traversed, stoking a need so urgent that Gina immediately leaned in and crashed her lips against Baby's forehead. Then she stood and wished Baby goodnight. It wasn't until she'd stopped to catch her breath in the hallway that she realized how fast her heart was pounding in her chest.

Gina went up to her bedroom, where she undressed, donned her pajamas, let her own hair down in the mirror, and began to brush it. She watched her other hand reach up and touch her bottom lip. How had the phantom pressure of Baby's forehead faded already?

After a dozen strokes, Gina's reflection yielded to images of Baby's wonder-filled eyes, radiant smile, and impossibly soft skin. She felt the urge to leap forward and kiss the apples of the girl's cheeks, the dimples on the tip of her nose and brow, the part in the center of her hair. She wanted to hold Baby and rock her to the rhythm of the brushstrokes. This desire to squeeze the girl safely in her arms was so overwhelming that it made her sick to her stomach. She had never felt anything so wild yet concentrated. She searched for a word that could possibly encapsulate this desire she had to keep the girl wholly, exclusively.

Her pale cheeks rouged scarlet in the mirror when she finally realized what to call it. This was love.

In Gina's world, love was an act, not a sensation. It was a brand you bore. Gina's name was an act of love. She had grown up among so many Michaels, Anthonys, Maries, and Annes that her brothers and cousins had required prefixes to be distinguished—"I'm looking for Patsy's Michael," or "Go give this to Antonia's Marie." Part of this was practicality, but laying claim to one's child was a way of loving them.

As the sole Giuseppina, she had never required a prefix; there was never a question that she was Giuseppe's girl. Her father wouldn't allow any nicknames, so she had dragged her full Christian name from childhood through adolescence into adulthood, fielding all manner of mispronunciations, belabored sighs at its length, and sideways glances at its ethnic-ness. She had borne it all because she knew that this was love—unconcealable and therefore, at times, awkward and embarrassing.

She had suspected that she might be in love with Eugene after he began to call her Gina. This was confirmed when her girlfriends began to tease her by referring to her as *Gene's* Gina. She was worried what her father might say, but if he ever did disapprove, he never let on. It seemed right that as her last name became her husband's, so did her first.

But this love she felt for Baby was nothing like that. This love was unspoken, unseen, expressed only through the clandestine contact of skin on skin. She had never desired to exert a claiming love onto a child of her own, yet now all Gina could think of was grasping Baby close to her body and shooing away the rest of the world—the Lucius Footes, the gossipy neighbors, even Eugene. She needed Baby to stay with her in her house. Without that kiss, she would have no reason to wake in the morning.

But she realized that it was not Lucius Foote or any of her neighbors who threatened the girl's time with Gina. Someone else had the power to take the girl away, and if Gina was to keep her here, she would have to speak with a specter.

Neither Eugene nor Baby would help her find Isaac Fox. However, her intuition told her that her husband was in contact with his brother. Hadn't Baby alluded to such a thing weeks ago? Now, Gina was happy to have the house to herself so that she could steal away to the study. She rifled through Eugene's desk, shuffling papers around and then around again as if the movement might shake out the information. She slipped her hand beneath Eugene's side of the mattress. She scrolled through the desktop computer's trash, the browser's search history, and months of emails in her husband's inbox. When Eugene was in the shower, she would confiscate his phone and investigate his messages and call log. She could not find a contact for his brother, nor any calls to a new number.

Sometimes Gina would stop and wonder why she was sneaking around behind her husband's back like a woman having an affair. She had always thought curiosity a puerile distraction, especially when she could depend so wholly on her intuition. Besides, hadn't she decided long ago that Isaac was better left untouched? Hadn't Eugene made as much clear with that withering look? But Baby had reignited the search. Gina didn't know what she truly knew anymore, except that she wanted to continue loving Baby, come what may.

As if responding to her newfound curiosity, the house shifted again. One evening, when Baby was out with Foote and Eugene was quartered in his study, Gina noticed a drawer in the entryway table on which the landline telephone sat. It had always been there, she knew, but the house had become so alien to her that the drawer seemed to appear out of nowhere. Inside, she found their family phone book, a lined pad of paper, a dead moth, and a small white envelope addressed to Eugene.

From the envelope, she extracted a folded piece of peachy stationery with a shy-looking cartoon girl in the corner, pouting with ginger pigtails and eyes half the size of her head. On it, Gina found a message: *Hello Cousin, I was looking through those old albums and thought you might like this. You and Gina should come down and visit soon! Love, Cousin Maryjean.*

Gina had met Cousin Maryjean once, on her wedding day. That was the only time she had met any of Eugene's family, who had come up to New York from Arkansas. She remembered Cousin Maryjean as a well-meaning but forgetful woman who, like the rest of Eugene's relatives, marveled at the quality of the silver in a way that prompted Gina to count the flatware afterward.

It was no surprise that Eugene preferred to keep his family at arm's length. Gina herself possessed a New Yorker's apprehension toward Southerners. Her primary association with that part of the country was a story that her father had recounted about a few of his uncles who had narrowly escaped being lynched after working in an integrated factory in Louisiana. She was glad that Eugene never asked her to take a trip down there.

Gina slipped a small wallet-size photo out from the envelope, depicting a father, a mother, and a young boy. Strangely, she recognized Eugene's mother before Eugene, the bouncy strawberry blond curls and the gray eyes she'd given her son. Six-year-old Eugene clung to his mother's visibly pregnant belly. Isaac Fox—the phantom brother, Baby's father, Eugene's original mystery.

Gina flipped through the phone book until she landed on Cousin Maryjean's number. The phone rang twice before someone picked up. "Cousin Maryjean? It's Gina. Eugene's Gina."

"*Gina!*" the woman's voice blared from the phone. "Well, well it is *good* to hear from you. Ed, it's Gina— Yes, Eugene's Gina!"

"Yes, hello, Cousin Maryjean—"

"How *is* Cousin Eugene? Is he there?"

"No, he isn't home right now. But he sends his love," Gina lied. The sound of a door shutting and movement on the stairs caught her ear. Her heart thudded against her ribs. "Maryjean, I was wondering if I could ask you about Isaac—Eugene's brother. Do you know where he is?"

"Oh, of course. I mean, he's down here."

The receiver trembled in her fist. "He's . . . down there?"

"Course he is," Cousin Maryjean laughed. "Why, did you want to see him?"

"I— Yes. Yes, I would." Gina heard the stairs creaking. She had to finish the call, but she couldn't help asking, "Maryjean, do you know about Baby?"

"What about her?" the woman asked.

She could hear Cousin Maryjean's breath against her ear, but Gina couldn't form words. She didn't know where to begin. She could hear feet descending the final set of steps. She whispered, "I have to go, Cousin Maryjean—"

"Should I call you back?"

"No!" Gina said, imagining if Eugene happened to pick up the phone. "I mean— Why don't I call you? Or I'll come visit?"

"Okay, hon'. Whenever you and Eugene make it down here, our doors are open. Goodbye—"

Gina slammed the phone onto the receiver.

"Who was that?"

Gina whipped around. Baby stood on the steps, looking down at Gina with inquisitive eyes.

"Nothing. No one," Gina said. "Actually, it was Cousin Maryjean." Baby's blank stare was enough to tell Gina that Baby didn't know the woman. But the woman had known Baby. Gina cleared her throat. "What are you doing back? I thought you and Lucky were on a date."

"We decided to cut it off early."

"Is everything alright?"

"Lucky was acting weird. He was telling me this story, and then afterward I told him—" Baby's lips moved, but no word escaped.

"Told him what?"

"Nothing. It doesn't matter. He just seemed . . . disappointed. Like he wanted me to say something else."

"Well, I'm sorry he didn't react the way you hoped he would," Gina whispered. She had a sneaking suspicion of what Baby might have told him, and the idea of Foote's ambivalence toward it triggered acid in her chest.

"I think I'll go to bed, now," said Baby.

"Goodnight," Gina said. Baby continued to stand there, watching Gina in the darkness with those moonbeam eyes. "Yes?" Gina asked.

"Aren't you going to—?" Baby cocked her head.

"Oh, of course! I'm so sorry, Baby." Gina walked up to Baby and pressed her lips against Baby's smooth forehead. She inhaled the smell of Baby's hair, like spring soil. "Goodnight, dear."

"I love you, Gina," Baby hummed.

Gina's voice trembled as she said, "I love you too, Baby." Baby smiled and skipped back upstairs.

"What did you do?"

Gina turned to find Eugene standing in the doorway to the kitchen. The shadows made it difficult to discern her husband's expression, though it appeared to be something between anger and fear.

He charged at her. "Why would you do that? I told you never to—" He grabbed her face, and though his voice sounded hard, his touch was tender. Still, Gina backed away.

"Eugene, she's just a girl. She wants affection—"

"She can get that from Foote."

"Don't be crude," Gina spat, marching toward the stairs, her back to him. She was unpracticed in arguments and did not want her husband to see her face.

"You will not touch her. Never again," he demanded.

"But I don't understand why," Gina huffed. "Because Isaac told you?"

"Because this is not about you, Gina. You are not a part of this."

"I'm a member of this household."

"And don't you understand that I'm trying to protect this house? Would you rather trust somebody like Foote with your home? With our community?"

"You know how I feel about him."

"Exactly! And that is why I'm doing something about him."

Gina turned back to Eugene. His face was still as stone. "What do you mean you're doing something? Now, Eugene, you'd better not be doing something foolish—"

"*I'm* not doing a thing. He's doing it all himself. You know the best way to catch a rabbit?"

"Eugene, what are you talking about—"

"A carrot."

Gina was quiet for a moment. "She's a person, Eugene. A human person. You know that, don't you?" But what Gina saw on her husband's face chilled her to the bone.

Nothing. There was nothing there. No remorse, no disdain, not even curiosity. Emptiness, as if she had been speaking gibberish to him.

"I'm going to turn in," he finally said, brushing past her.

"Did you ask Isaac to bring her here? Did you know about her?"

"Goodnight, Gina," Eugene said. Then he cleared his throat—gravel on tin—before spitting some phlegm onto the floor and mounting the steps.

A scream seemed stuck in her throat. She tried to think of anything she could say to get Eugene to turn around. But she had never demanded anything of him for their entire marriage. Her intuition came up dry as her husband disappeared up the steps.

Her eyes drifted down to the mess he had made on the bottom step. Even in the dim light, Gina could see Eugene's spit was charcoal black.

The voices in the car are singing as my One and Only smashes his skin into mine. Once he is inside me, I claw the fabric off my shoulders, his chest, our stomachs. I press my thighs into his waist and my arms against the back of the seat, once an animal's hide. The heat of our bodies glues the seat's leather flesh to my flesh and his flesh. Our clothes giggle, the hard buttons snicker, the leather chortles, and I throw my head back and laugh with them. I laugh so hard my body quakes.

My One and Only gazes up at me, searching for that thing. Sensation! Feeling! We chase it together, he and I. We sprint toward it, fueled by overflowing anticipation.

Yet it eludes us. And then the sex is over.

But something has changed in my One and Only. I can see that hunger-like thing he holds in his eyes, only greater than before. Hungrier. When I try to slip off his lap, he holds me still. Something inside him threatens to bubble over.

Then he says he wants to tell me about his birchbark.

Lucky

•

Lucky and Bernie Orson had been tight back in the day. The jaunt into Old Man Farmer's yard was just one of many troubles that the two got up to. Like many of their comrades, they dabbled in petty theft and pranked the girls that they liked, daring the world to react against their boyish intransigence.

Unlike Lucky, who suffered little more than an "Oh, that boy—" when slipping away from any situation, Bernie maintained his good graces in Briar Heights through an equal balance of good deeds and transgressions. If he was caught loitering outside the Catholic girls' school with a bottle of tequila or blasting music out of his car late at night or forgetting that he was supposed to take someone's sister out to the movies, the affronted parties reminded themselves that he had also shoveled every car on Jefferson Street out of the snow and had driven Mrs. Steward to the hospital when she fell and had walked their cousin the mile and a half home after the cops had shut down a house party.

During his seventeenth spring, Bernie shed his winter layers to reveal broad shoulders and sculpted arms that made wearing T-shirts so uncomfortable, he opted for tanks exclusively. The last of the baby fat had melted from his face, leaving behind divine cheekbones, a flint jaw, and broad lips that became an exciting subject of discussion in the girls' bathroom, not to mention the booming baritone that emitted from them. The guys would pick vague fights just to tussle or try to clown him for looking pretty and acting quiet. Bernie's transformation did not go unnoticed by his friend, either.

When Lucky made clear his intentions of leaving Briar Heights far behind him, there was no question that Bernie would follow. "When we're up out of here—" Lucky would begin before letting his imagination run wild over all the money they would make, the sights they'd see, the adventures they'd have. They would rip the world out of everyone else's hands to mold it into their own.

Once, Bernie asked, "What if we end up going different directions once we get out of here?"

"What do you mean?" Lucky asked. He was sitting in the passenger seat with his knees up against the glove compartment. Even though they were parked, Bernie had his hands at ten and two on the wheel.

"I don't know. We always talk about hustling together, but what if it doesn't work out like that?"

"We just won't let that happen," Lucky said. "We make the rules."

"I'm just saying 'what if,' that's all."

"And I'm saying 'never,'" Lucky huffed, turning to meet Bernie's eyes.

A lopsided smile grew on Bernie's lips. "Yeah. Never."

As their senior year progressed, the two solidified the details of their escape. Dates were set, provisions were secured, and nights were spent fleshing out the details of their near future. The typical high school milestones set before them passed largely ignored. It wasn't until Lucky's mother asked him who he was taking to prom that he realized it was already May. All but one of the handful of young women who had impatiently waited for Lucky to ask them were finally disappointed but, in any case, relieved.

The night of senior prom, Lucky slipped a wide box from beneath his bed, where it had been gathering dust since he had last peeked inside it years ago. He shimmied the top off the box and marveled at his father's vest, its deep violet hues, shimmering paisley design, and the five mother-of-pearl buttons that trailed down its center. It was garish, unstylish, and loud, but it was *a look*. He'd never had an occasion to wear it, but prom was going to be his and Bernie's swan song to Briar Heights, so it was now or never.

When he stepped out of his bedroom in his rental tux and father's vest, his mother shut her eyes tight. A full minute passed before she finally allowed herself to look at Lucky, who patiently stood before her. "You look just like him," she choked out.

The two couples carpooled in Bernie's car. Lucky could not recall a single interesting word that either of the girls exchanged with them; rather, he had focused on Bernie in his uncle's black tux and the yellow carnation boutonniere his date had given him. Though Lucky's date was a great dancer, he kept stealing glances over her shoulder to his friend. Bernie's girl was all over him the whole night, not the least because other girls certainly would have cut in if she let her guard down. Lucky didn't know her very well, but he quickly decided that he disliked her. Bernie also seemed unimpressed, though Lucky couldn't get a moment away from his date to confirm. Whenever Bernie and his date danced past, it left a deep sinking feeling in the pit of Lucky's belly that he couldn't exactly explain.

After they dropped their dates back home, Bernie and Lucky drove around, talking about nothing and everything. Bernie seemed even quieter than usual. Lucky was so focused on holding the conversation that he barely noticed they had hit the highway. A few minutes after midnight, they passed a sign for a town ten miles north of the Heights. He whipped around to Bernie, ready to demand where they were heading, but was met with an expression filled with mischief and determination. *Escape*, it said. Lucky nodded and relaxed into his seat, never letting the conversation drop.

Two hours later, the highway fell away to an older road, and the endless stretches of night on either side were swallowed by woods. Bernie turned down one road, and then another, and then a third, which led to a wide clearing encircled by trees. Bernie shut off the engine but kept the headlights on to illuminate the campground as the two stepped out to stretch their legs.

"My pops took me here a couple times to go hunting," Bernie said.

"It's a nice spot," Lucky nodded, allowing the brisk late-spring breeze to caress his cheeks. That night, the two friends reclined their seats and slept gazing through the sunroof at the stars that hid from the city's view. Lucky slipped into sleep with the sound of his friend's steady breathing beside him.

The next day, Lucky awoke to a chorus of birds and rustling of other creatures deep in the forest of birch trees. After the two relieved themselves at the edges of the clearing, Bernie gave Lucky a tour of the site. Neither wanted to muddy up the borrowed and rented tuxes, so they didn't go too far into the brush, but Bernie was able to identify various points of interest in the nearby wood. Here was an old fox hole. This stump had been here the last time Bernie had come, but the large community of mushrooms consuming its decaying flesh were new. Young deer had made these marks on the birchbark. These marks had been made by a bear. This eagle's nest was at least four generations old—and that was the mother staring down at them from two trees away.

When their stomachs began to rumble, Bernie drove them to a diner in the closest town, which mostly catered to folks heading to the boundary waters. They sat at the counter, where the waitress looked them up and down in their day-old black ties and smirked. "You with a limo company or something?" Lucky tried shooting her a dazzling smile and cracking a joke, but she just sniffed at it. Two young Black men in tuxes in this joint was too bizarre for even his charms to account for. What eventually won her over was the sheer amount of food they ordered, not to mention the generous tip. She even threw them a "You two come back, now," as they left.

The wind had picked up, and their dinner jackets flapped like capes behind them as they ran for the car. "Should probably head home soon," Lucky suggested. "Our moms'll skin us either way, but sooner we get back, less time they have to get creative."

"Yeah," Bernie agreed, staring at the stretch of road that led to the highway. "Maybe swing by the campsite one more time?" Lucky nodded in agreement as Bernie revved up the engine.

Turning into the campsite, Bernie hit the brakes. The wind had blown one of the white-and-black-striped trees across the road. "Yo!" Bernie laughed, shutting off the engine and hopping out of his seat. "That's a nice piece of birchbark. Do you know how much we could get for this in the city?" Lucky nodded as Bernie sized it up. "Looks just small enough to fit in the back. Come help me." Bernie crouched on his heels and started to strip the thin branches off of the trunk. Once the two had cleared the specimen into a handsome log, they hoisted it up and attempted to maneuver it through the car's back door.

"I'm gonna have to lift—"

"Okay, just watch my side," Lucky said. The trunk jabbed him twice in the stomach. "Hey, man!"

"Sorry! Okay, now, move—"

"Wait—" The trunk was pressing into Lucky's diaphragm again.

"Watch the car!"

"Man, just wait—"

"Just a little—there!" Lucky felt the trunk scrape across his vest and heard a small snap as Bernie pushed his end through the door: One of the mother-of-pearl buttons had been ripped off. Lucky dropped to his knees and searched through waves of leaves blowing this way and that for a shimmer of white.

"What's up?" Bernie asked.

"My button! One of my buttons snapped off."

"Oh, man. The rental didn't come with extras?"

"The vest! It's my dad's vest, man. It's the only thing I have—" Lucky's voice broke as his fingernails scraped through the dirt and dead leaves. Without another word, his friend dropped to his knees beside him. For the next few minutes, they silently looked, smoothing out the ground and overturning every leaf and pebble. Lucky's eyes and nose burned from the dusty wind. Then Bernie lifted something up to the sun.

"Is this it?" Bernie asked. The opalescent button glinted back at him. Lucky grabbed it from Bernie and shoved it in his vest pocket.

"Oh my God, man, thank you," Lucky huffed, catching his breath.

"I'm so sorry about that, man," his friend said.

"Nah, bro, it's fine. I owe you . . ." Lucky said. He could see that Bernie was breathing just as heavily as he was. His chiseled face was covered in flecks of dirt and sweat. His lips were parted, exhaling staccato sighs, so close that Lucky could feel his breath on his cheek. "I owe you . . ." The wind had lulled for a moment, and everything was quiet except for their breathing. As it picked up again, the look that Bernie gave him was loud enough to drown it all out.

Then, Bernie was on top of him, the wind and leaves swirling around them, their breath joined. When Lucky opened his eyes, all he saw were flashes of black and white above him—eyes, pupils, wanting lips, teasing teeth, bow ties loosened, shirts and pants undone, his fingers grasping his friend's chest and tangled in his curls, and the many towers of birchbark.

Afterward, seated once more in the back of Bernie's car, all Lucky could think to say was, "Crazy, man."

"Crazy," Bernie agreed, and if they had left it at that, then maybe it would have been possible to keep their plans set, to stick with the promise that they had made to one another.

But then, Bernie said, "What if—"

Lucky shot his friend a glance, and Bernie shut his lips. But the look on his face said everything.

Bernie's what-if hung between them as they drove back to Briar Heights. Lucky weighed it, studied it from every angle. As much as he might want to indulge it, explore it, he knew it was too dangerous. Too volatile. A what-if like that would eviscerate the gift that he had carefully cultivated all these years. That gift was his key to success once they left Briar Heights.

The trouble was, now that it had been said, the what-if was among them and could not be ignored. Lucky knew that pretending otherwise, while still pursuing their plan, would blow up in his face. Lucky also knew that escape had always been his idea. On his own, Bernie would stay, see to his obligations, rack up debts and pay them off, settle into the inertia of Briar Heights. Bernie would not come after him.

Bernie dropped Lucky at his place. They exchanged chaste farewells before Lucky watched Bernie drive away. Ten hours later, Lucky was on a bus out of town, alone. As he leaned his head against the window and closed his eyes, feeling the rumble of the road beneath him, all he saw were visions of birchbark.

Baby was stroking Lucky's neck with two fingers as he finished this explanation, the way that children are told to pet puppies and kittens. They were sitting in Lucky's car, parked across the street from the Foxes', beside the two trees that Baby seemed to enjoy so much. Their clothes were still rumpled, and the air smelled of sex and warm leather. She was quiet for a long time, which Lucky mistook for processing. His heart pounded in his throat as he wondered whether this had been a mistake, whether he should have kept this story shut up, as he had always sworn he would.

He finally muttered, "So . . ."

"Is that it?" Baby asked.

He scoffed and looked at her. Her wide eyes looked sincere, not coquettish or sarcastic. Lucky laughed and shook his head. "Well, whether or not *you* think it's a big deal, don't ever bring it up again, okay? Just . . . forget I said anything about it."

"Do you still think about him?" she asked. Lucky exhaled before he nodded. Baby smiled and stroked his knuckles. "And other men?"

He nodded.

"But you've never touched other men?"

"Why are you asking me this?"

"Well, why not?"

"Because," Lucky said. "It wouldn't . . . work."

"Oh, you mean your trick."

"My trick?"

"Yes. No, what'd you call it? Your gift," Baby hummed. "Why wouldn't it work?"

"It just wouldn't."

His gift only worked as long as he remained uncomplicated, fit easily into the neighborhood's idea of who he ought to be. If he ever overstepped, no amount of genial charm or red-carpet smiles could keep him from being branded a liar, a shape-shifter. There was no way for the birchbark to fit into the identity that Lucky had constructed in Original Hill.

"But doesn't it hurt?" Baby finally asked. "Not being true to what you want?"

"But everybody's got something like that, right? That's part of being human," Lucky said, glancing back at Baby. "That doesn't bother you? That I've been with—"

Baby shrugged. "Should it?"

Lucky scoffed again and leaned in to kiss Baby's lips. He held them against his, running his tongue along their softness. Sex had relieved nothing. He was hungrier for her than ever. He bit her lips between his teeth, grasping her head in his hands, trying to press her into him. But he still couldn't fully feel her there, even as his hand squeezed her tighter.

Finally, he released her, both breathing heavily in the

darkness. Her mother-of-pearl-button eyes glinted back at him. He wondered if the neighbors were watching the car from their windows, waiting to catch a glimpse of her. Even the little bit of light from the neighbors' porches seemed to bend toward her. "You know, I've never met another person like you," Lucky sighed.

Then he cleared his throat. "I told you this because I wanted to let you know that I've got shit in my past I don't talk about. And that you can tell me about stuff in your past you don't want to tell other people about," Lucky said. "So, do you? Want to tell me? Anything?"

He felt like a little boy begging. He had given her his deepest secret; now, he needed hers. Something moved in the dark of her pupils, straining to be released. Lucky wondered what it could be. Good, bad, damning, revelatory, mundane, heartbreaking? All he knew was that he wanted it. He needed to cross that last bit of distance, finally be permitted inside.

He was so raw to her that what she told him sent a shock through his system. Mistaking his confusion for disappointment, Baby immediately marched out of his car back to the Foxes' house.

In a million years, Lucky had never expected her to say something like, "I want to knot my roots with yours."

I am in my bedroom, where the mirror is droning on to its wooden frame about the shores where it was once many grains of sand. The wood clearly does not care, having been a tree and therefore generally uninterested in beachfronts. I hear my Goodnight Kiss pacing through the floor below me. She is upset. I am not entirely sure why, but I think it has to do with Father.

I am still thinking back to the story that my One and Only told me, about the sort of touch that he desires and does not allow himself. His birchbark. I know, now, that it is not only me. Anyone's touch can be dangerous. Even after so many years, Lucky is stuck to that touch.

I want to touch and stick, but I have not discovered that sort of touch yet. Not from my One and Only, not from my Goodnight Kiss. When our skins part, I am alone again. I want to know about stuckness. The only thing I am stuck to is this road, and that is different. It frustrates Lucky, my adherence to this road. He would prefer I not fade when I leave it, and I know he wishes that I could cross the highway. But I do not need to leave. Everyone that I love is right here.

The voices are talking about me again. I have tried to speak with my One and Only and my Goodnight Kiss about the voices, but I don't think they understand. He hardly listens, and she tells me I have an "expansive imagination." Sometimes, though, I do think she can hear the voices in the house. She will stop in the middle of a room and touch her hand to a wall.

I have asked the voices why people do not hear them, but they say it is a human thing and then get back to their conversation. It is a beautiful thing to be human, to be a person. *When Gina tells me things like, "You're still an adult human being," it feels like the highest compliment. When Lucky says things like, "I've never met another person like you," I hold on to it tightly and never want to let go. I cradle it in my hands like a newborn thing, and I want to nurse it until it grows strong. Father does not care as much about being a human person. He is more concerned with souls.*

I hear the front door shut beneath me as my Goodnight Kiss leaves. Where is she going so early in the morning? Is she upset because the house has become more interested in me? I'm not sure what I have done differently to attract its attention. The voices ignored me before, but they talk about me now. When I try to talk back, they do not listen.

No one listens.

Gina

•

Summer was holding strong in Little Rock. A burst of hot air whipped Gina's cheeks as she exited the airport's overpowering air-conditioning into the late-afternoon sun. Aside from a trio of men in military uniforms chatting ahead of her, there were few people on the arrivals platform. She shaded her eyes from the low sun, finally locating an ancient pickup truck idling at the far end of the platform. She rolled her suitcase over to the truck, craning her neck ahead of her until she could catch a glimpse of the driver.

Behind the wheel sat a strawberry-red man jabbing at some game on his phone. Decades of sun damage had left his face peeling almost as badly as the paint on the truck. Faint tufts of ash-white hair poked out from beneath the U.S. Marines cap fixed securely on his head. As she approached, his blue eyes shifted from the phone to her.

"Gina?"

Gina nodded. "Cousin Ed?"

Cousin Ed hoisted himself out of the truck and wrapped her into a bear hug, filling her nostrils with the smell of tobacco, before stepping back to get a good look at her. "Aren't you something? Can't believe Cousin Eugene's been hiding you away all these years."

"Yes, well, I thought I would fix that." Gina chuckled, patting the sweat at her collar with an airline napkin. She very much wanted to be on her way. She had already come this far: purchasing the plane ticket, then packing the suitcase, then taking a cab to the airport, then boarding the plane, then boarding her connecting flight in Detroit. But Cousin Ed did not seem to sense Gina's urgency. He scratched beneath his cap. "Shame Cousin Eugene couldn't make it. I don't think we've seen him since y'all's wedding."

"Yes, well, he couldn't get away. I just happened to be in this neck of the woods visiting family," Gina lied.

"It's been, what, twenty years?"

"Thirty-five. Almost."

Cousin Ed let fly a low whistle. "Maryjean would've really liked to see him."

"Maybe some other time." Gina smiled. Finally, Cousin Ed threw open the passenger door for her. He spat onto the asphalt before climbing back up into the truck and shifting into drive.

As they drove onto the highway and out of the city, Gina felt a cautious thrill. For almost as long as she had known Eugene, she had imagined meeting his brother, sometimes approaching him with curiosity, other times with anger. Sometimes he was a mirror image of her husband, and others he looked the part of the vagabond. She hadn't realized until now how large this faceless ghost had loomed in her marriage since the start—that knowledge of something in the periphery that was not to be looked at directly. It had been her first real test as a wife, following her intuition rather than submitting to crude curiosity. Yet here she was about to tear away the curtain.

Though Gina had only left Baby this morning, her stomach twisted as she thought about the miles between them. She dabbed away more sweat, which she told her herself was only a reaction to the Southern heat, though her intuition suggested more. She needed to get back to Baby. But first Gina had to know what scheme these brothers had hatched to send Baby to Original Hill, and what she could do to protect the poor girl and keep her there.

As they pulled up to the quaint little house, Gina was greeted by a jolly older woman who filled the entire doorway in her floral apron. "Well, now, look at you!" she howled, wrapping Gina into a bone-crushing hug. "Come on in. I'd like you to meet somebody."

Gina inhaled deeply and nodded, stepping into the house. The kitchen was clearly Cousin Maryjean's domain, all linoleum and aluminum cushioned in peachy frills. The window above the sink was shaded by pink gingham with Raggedy Ann and Andy winking coyly at one another. The bulging eyes of ceramic puppies, monkeys, deer, bluebirds, and cherubic children oversaw the room from nearly every surface. The only pair of eyes not attached to a cutesy face were those of a blessing Christ, whose portrait hung just over an archway that led to a small TV room.

As Gina sat at the kitchen table, another pair of buggy eyes entered the room. "Cousin Gina, I'd like you to meet Princess Pepper here," Cousin Maryjean said, lifting a sand-colored shih tzu into her arms, pressing their noses together until the dog began to lick her ravenously. "'Round here, she's just as much a part of the family as anybody else."

Gina smiled politely at Princess Pepper as she continued to dab at her neck with the same napkin, though the paper was beginning to tear and pill in her hand.

"Where'd you say you were flying out of? Tampa?" Cousin Maryjean offered a blondie from a mouse-shaped cookie jar, which Gina declined.

"No; Detroit."

"Detroit's a rough city, ain't it? Though I'm sure the airport's alright—"

"I'm sorry, is he upstairs?" Gina interrupted.

"Upstairs?" Cousin Maryjean frowned.

Gina's stomach twisted. "You said you wanted me to meet someone—?"

"Princess Pepper's right here," Cousin Maryjean said, looking down at the dog sniffing at her house slipper.

Gina wasn't sure whether to laugh or cry. She felt as if she'd stumbled into some kind of riddle. "Cousin Maryjean, when we spoke over the phone, I asked about Isaac?"

"Of course! You wanted to go see him."

"He isn't here?"

Cousin Maryjean looked at the cookie jar she was holding, then chuckled. "Oh no, honey. We don't . . . Well, the family doesn't do it that way."

"Well, would it be possible to see him tonight? I really wasn't planning on spending more than a day—"

"I really wish Eugene'd come." Cousin Maryjean sighed. "Person ought not to keep his kinfolk at bay the way that he does."

"I think there's a lot I need to talk about with Isaac—"

"Man can't come down for a day to visit his own brother."

"I know they have a complicated relationship—"

"Complicated? They never got to know each other." Cousin Maryjean whipped around, swinging her hip against the edge of the counter. "Even at his daddy's funeral, Eugene couldn't be bothered to visit with family. I played hostess the whole time—and was happy to do it, don't get me wrong. His mama was like a big sister to me, you know. I'll show you!"

Cousin Maryjean turned and rushed up a flight of stairs before Gina could stop her. With a soft groan, Gina tossed aside the disintegrating napkin and plucked another from the center of the table. Alone in the kitchen, still sweating like a pig, she felt watched by a thousand bulging eyes. She had to get back to her own house, back to Baby.

She was seconds away from bolting out the door when Cousin Maryjean returned to the kitchen and dropped a photo album onto the table. On the cover was a small inlaid piece of paper inscribed with beautiful cursive: *Baby and Friends.*

She looked up at Cousin Maryjean. "Baby?"

"Eugene's mama, of course."

Gina hesitated. His mother's name was Babette. "I didn't know anyone called her Baby," she murmured.

"Oh, we all did. Didn't you ask about her on the phone?"

"I asked about Baby."

"Eugene didn't have much time to know her," Cousin Maryjean said somberly. "After she died, his daddy packed up and moved north. Just left in the night, not a word to anybody else. Apple doesn't fall far from the tree, I guess."

Cousin Maryjean opened the album and flipped through black-and-white photos of smiling and giggling women in 1950s hairdos and dresses. She pointed to herself a few times, an awkward child holding the glamorous teen Babette's hand, though Gina was more interested in the dresses Eugene's mother wore. She was sure she had seen the same ones on Baby.

Gina flipped past newspaper clippings that referenced Babette's participation in high school sock hops and friends' weddings, stopping at one especially large photograph. She saw a group of teen girls much like the other photos, only their debutante smiles were contorted into vicious screams. Babette was at the front of the crowd, a visible vein bulging from her forehead and an accusing finger stretched out before her. The finger was aimed at a young Black girl in sunglasses, strolling past the roiling mob of white teenagers as if they were willows swaying in the breeze. The caption at the bottom read: *Local students protest integrating high school.*

Gina studied the target of the white girls' ire. It wasn't that the student looked like Baby at all, but Gina swore there was something she recognized. Was it the mouth, that set line of disregard for those protesting behind her? Gina felt a stabbing pain in her abdomen alongside an irrational desire to grab the girl in the photograph away from Eugene's mother.

"Has Eugene seen this?" Gina asked.

"Oh, sure. Eugene's mama was very politically involved," Cousin Maryjean said, nodding at the clipping. "Probably where he gets it from."

Gina stood abruptly. The legs of her chair scraped against the linoleum, spooking Princess Pepper. "Cousin Maryjean, please, I would really like to see Isaac tonight. It's very important."

Cousin Maryjean pursed her lips. "Sure you don't want something to eat? I'd'a thought you'd want some rest."

Gina stood with her fists by her sides, trying to ignore the sweat dampening her forehead and clavicle. "No, please, I would much rather see him if I can."

"Place closes at sundown, Maryjean," Cousin Ed shouted from the TV room. "Gotta go now if she wants to see him."

"Well, alright," Cousin Maryjean sighed. "I'll change into something decent."

As Ed drove the truck, Gina sat stiffly in the back seat. She should not have come here. She understood why Eugene had cut ties with these people. Of course, Gina had suspected that kind of thing down here, but the fact that even Eugene's own mother—well, it was shameful. Just shameful. And now she was stuck in a car with people she hardly knew aside from their backward ideas. She should have left these Foxes alone, trusted her intuition, trusted Eugene.

But Isaac had to be different than these Foxes, didn't he? If he had a child who looked like Baby? It was clear that Cousin Maryjean either didn't know about or refused to acknowledge the young woman's existence. Were they the reason that Isaac had kept Baby secret, for her own protection? But then why had Eugene cut ties with Isaac, too? All Gina could think was that Eugene had told her that she was not a part of this, and maybe he was right.

Gina did not catch the name of the facility as Cousin Ed drove through its gates. Beautiful expanses of green lawn stretched out on either side of the freshly paved road. "'Bout here should be alright," Cousin Maryjean said, and Cousin Ed pulled over. There were no buildings in sight, only a few statues and fountains here and there. After following Cousin Maryjean and Princess Pepper a few steps into the lawn, Gina realized where they were.

Passing weathered tombstones, newer reflective graves, and genuflecting angels, Gina combed through every conversation she had ever had with her husband about his brother. There had been no mention of Isaac's death, no hint that his daughter was an orphan. Why hadn't Eugene just told her the truth? Had he even attended his own brother's funeral? Was he too ashamed by whatever dispute had caused their decades-long rift?

A pang of despair stung Gina's heart as she realized she would never know what had really happened between the two brothers. Oh, she might one day pull it out of her husband, but it would only be half of the story. Whatever truths lay solely in the other half were now buried.

But Baby must know something. Gina felt a small

flutter of revival, a phoenix poking its naked head from the ashes. Now that she knew the situation, Gina was sure that she could encourage Baby to tell her Isaac's side of things. Together they could trade notes on the two brothers, put the full story together. She and Baby could salvage a beautiful truth out of these brothers' wreckage.

As Gina drew closer to the graves, studying the details, she felt her budding dream falter. The first grave belonged to Eugene's father and the second to his mother, Babette. The third headstone was much smaller than the others. An infant's gravestone. *Isaac Fox. December 10, 1965*. A single day for the single day of the brother's life.

Gina had finally looked directly at the ghost in her periphery. But there was nothing there, and there never had been.

It was so simple, so obvious. There had never been an estranged brother, not really. Everything that she had intuited as Eugene's shame, protection, pride—it had all just been a lie. She didn't wield a sharpened intuition; she was a silly magician's assistant, laughing and clapping at Eugene's sleight of hand without being in on the trick. If Isaac was a lie, then what other deceit had Eugene been getting away with? And all because of Gina's blind faith in her intuition. Oh, God! Staring at the solid gravestone, everything that she had built over thirty-four years came down around her, brick by brick.

There was only one piece still standing in the middle of it all: Baby. Who was she?

Gina felt numb as Cousin Maryjean led her back to the truck. Her blouse was damp with sweat, and her body trembled slightly. As they drove away from the cemetery,

Gina could only think of that beautiful girl. She reached for the shredded threads of what Baby had told her. She had a father, that much Gina knew, whom she loved and feared and wanted to protect. She had come from somewhere she did not want to return to, a place of confusion with no beautiful gardens. The neighbors had all looked at her with such suspicion, but she had won them over.

But that was her own story, Gina realized. How was it possible that after living under the same roof for months, all she knew of Baby was her own reflection in the girl?

That's when Gina smelled it, the strange odor that had enveloped her house. Miles from home and months later, the stench was still unmistakable.

"What's that smell?" Gina demanded.

"Recreation," Cousin Ed said.

"What?"

"That swamp out there," Ed said, torquing his head to the left. Gina looked out the window at a large stretch of rich, dark land dotted with verdant greenery. "Used to be a town out there called Recreation before it got swallowed up."

"When we were kids, there was a story folks used to tell about it, remember?" Cousin Maryjean hummed.

"Oh, sure! See, back in the twenties and thirties it was a colored town, but when the men came home after the war, folks needed more space to raise their families. Well, the county took the land, moved the Black folk out, and built a nice little town for the white folk and named it Recreation. Anyway, story goes that a man from Recreation came walking along one day, and by the side of the road he sees this Black girl—dark as anything, but beautiful. She seemed to have hurt herself—some said it was a twisted ankle, others said that she was running from somebody who roughed her up. So he takes her back home.

"Now, as you can imagine, the neighbors weren't too keen on this man bringing home a darkie. So the man takes her to each and every house in Recreation and makes her shake their hands, just to show what a lady she is. And something happens to these people. They start coming by his place more and more often, asking if they can see his lady. Now, at first the man's ecstatic—he thinks his little plan has worked. But then he starts to notice strange things about her. Like, she can't go out in the heat of the summer for too long, and when she comes back inside, she seems a little muddled—not just her head, her face and her body.

"Meanwhile, one of his neighbors, this old crone, well, she's been stewing about this Black girl that's come into town. She wouldn't even come to the door when the Black girl did her round shaking everybody's hand. So, this old woman, she goes to the county sheriff and says there's something unnatural going on in Recreation. She says, why doesn't he get some of his boys together to set things right? So the sheriff does, he gets some of the men together and they all go to do what they need to do in Recreation.

"They drive around all night looking for Recreation, but they can't find it. By the time the sun comes up, they realize that it's gone. The whole town. Like it never was. And in its place, one big, wide tar pit."

"She was a tar-baby," Cousin Maryjean piped in. "Like

in that Br'er Rabbit story, you know? Only she was a tar-baby come to life."

"Some folks said that one of the Black folk who got kicked out of Recreation was a conjure man or a voodoo priest, and he made this girl to destroy the town as revenge."

"That's quite a story," Gina said.

"Well, it kept us kids from playing around the swamp. Lots of quicksand and sinkholes and things around there—not tar pits, but you know, that sounds flashier."

"There did really use to be a town there, though," Cousin Maryjean insisted. "That part's true."

As Gina stared out at the wide expanse, she imagined it instead covered with houses and a paved road. She conjured up the neighbors, carrying groceries from their cars and trading gossip over their picket fences. She pictured a house at the very end of the road, with a beautiful walled garden. And on the garden wall, a young woman in a dress. Then Gina saw the house and the garden sink into the ground, until there was nothing left but this swamp. The knot in her stomach twisted.

Gina lurched forward and grabbed Cousin Ed's shoulder. "Take me to the airport. I have to get home now!"

I used to sit on the garden wall and eavesdrop on the thousand conversations around me. I listened to the debates between the minerals in the concrete, the manifestos of insects and grubs burrowed in the dirt, the gossiping between tomatoes twisting their vines up the chatty brick wall. The voices hardly stopped for breath, and they all ignored me. The few times that I did try to join in, none of them acknowledged me. So I stuck to listening.

This is how I learned of the love affair between the two oak trees across the street. Each tree's trunk is enclosed in a neat square of soil, bordered and separated from its neighbor by a stretch of concrete. I would giggle at their bickering and blush at their teasing. I would grow teary-eyed at their nostalgia for the tree farms where they had grown from saplings. I attended, with bated breath, as they hatched their plot to defy the stone cages into which they had been set, to reach out and finally touch one another.

One of the oak trees has already succeeded in arching its root through the concrete about a quarter of the way to the other. This had taken thirty years, not long at all for an oak tree. The other has been negotiating a large stone sealed beneath the sidewalk, forced to curve its roots around the obstruction. I dropped into this drama long after it had begun, and yet the lovertrees' desire sounded no less urgent than a freshly blooming romance. I was often so enrapt by their voices that I realized I had forgotten to breathe. I couldn't help but wonder if someone out there was trying to reach their roots toward me.

I tried to show my One and Only my lovertrees, once. I got him to press his hand against the root, but he didn't hear it. People only seem to listen to other people.

I first heard the voices after I woke in the room upstairs. I thought that I was in a forest because the voices around me all talked about having been trees, trading stories from different soils or reigniting rivalries from old groves. Those who hadn't been trees spoke of burrowing into their meat and homemaking beneath the surface. It must be a very old forest, I thought, as they all reminisced of a distant past.

But when I lifted my head, I found myself encased—four walls and a ceiling and a floor and a window letting in a thick bar of light that hit a tall door, and many dusty boxes all around me. That is when I realized it was the wood in the walls and the floor and the door and the cardboard boxes that were speaking. All had once been trees, and they recalled that time in congress with everything else inside the room. Everything but me.

Before I could ask the voices where I was, a majority of them, all at once, registered that someone was coming. My ears tuned toward the sound of footfalls from the other side of the door. I scampered backward, shoulder blades knocking against the boxes behind me. But when the door opened, I saw that it was only Father.

I knew him the way that everyone knows their father when they meet him.

Father brought with him new voices, hanging on to him and inside him. He stood in the doorway for a very long time, looking at me the way that some people look at a beautiful stone or a striking phrase. I only gazed back. Finally, his fatherly voice boomed above the rest, "You must be hungry."

He left and returned with a peanut butter and jam sandwich and a glass of water, which I ate and drank ravenously. It was only then I realized I had been holding something since the moment I woke, and that something was hunger, and that hunger could be sated by the peanut butter and jam, which was perfectly salty and sweet. Father watched me eat and rubbed his chin without saying a word. I didn't mind his silence because I could listen to his pant leg, which was discussing whether having grown up in a cotton field or an indigo farm had been a more fruitful youth. When I finished eating, Father and I sat together, silent and still, until the room grew dark and the shining sun outside was supplanted by a low, buzzing light.

As we sat there, I began to understand that I was holding something else too, something like the hunger. To sate it, I reached out to touch Father's hand. He yanked his arm away and looked at me like a vile, rotting thing. "No," he said fatherly, and left. Then I was alone again with the voices that ignored me. I still held my hunger-like thing, but I was holding something new too, something that made me want to crawl up inside myself like the dead beetles lying in the corners.

Later, Father would tell me that my skin was dangerous, my touch horrific. Then I understood the weight of what I held.

I cannot say exactly how long I stayed in the room upstairs. I spent most of my days watching the sun move across the floor, listening to the boards and the glass and the silverfish and the dust mites conversing with one another, and waiting for Father. He would come at night, and we would sit an arm's length apart. He would bring food and remove my empty plate and used pot. Sometimes he would ask how I was feeling. I would answer with smiles and shrugs. Anytime I tried to locate a voice within myself, some mortifying growl or squeak escaped instead. Some mewling thing. But most often, Father and I would sit in silence together. More often than that, I was alone listening to the voices.

It was much better than the place I was before, the darkloudhot place. I should never have been there. It was a wrong place, not somewhere to put a person. No voices there, only that horrible roar that drowned out all substantive thought. I was grateful that Father took me out of that place and brought me here, even if it was only a small, dusty room.

Before the darkloudhot place, there was another place, but I hardly remember it. All I remember is the sound of my mother's voice. She is saying my name. No, not my name. Something else. Not sure. It's hard to hear her with that terrible roar, breakage and crumbling and death. I think she's the one who put me in the darkloudhot place, and I'll never forgive her for that. It was a wrong place, not somewhere to put a person.

Soon, I became accustomed—well, bored—by the reminiscing of the walls-once-tree and the floor-once-tree and the boxes-once-tree. This was long before I knew the joys of the garden's conversation, before I had even laid eyes on my lovertrees. I was annoyed by the circuitous discussions that occupied the stale room. With nothing else to do, I explored the boxes.

I found them filled with lovely dresses like the one I wore. There was a smudgy mirror in one box, which is how I first became aware of my reflection. I fell in love with the way the pinks and yellows of the fabric played against my dark skin, how my hat pushed my hair forward like a celebration. I saw for the first time the dimples at the center of my forehead and chin and on the tip of my nose. When my reflection smiled, I saw the little space between my two front teeth. I saw that I was my own reflection, that everything on one side was just the same as the other with a line drawn down the center.

But eventually my reflection lost its novelty, too. I began to dream of reaching for the doorknob, turning it, and throwing open the door. But I could never settle on what would be on the other side. Sometimes it was Father, ready to scold me for my disobedience. Sometimes it was a plate towering with food, and others, a pot towering with excrement. Often, the door opened into the groaning maw of the darkloudhot place, and that roar began to drag me back to it. I could tell from the voices on him that Father had hurt himself greatly to save me from that place. He had made himself sick to bring me here, and I could not bear to imagine slipping back there out of my own foolishness.

One day, searching for some entertainment in the boxes, I came upon a smaller box, glossy and new, unlike anything else I had found in the room upstairs. I delicately separated the top of the box from its bottom and found a small card laid atop some colorful tissue paper. When I turned the card over, it simply read, To Baby.

It was a gift—a gift to me! I remembered, then, that this was the not-name my memory-mother called me. Baby. *I eagerly threw aside the colorful tissue paper and found a beautiful pair of white gloves. I carefully slipped them on, pressing my fingers and forearm into them snugly. I held my gloved hands out in front of me and admired the way that they reflected the morning light. I did not consider until much later who might have gifted these to me.*

When Father next visited, I showed him the gloves. "Now I will not be in danger of touching anyone," I said. My voice was still embarrassing, but I was too excited by my discovery to keep silent. "May I leave with you now?"

Father was quiet at first, though I saw the glint of an idea in his eye. Finally, he nodded. I nearly leapt into the air with glee, but his stern expression stopped me. "But you must never take them off," Father warned me. "You can never touch anyone or let anyone touch your bare skin, except for One, and Only one, man. And he has to touch you first. Understand?"

I nodded as tears of gratitude pooled along the tops of my cheeks.

"And you cannot tell anyone that I am your father," he said. If anybody asked, I was to say that he was my uncle. I was so excited for him to take me from the room, I did not think to ask why we were playing pretend. For the first time, Father took my hand. I buzzed at the new sensation, feeling the faint warmth of his heat through the glove. His face was deathly serious, but I could hardly contain my joy as he guided me through the door.

After I left the room upstairs, I found that the whole house was filled with voices, and even more outside. Listening to the symphonies of the world from that garden wall, I learned how often things were crashing into one another. There seemed to be unending combinations of pushing, pulling, attachment, collision, grazing, enwrapping, and divorce, all of it apart from me. I knew the pressure of my father's hands through cloth, of Gina brushing by and fluttering the fabric of my dress. But to meet another's flesh with my own— What was that like?

I began to wonder more and more about my One and Only, the single person that I would one day be able to touch. I dreamed that this person might recite love poems and release gentle pheromones into the air just for me like my lover-trees across the street.

When Lucky did finally appear, I was glad to complete Father's prophesy. I ran my hands over every acre of Lucky and let him feel every inch of me. I urged him to press his fingers into my depths, as I had submerged my hands into the deep brown soil of the garden. His poking and palming certainly elicited new sensations, but it never satisfied. I never stuck.

One misty morning, I was walking around the garden and discovered a bush bursting with blackberries. To avoid staining it, I removed my glove and reached to pick a berry. The moment that my finger made contact with the fruit, I felt a sharp pain from one of the bramble's thorns and the soothing wetness from a drop of dew that fell onto it. I pulled my finger back and shoved it between my lips. All at once I felt the sharpness of the thorn, the slickness of the dew, and the pacifying undulations of my tongue, each unmediated by my glove.

Some things you know and some things you have to be told. I can't explain it. I knew that Lucky was my One and Only and that Father was my father—they defined themselves. I know that I cannot cross the highway or stray too far from this road—these truths I feel in my body, down to the soles of my feet. If I venture too far away, my bones become jumbled and my thoughts become viscous. It's horrible. The road is a truth that I cannot disobey. But I had to be told *about the danger of a touch.*

After Gina touched me with her Goodnight Kiss, I was not pulled back to the darkloudhot place. But I did not stick to her either. Every evening, I still felt the weight of my hunger-like thing. I realized that the things you know, you cannot change or disobey . . . but the things you are told*? Even if the telling comes from your father? Well.*

So I made up a game, removing my glove and grazing the warm satin of skin as swiftly as I could without anyone noticing. I quickly moved beyond the garden and the house and Lucky and Gina. I would slip off my glove and sweep my fingers against a waiter's knuckles as he placed the check on the table, or through a neighbor's hair as she passed at the market. I petted the dogs through white fences and tickled the bottoms of babies' feet. I couldn't be too obvious, as I was afraid Father might send me back to the darkloudhot place for my disobedience. I got very good at this game. I'm sure I've touched every person in this neighborhood, except for Father.

I want to, so badly. I care for him so much, and I know he cares for me in ways that Lucky and Gina cannot. We were together from the start. He brought me here from the dark-loudhot place. I know that he needs me, and it is so good to be needed. It is good to not be a person who can be put away in a wrong place and forgotten. I want to show him my gratitude. And I feel—I cannot explain it, but I feel—that he can take away this hunger-like thing I am holding. He brought me to the world, and he can make me stick to it.

But I do not touch him, ever. I do not want him to look at me like a vile, rotting thing again. It would destroy me. So I leave him out of my game.

And still, I hold my hunger-like thing. I return home to hear my lovertrees whispering sweet nothings and promising to embrace one another when the time comes. I wonder, if they ever do finally reach their roots to one another, will it all have been worth it? Or will they discover that the touch of another does not possess the weight and permanence they think it does?

A touch is so fleeting. I have touched so many, now, and have not stuck.

Lucky

•

Lucky flicked his lighter with his thumb. He wanted a cigarette badly to calm his nerves, but there was no way he'd be caught smoking in the middle of Orchard Street in broad daylight, especially not across from his opponent's house. He tried to concentrate all his nervous energy into the tiny flame that emerged and disappeared with each click.

His phone vibrated in his pocket—angry, drawn-out caterwauls that seemed to never end. Probably Stu calling to deride him for missing some interview or photo op. At the last campaign meeting, Stu had ridden Lucky's ass for his ongoing absences. "Don't you want to fucking win this thing?" Stu had ended the meeting on the spot when Lucky responded, "Language, Stu."

What else could Lucky have said? Of course he wanted to win. Losing the election meant that he had lost his hold on the people of Original. But Stu wasn't on the ground in Original Hill. He didn't see that Ms. Branch and

Dr. Wood had stopped waving at Lucky's car as it passed. He couldn't have noticed that Mr. and Mrs. Ives's evening stroll now solely looped this block of Orchard Street or that Bush had stopped stocking chips and toiletries in his store, filling the shelves with bags of candy and packaged sweets. Something was shifting, and Lucky had to hurry up and figure out what it was so that he could shift with it. That was more urgent than some meetings at City Hall.

Lucky released the lighter to kill the flame before flicking it back to life. When *was* the last time he'd been to City Hall? His memory was a haze, probably because he hadn't gotten a good night's sleep in weeks. His only recollections of the last few days were Baby in pieces—her leg tucked beneath a chair, her arm against the leather seats of his car, her chin perched just above his shoulder, not quite resting on it. These memories—or were they dreams?—emerged from the fog in his mind's eye, dispersing again before becoming fully formed.

Ever since he had told Baby about him and Bernie beneath the birchbark, something nagged at him—maybe he'd been played. Was it possible that this game was just an elaborate ruse for her to get information to Fox? He had trusted her with a secret that could ruin him, and she'd given him nothing in return. Forget a secret—what did he really know about her at all? Only that he wanted her more than anything, more than air! The notion that he had fallen for some trick haunted him, but spending even a day without Baby was unthinkable.

The Foxes' front door opened, and Baby stepped out into the afternoon sun. Lucky had to stop himself from running to her and sweeping her into his arms. Holding her gloves in hand, she wore the same floral prairie dress she'd worn at the Midsummer Soiree. It took all his willpower to wait until she was only a few feet away from him to close the distance. He gripped her hips as their lips met. He kept their mouths locked together until his lungs ached for breath. Still, he might as well have been kissing her through a pane of glass.

"We're going to see a friend of mine," Lucky said, slipping into the driver's seat. Auntie Riri would know if there was something duplicitous hiding in Baby's quiet nature. He had no idea how he would respond if Baby *had* been playing him all this time. He would cross that bridge when he came to it. Speaking of . . .

Lucky knew Baby wouldn't like crossing the highway, so he tried to distract her by cracking jokes and getting her to laugh. Even so, when the car stopped at the Orchard Street Bridge, Baby's head whipped forward. Her brow furrowed and her large eyes widened.

"Lucky—"

The light turned green and Lucky hit the gas.

"Lucky, don't! I can't!"

The engine snarled as they accelerated over the bridge. Baby pressed her back against the seat and threw up her hands to cover her ears. Out of the corner of his eye, he could see her squeeze her eyes shut and grind her teeth. Then her whole body rippled in some strange, erratic spasm. But by the time Lucky could look at her straight on, she was just as stiff and erect as before.

A car honked and Lucky slammed on the brakes. They were across. Baby opened her eyes and relaxed, looking uneasy but unharmed.

"See?" Lucky chuckled. "That wasn't so bad."

A few minutes later, they were standing hand in hand outside Auntie Riri's house. When the old woman opened the door, she was wearing a deep scarlet dress and a string of buttery yellow pearls. She had ironed and curled her hair into streaked silver clouds, and a slash of crimson lipstick stained her lips. As her eyes fell on Baby, they seemed to lose focus in a way that Lucky worried might mean disapproval. He puffed his chest out, prepared to defend Baby against whatever critique might be thrown at her. "Auntie Riri, this is Baby. Baby, Auntie—"

"Come on in, now," Auntie Riri interrupted. Her voice was small and distant, so far from its usual authoritative pomp that Lucky wondered if he was imagining some echo from a neighbor's radio. The old woman turned and faded into the interior of the house. Lucky tried to brush aside the awkwardness with an easy smile as he pulled Baby over the threshold.

The moment that Baby entered the house, Lucky felt her tense. Her hand slipped from his as she turned to watch the door closing behind them. He guessed it had something to do with the strong smoky smell. "I told you there's a funk," he said. "Don't worry, though. You get used to it." That last part was a white lie, but he felt the need to reassure Baby. As they sat down at Auntie Riri's kitchen table, Baby eyed the walls and the ceiling, taking in every detail of the room. Her palms spread flat and wide over the table, pressing into it as her gloves lay in her lap.

Auntie Riri slid plates with steaming pork cutlets and heaping piles of applesauce and buttery sweet potato in front of Baby and then Lucky. Lucky's stomach roared with approval, though Baby glowered at her plate like it held a dead cat she was about to dissect. Lucky leaned into her and whispered, "Girl, what's the matter?" But Baby remained silent.

"You both seem quiet," Auntie Riri hummed, tapping some sweet potatoes onto her own plate.

"Baby's just a little shy, is all." He shot Auntie Riri his red-carpet smile and grasped Baby's wrist. Every muscle in her arm was pulled taut like a violin string.

"Quiet isn't bad at all. Not at all." Auntie Riri smiled. "You can get pretty far not saying much. Just because folks don't talk doesn't meant they don't listen. Eat up, now." She nodded, taking her seat at the other end of the table. Baby cautiously lifted her fork and began to scoop the food into her mouth. In no time, she was shoveling the delicious meal down, which Lucky took as a sign that whatever had raised her hackles had passed.

Auntie Riri sat across the table without touching her own plate. "Yes, listening can get you pretty far," she said. "My grandfather was a barber for the white men. Had a shop by City Hall, and he would *listen* to the politicians while he cut their hair. That's how he heard about a huge plot of land that became available for cheap right here. He and his brothers were able to buy it up as soon as it went on sale. They sold it off to their friends and neighbors. Doubled the size of Sankofa."

"Why didn't you ever tell me that, Auntie Riri?"

"Oh, don't be foolish. Of course I've told you about him. Granddaddy all but built Sankofa."

"If you have, I sure don't remember." Lucky looked up from his plate, but Auntie Riri was watching Baby.

"Well, I guess some memories I like to keep in the family," Auntie Riri muttered. Then, even more quietly, "You like those sweet potatoes?" Baby said nothing, sucking on the tines of her fork. "I always wanted her to try my sweet potatoes."

Lucky frowned. "Auntie?"

"Baby . . ."

Baby dropped her fork on her plate and turned to Lucky. "We have to leave."

"Baby, come on—" Lucky said, trying to lean into her. His wrist brushed against the overheated radiator, and the jolt of pain rocked him back. "Aw, shit!"

"Let's go," the girl insisted, wringing her gloves in her fists.

"Just, hold on—" Lucky said, gripping his throbbing wrist.

"Baby?" Auntie Riri interrupted, her eyes fixed on the girl.

Baby stood abruptly, letting the white gloves drop to the floor. "It's you!" she gasped. "You—you—nasty woman!"

The crystal hatred in Baby's eyes shocked Lucky. He nearly grabbed her arm and yanked her back into her seat. He expected Auntie Riri to banish them both from her kitchen, but instead, a tinge of pink entered the old woman's eyes.

"I tried," she said. "I tried for so long, baby—"

"You put me in that place, and you left me!"

"No," Auntie Riri insisted, standing. "No, no, I brought you back."

"My father brought me back."

Auntie Riri furrowed her brow. "Your father? You've never met your father."

"Yes, I did. He—he brought me here, to my house." Baby pointed in the direction of the highway.

Auntie Riri's lips quivered for a moment. Then the crimson slash widened into a large red oval as she began to laugh. "That white man? Honey, you don't know much. He's not your father—"

"Yes he is," Baby barked back.

"That man? *That* man?" Auntie Riri's bosom shook as she continued to laugh.

"Stop laughing!" Baby shouted, her voice cracking.

"You go on and ask him, then. You ask him where you came from and who told him how to get you from there."

"Stop it!"

"Ask him what you are to him. You don't know—"

"I know that you're a lying, nasty, awful woman and I never want to see you again!" Baby screamed.

Lucky was speechless. Reality seemed to be speeding ahead, quickly leaving him behind. He had never seen Baby so furious, nor Auntie Riri so deeply hurt. And how could they possibly know one another?

Auntie Riri had gone quiet, her lips tightened into a dangerous, crimson gash. "What do you know, little girl?" Auntie Riri huffed.

Baby turned to Lucky. "Lucky, please. Let's leave."

He looked between the two women, unsure what to do. But there was an uncharacteristic desperation in Baby's eyes that told him she sensed some real danger. So he nodded and stood by her.

Auntie Riri's steely gaze could have crushed Lucky. The old woman whispered, "I'll show you how much you know—"

Then, suddenly, Lucky was splayed across the floor. The old lady had pushed him down! Head swimming, he looked up in time to see Auntie Riri shove Baby's naked palm against the radiator.

"Baby!" Lucky roared.

A putrid smell filled the room. But it wasn't the smell of burnt flesh. It smelled of something mineral. On the radiator, a slick, thick, darker-than-molasses substance now marked the spot where Baby's hand had been.

Baby cradled her hand against her chest, looking more shocked than hurt. Slowly, she opened her fist. In her palm was the same viscous substance. Only, it wasn't *in* her palm, so much as it *was* her palm. Just as Lucky found a name for the substance, he watched the black tar resolidify back into the skin of Baby's palm.

The air left Lucky's lungs. There was no rationalizing what he had seen, but neither could he deny it. The only consolation was that this girl—Was she a girl? Was she even a person?—appeared just as terrified as he was. Lucky tried searching Baby's mother-of-pearl-button eyes for some answer, but she only stared at her hand. He willed her to meet his gaze, but when she finally raised her head, she locked eyes with Auntie Riri.

"Ask him what you are," Auntie Riri whispered. For a moment, the room was so quiet, Lucky felt that the house itself was holding its breath. Then Baby took off through the front door.

Lucky's legs fell out from under him as he pursued

her into the streets. Why was he following her? He wasn't sure he wanted to have anything to do with her, whatever she was. But he didn't seem to have a choice. She tugged at him with an invisible tether as she flew barefoot over the asphalt to the Orchard Street Bridge. He blinked, and she was instantly on the other side. He had no time to wonder how before he was yanked across, too.

As they ran through the Village and past the houses that lined Orchard Street, Lucky could feel the neighborhood's eyes on him again. He tried to slow his stride to a casual saunter, but anytime Baby got too far ahead, he was wrenched forward, forced to pick up his pace. As familiar faces turned their direction, Lucky realized the neighborhood wasn't watching him. They were watching her.

As they approached the Foxes' house, Lucky finally caught up with Baby. He grabbed her arm and nearly shuddered at how good the contact felt. He flipped open her palm. But there was no burn—no flesh wound. It looked like normal human skin. Wasn't it?

Lucky met her eyes. "Baby, please," he said. "I need some explanation here."

"I don't know," Baby said, tugging at her arm. "I need to speak to my father."

"Your father? Baby, just tell me what the hell is going on." The whole neighborhood was watching. From their yards, from their windows. He could feel it.

"Just go away. Please!" Baby shouted.

"This is some freaky shit—"

"Then just go!"

"I can't." He was gripping her forearm hard now. He couldn't let go, not if it meant losing this feeling. But she pushed him away and ran into the house at 1 Orchard Street.

A small crowd was making their way up Orchard Street. Concerned neighbors or snooping gossips? Either way, Lucky couldn't stick around. It wasn't right for him to be seen chasing after his own woman, for her to be seen fleeing into his opponent's arms. He could feel the veil slipping, and he had to step lightly. If he was clever, he could disperse this crowd with a few words and then get the hell out of here. And then the whole business with this girl—or whatever she was—would be behind him.

But the only direction his feet would carry him was toward the Foxes' front door. As vehemently as he told himself to leave, the tether pulled. Any attempt to go the opposite direction was thwarted. This was worse than the stomach cramp or the dreams; this was a physical impossibility. He could not leave.

His heart dropped into his stomach as he watched the Foxes' house draw closer and closer. Had this been their plan all along? Had Old Man Fox brought Baby here to reel Lucky in? And then what? The only way to find out was to open the door. If he did, Lucky couldn't be sure that he would be able to leave the house without Baby. But it was too late for that. He was stuck to her. He gripped the doorknob and turned.

Stepping into the foyer, Lucky caught the tail end of Gina Fox demanding, "—if she's not your niece then who the hell is she, Eugene?!"

Fox's wife was standing at the bottom of the stairs wearing her coat, her face bright red. Baby stood on the other side of the steps. Both of them stared up at Old Man

Fox, at the top of the stairs in his burgundy suit. His hand gripped the banister like a falcon's perch. His stony glare shifted from his wife to Lucky. For a moment, no one moved. No one spoke.

Then Baby took a step forward and asked, "Father, what am I?"

Bitumen

Fox

•

You are not a sick man. Gina refers to it as a "health scare." This maintains the seriousness and alarm of the episode but lacks any teeth. You both noted the doctor's diagnosis—*not* a heart attack, he assured you, definitely not that. According to him, this kind of thing "isn't surprising for a man your age." But you *were* surprised.

You are not a sick man. But now Gina has you on some low-sodium-high-vegetable diet she read about in a magazine, and she watches you like a hawk every time you climb the stairs. So you lift weights in the garage. You reach your fists into the greasy, black guts of the sedan when the engine needs a tune-up. You carry heavy pumpkins and squash from the garden into the kitchen. You never let anyone see you break a sweat. The neighborhood tells you you're in great shape and doesn't even add *for a retiree*. And still, when you tell Gina that you plan on running for city council against Foote, she worries how it will impact your health.

She does not understand that you have already done everything you can from your current position. You have tried to seed skepticism toward Foote, suggesting to your neighbors that someone should look into his background, his credit, a possible criminal record. You have scoured the bylaws of city council and made calls to other representatives regarding Foote's fitness for the role. You have spoken with Bush and Burdock and Thorne about the dangerous precedent this election might set, the sort of people who might be attracted to Original in the future. But no one seems interested in questioning Foote's presence in the neighborhood, and you are left listening to your own echo. So you alone can stand in the way of Foote taking over everything that you built.

The campaign is not what you'd hoped it would be. You can tell that the neighbors who once reelected you again and again now wish you had just stayed retired. But you fight harder, you strategize. You still never let them see you sweat. You've been on this campaign trail many times before, but you just can't burn the midnight oil anymore. The meetings have to be shorter. You have to write out more detailed talking points. You'd thought that your decades in service of this neighborhood would speak for itself. But they want young blood, and you don't have that.

Foote is young, attractive, and healthy. He knows it, too. Every time he sprints past your window, you know he is taunting you. The neighbors love that he walks everywhere. They love his teen-heartthrob smile and boyish charm. You have experience, but he has muscle and sinew and libido. He has beautiful girls on his arm at every event. When you watch him walk by, brisk but easy, you almost salivate with envy. He doesn't break a sweat, but he isn't even trying. And people can tell the difference.

You have to find some way of keeping up with Foote. So you find your way to the woman named Rhema.

You have been aware of the woman for many years, though you have not spared her much thought until now. Protesters had dragged the elderly woman to at least two city council meetings during your time, wearing what you assumed must be her church outfit: a faded salmon dress with a starched collar and a small hat to match. The podium microphone had to be adjusted to meet her small stature. She would kill twenty minutes of her allotted ten muttering through a statement about the seventy-year-old neighborhood of her youth. You felt sympathy for the protesters, who must not have realized that if *this* was the only person they could find to vouch for "Sankofa," it was doing their argument more harm than good.

The Rhema woman was followed by a protester who argued that the city had targeted the "Sankofa" neighborhood because of its racial makeup, and therefore reparations were owed to the city's Black community. Then a representative from the city would present evidence that I-94's route was designed with the intent of creating minimal disturbance for the city's "highly productive" neighborhoods, and that it had offered to assist with the relocation of qualifying residents. The Rhema woman would sit quietly, her hands in her lap or grasping a small purse, her foggy eyes fixed to a point in the floor.

But the woman's name came up in another context. It was a specific breed of woman that whispered the name Rhema during club events, those women who had always just read some article about how much healthier humanity had been before the advent of such-and-such medicine, who were suspicious of vaccines, who wasted their money on "holistic treatments" and "women's multivitamins." You roll your eyes at these neighbors who sneak away to get folk medicine from an old woman at the edge of town, and yet, here you are on the same woman's doorstep. It seems you just keep surprising yourself.

You do not recognize her for a moment. She is wearing a headwrap with some sort of African print and hammered gold earrings that depict a goose looking at an egg on its back. When she asks what your business is here, you reintroduce yourself and say, "I was wondering if I could talk to you because— Well, because I believe that you can help me."

Her sharp eyes sweep over your face, and you feel as if her gaze is penetrating beneath your skin. Then she says, "Come in, Mr. Fox."

Upon entering, your nostrils are assaulted by a rank and smoky odor. Your fist flies to your lips to stifle a cough. The smell reminds you of construction sites back in New York. But there's something else, too, something that brings you back to Arkansas—the smell of old rot. Rhema is not fazed by the smell and shows you into a modest kitchen. She offers you coffee, a welcome relief from the odor emanating from the walls. She sits across from you with the blankest stare you've ever seen.

"Ma'am, as you may know, I'll be running for city

council this November. Up until a few years ago, I held that seat for over a decade, and I have been a steward of Original Hill's community since long before. I've represented it and captained it through tough spots to the best of my abilities. But I'm no spring chicken." Your tongue runs across your bottom lip. "About a month ago, I had—well, my wife likes to call it a *health scare*. My mother died when I was a boy and I've already outdone my father by ten years. Political life is hard on the body. I have the conviction, you see, but my body, it's . . . I've been told you might be able to give me something to help."

Rhema's eyes remain blank, two dark pools looking back at you. Finally, she says, "You are running against a much younger man."

"Yes, ma'am. But I don't think he has the same dedication to this neighborhood as I do."

"Why?"

"Well, how could he? I've been here for thirty years; he's been here five. He's hardly gotten his feet wet."

Rhema nods. "Of course. Lucky's priorities are a young man's—selfish, unmoored, unserious."

"Exactly! See, folks who've been around as long as you and I can see these kinds of things—"

"And what about you? What are your priorities?"

You are about to regurgitate some campaign jargon, but her eyes dare you not to. You need to give her something deeper. "I'm trying to keep this neighborhood from losing its soul."

She purses her lips. "It's very hard to lose a soul, Mr. Fox. Bury it? Maybe. But lose it altogether?"

"I know it's happening."

"You're so sure you know what this place's soul looks like?"

"I'm old enough to remember the original Original Hill when it was nothing but the I-94. When my daddy moved up here, there wasn't much, but we were proud of our community. We wanted folks to feel like they could lay down roots here, make a home. Now, that's not enough. People want trendy, flashy—they want the whole world in a few blocks . . ."

"They want Lucky."

"Because he's shiny and new! Of course, as a young man, I was attracted to novelty as well. I had to go away to appreciate Original Hill for all it was. But I came back because what we have is worth keeping. And if we don't claim it, we'll lose it, to Foote and who knows who else."

"And what would you do to save this neighborhood's soul, Mr. Fox?"

"Whatever it takes."

Rhema nods. "You say you remember the original Original. But I was here before Original."

"You want me to back these reparations talks? I'll do it. The minute I'm elected, you're on the docket. Now, I can't guarantee much, but since you were a flesh-and-blood resident, I'm sure we can get *you* something. Something to fix up this house—or find a brand-new one if you like."

You're against extending these sorts of promises to most, but who knows if a woman her age is even going to make it to November. Rhema smirks and places her right wrist in her left hand. "I cannot give you what you've come here for. Besides, one body made stronger will not do much to solve your problem."

"What do you mean?"

"Even *if* you win against Lucky, only more like him will come. Just as ambitious and flighty. And if this neighborhood is already welcoming them, drifting away from its soul? As you said, we're no spring chickens.

"But there is a way to make Lucky less slippery, to make him show his true nature. You can make this neighborhood recognize its soul again, and then all of Lucky's smoke and mirrors will lose their power."

"How?"

The woman hums. "Mr. Fox, do you know what it is I give your women—Original Hill women, I mean—when they come to me?"

"Some kind of medicine?"

She shrugs. "Sometimes. More often, I tell them stories, and that is enough. I would like to tell you a story, Mr. Fox. Then it will be up to you if you are willing to do what it takes to protect this place you love so much."

It is a funny little ghost story she tells you. Though you leave her house denouncing the visit as a waste of time, the story elicits a lingering sense of nostalgia. Sitting in your office that evening, your mind drifts back to Arkansas, when you were just a boy no older than six. The nights come back faster than the days—the musty smell of the thin cotton comforter, the sound of your daddy's snoring through the walls, the roar of crickets and cicadas and

God knows what other calls that escaped the woods just outside your window.

You remember those woods more vividly than the house you grew up in. The trees were so densely packed that you could not estimate its depth. They reached their shadows through your bedroom window at night, inspiring nightmares and tickling your imagination. You remember your mother, her stomach inflated like a balloon with your brother inside, sipping tea from a tall glass and staring out at the wood as you played in the grass at her feet. "It's so nice to be by a wild place," she used to say.

You remember the flashes of red and white, red and white, red and white, thrown against the trees as the ambulance took your mother away. She was white as a sheet, except for her fingers, which were crimson and stunk of iron. It was night when that ambulance cried into the darkness, fainter and fainter. It was night when they laid your mother and brother in the ground beside one another. It was night when your daddy turned the house inside out, threw a tarp over your world, and tied it to the back of his truck. You dozed off in the passenger seat, and by the time you woke up, you were already driving through Missouri.

You returned to Arkansas only once because your daddy had insisted on being buried in the family plot rather than up north in Original. By then, you were in your thirties, and you had lived a life far away from there. You were gainfully employed in the greatest city in the world, and you'd already met the girl you were planning on marrying. You did not remember much about Arkansas, and what you did, you didn't like. You went so far as to resurrect your brother through some carefully worded phrases in order to deter Gina from accompanying you to the funeral. You had planned on telling the truth about Isaac, but you would soon find that keeping him alive could be convenient. You are not a dishonest man; everyone lies to their wives.

The funeral was a whirlwind of droning eulogies, reacquainting with family, heavy food, hastily made decisions, and seeking shade from the unforgiving Southern sun. You contributed a meticulously prepared and well-spoken speech, and you accepted everyone's condolences with grace. But the twang in your cousins' voices itched your brain, and you forced yourself not to sneer anytime someone spat their chew into the grass. Every word embarrassed or infuriated you as they drawled on about how brave you were to face the dangers of the "inner city." When your cousin Maryjean tried to show you a photograph of your mother at some pro-segregation rally, it was the last straw. You were not cut from the same cloth. In that moment, you knew that you had buried your last connection to this place.

The evening before you left, you snuck away from the family and returned to your childhood home. The house was occupied, but you walked past the whitewashed gate and around the back. The woods behind the house still towered over you. You were used to bastions of steel and glass climbing into the heavens, and yet these giants of dark gray wood took your breath away.

Standing before the wild wood, you contemplated walking into that seemingly impenetrable thicket, not stopping until you'd come out the other side. Instead, you turned back toward the road. The next morning, you left with only a box of your mother's keepsakes from Cousin Maryjean's attic. You let her keep the photograph.

You sit at your desk and think back to that wall of trees, partition and threshold. You think back to the girl in the fairy tale that the old woman told you. *She lives in that wood, as all wild things do.* You're not sure where that thought comes from. Then before you know it, you have dozed off.

Your mother appears in your dream. She is still very pregnant, but somehow you know it is not Isaac in her belly. It is someone else. She is not in your house in Arkansas but the house in Original Hill. You watch her shuffle between the kitchen and the garage, gathering items from the cabinets: gardening gloves, an N95 mask, a large white plastic bucket, an old broom that she snaps in half over her knee. She does not notice you watching as she carries these things to the attic.

A few days later, you open your front door and find a cardboard box filled with two thirty-two-ounce canisters of turpentine, along with an invoice from an art-supplies store. You have no recollection of ordering these. When you take the box to the attic, you find a pile of the exact items your mother had retrieved in the dream.

A gallon of birch pitch arrives the next day. The Rhema woman's voice emerges from your memory: "Must be birch. Pine tar wouldn't do." You check your email; you ordered the tar from a wholesaler that sells it for soapmaking. This time, Gina catches you carrying the can up to the attic. When she asks you what it is for, you tell her that you've decided to do some repairs on the roof.

She fails to hide her apprehension as she asks, "Are you sure that's a good idea with your heart?" You wave her off and carry the tar up to the attic.

You try to set it down gently, but it thuds against the hardwood floor. You are breathing heavily, and your heart is pounding against your eardrums. Your vision adjusts to the low light, focusing on the collection of objects in the center of the room.

"The man gathered four materials: tar, turpentine, bone, and breath," the Rhema woman had said. "The first two were easy to acquire. The third was trickier, but he knew where to start: a large bridge not far from his home. Its concrete was rife with fissures sprouting flowering weeds. Embedded in the cracked foundation, he discovered a stone with a cross etched into it. There, he began to dig."

You shiver recalling the old woman's tale. You decide to throw a tarp over these items and make your way down the steps as swiftly as you can. On the way to your office, you pass the bay windows that face Orchard Street, and you catch sight of Foote. He is wearing his usual gray suit and strolling past with a hop in his step. You expect him to disappear after he turns the corner, but he stops and leans against your garden wall. He bends down and lifts his leg to adjust something, maybe his pants or the heel of his shoe. You watch the strong curve of his back move with ease, his brown hand grasping the redbrick wall. If you look hard enough, you can see the muscles and tendons of that hand flexing, groping. He places his foot back on the ground and walks on, but you find yourself unable to tear your eyes away from that spot on the wall.

That night, you dream of the man from the old woman's story. He is older than you imagined. He scratches at the concrete beneath a bridge, tearing away fistfuls of dandelions and thistle. His fingernails are filled with dirt, gravel, and oil. Blood stains his fingers as he claws against stone. The muscles in his arm and shoulder shudder beneath his stained shirt. He huffs and snorts like an animal.

You watch as his digging widens a crack in the concrete, his hands grasping against the gaping dark. You wonder what he is so desperately searching for. Soon, you see it. It emerges out of the concrete, hard and round and bigger than your head. It is caked in decades of soil, which flies off in gritty clouds. After a minute, you recognize it is an old hatbox.

The hands pull the hatbox from the concrete and feel its weight. Something slides around inside of it, and the hands slowly lift the lid. Your heart pounds in your ears as the hands reveal its contents to be—

You wake in bed beside your wife, sweat dripping down your brow. You try to settle back into bed but find your feet uncomfortable. It takes you a moment to register that you are wearing your shoes.

Gina notices your nerves the next morning over coffee. She asks if you are feeling alright and you tell her it was just a bad night's sleep. When she tries to nudge with follow-up questions, you tell her that you should get started on the roof and make your way up to the attic. You cannot stomach Gina's probing right now. She wants to blame everything on your stupid heart.

When you flick on the attic light, you see the dirt-covered hatbox beside the other materials. You rush back to your office and stay there until dinner.

Gina is asleep when you hear something moving in the attic that evening. You get out of bed to investigate. Peeking past the attic door, you see someone hunched over the materials. You recognize the man from the old woman's story. He is wearing workman's overalls, a ratty old shirt, his winter boots, and Gina's gardening gloves. He is prying the top off the can of birch tar, and once he wrenches it loose, a burnt, phenolic scent wafts from it. He grunts, affixes the N95 mask over his nose and mouth, and then tips the gallon of tar into the large plastic bucket.

You watch ribbons of viscous tar pour out, doubling up onto themselves as they hit the basin. Even with the mask on, the rank smell fills the man's nostrils. Some tar drips down the side of the can and onto the gloves as the man shakes out the last drops. The thin black threads glimmer in the attic's low light.

As he turns to grab the canisters of turpentine, you notice a streak of black across his thigh. Rubbing it off his overalls only succeeds in spreading more tar to his glove. He curses under his breath, snatching up the first canister of turpentine. As he empties it into the bucket, a whiff of sweet, piney air sneaks past the fabric of the mask.

He goes to grab the second turpentine, but the tar on the glove has fused to the first can. He grips the metal with his other hand and yanks, grinding his teeth. Finally, the can tears away from the glove with a sickening rip that leaves fuzzy brown fibers adhered to the metal. Then he dumps the second canister of turpentine into the bucket.

The man lifts the hatbox and removes its lid. He lets its contents sink beneath the surface of the concoction.

You notice movement inside the bucket. You squint through the darkness, but now everything is still. The smell begins to grow stronger through the mask. And then you see it again, a small ebb and flow in the thick liquid, as if the tar is starting to simmer. Maybe this is some sort of chemical reaction between the pitch and the turpentine. Or, more likely, you have been asleep in bed all along, and this is all some dream. But you do not wake and instead watch the man insert the broken-off broom handle in the mixture and stir.

"He poured his intentions into the tar," Rhema had said. "His hopes for it. His fears."

This dream is so vivid, you can feel the gloved hands chafing against the wooden handle as the tar is stirred. The more it is mixed, the harder the tar resists, and the more the muscles must strain to get the tar moving. Bicep, shoulder, and back all groan against the constant rotation of the tar.

Suddenly, an angry bite stings the underside of your wrist. The broom handle drops against the side of the bucket. The smallest fleck of tar has landed on the exposed skin between your glove and shirt. The flesh around the minuscule droplet is already growing an angry pink. The mixture has burned you.

Inside the bucket, the tar is boiling. Fat, dark bubbles rise to its surface and burst before sinking back down. You slip your shirt sleeve down your arm to close the space of throbbing, exposed skin. Then the stirring resumes.

As it thickens, the concoction fills more and more of the bucket. The heat makes your eyes and cheeks ache. The meat of your neck screams as more rogue flecks of tar hit it. The mask is no match against the stench. Noxious air swirls in your nostrils and lines your lungs. No amount of coughing or clearing of your throat can excise it.

You beg the man from the story to stop this, but he will not, even as the thickening tar demands more strength, as it begins to feel like mixing hardening cement. The muscles oscillate between soreness and sharp pain. Sweat pours down from the forehead and neck into the bucket.

Then the concoction changes. A few laborious turns form the dark liquid into a smooth, wet ball in the center of the white plastic. The man from the story sighs and collapses onto the bucket, and you wake in bed to the gray morning light.

You ease into the soft mattress and pull the comforter against your quivering shoulders. Your entire body is sore, your arms stretched like taffy. Your eyelids begin to droop back into sleep when Gina enters the room. "Dear, I tried washing your work clothes, but I think there's something—" Her voice stops. Then she gasps, "Is that *you*? Get out of the bed! Right now! If that smell is you, take a shower!"

You allow the scalding water to massage your body. Your mind wanders back to the shiny black ball at the bottom of the bucket in your dream. Drying yourself, you notice a pink scar on your wrist, in the same place the tar had burned the man. The Rhema woman's voice comes to you once again: "Seven nights. It took seven nights to complete the task."

A wave of exhaustion hits, and you return to bed. The shower has done nothing to eliminate the smell, but by the time Gina returns to discover this, you are fast sleep.

You are not a sick man, but you are overcome with some sort of flu. The aches and exhaustion of your body speak for themselves. Because of the persistent smell, your wife timidly suggests you sleep on the sofa in the parlor. You are so exhausted you hardly notice the difference. Soon, the entire house is filled with the stench regardless of which room you occupy. Gina lights every candle in the house, opens the windows, and sprays the walls with air fresheners. Finally, with no other recourse, she flees the house, citing errands and appointments at the club. When she is gone, you sleep through most of the day dreamlessly. But at night, you continue to dream of the man in the attic, stirring the tar until it solidifies into a smooth ball.

After nearly a week, you can hardly move your body. Your bones feel like they have been broken and refastened a dozen times. When you demand your arm to lift and scratch your chin, it does so slowly, like a rusted hinge. Small red welts have risen along your neck, and you taste iron and sweat all the time. You can hardly keep your eyes open for ten minutes. *My God*, you think, *I am a prisoner in my own skin.*

You hardly register Gina perching on the couch beside you. "I think you should see a doctor."

You tell her, "I'm feeling better already. Just want to get a few more hours of rest."

"Tomorrow, Eugene. You are going to the doctor *tomorrow.*"

You nod, though your head seems to move of its own accord. When Gina leaves for her errands, you lift your sore body off the sofa. Every muscle cries in protest. You pull yourself up the stairs to the attic. The afternoon sunlight filtering through the dusty air makes everything in the room appear like an old photograph. You slowly approach the plastic white bucket. The black tar ball glistens in the center, just as the man had left it. The slick dark surface reflects your gaunt face back at you.

The mask and gloves sit beside the bucket. You consider waiting for the man from the story to return, but in the end, you don the protective gear yourself. You remember the old woman's story well enough.

Fingertips sink below the ball's obsidian surface. The hand pulls until a chunk of tar tears away with an unnerving squelch. The substance acts like wet sand in the palm and is heavier than expected.

You notice that the contents of the hatbox seem to have completely dissolved into the mixture.

The hand smacks the substance onto a cardboard box covered in a tarp, waving away the resulting dust before forming the tar back into a ball. It takes many rounds of trial and error to get the tar to stick to itself rather than the gloves. The hands form the rest of the tar into a head, which they place atop the round body. You can feel the burn of lactic acid broiling in your arms and shoulders each time the hands pull and yank and knead. You are in no condition to do any more physical activity. You become nauseated and lightheaded, though it is unclear whether this is from the overexertion or the substance's strong odor. By the time the hands have scraped the last of the tar from the bottom of the tub, the sun has set.

There is a knock at the door. You run to it just as Gina cracks it open. "How are you feeling, dear?"

"Much better," you say, trying to fill your voice with a strength you do not have. "I thought I'd better get back to the roof."

"Oh." Gina nods. "Well, would you like to come down for dinner?"

You follow Gina downstairs, making sure to close the door tightly behind you. Dinner is quiet. You eat as much as you can even though you have no appetite. Staying upright in the chair is a chore. Gina holds a napkin over her nose between each bite.

"I'll see if Dr. Wood has any availability tomorrow," she says at the end of the meal. "It's that *smell*, I just can't imagine—"

"I have everything under control," you say. Gina sighs and takes your half-full plate away.

When you return to the attic, the stacked balls of tar face you in the low light. "She'll need eyes. Buttons would be good for that," the old woman had said. You snap two large white buttons off your shirt and press them into the tar figure's head.

"Ears, too." You rummage through some of the boxes until you find an old coat. You break the buttons off and press them onto the sides of the head.

"She'll need something nice to wear." Your tired eyes

fall on a box in the corner labeled "Babette Fox." You open it and find the keepsakes that you brought back from Arkansas years ago, including a stack of sundresses. You fan out the blush-and-canary dress on top and place it around the tar figure.

"She ought to have something to cover her head, too." You are at a loss until you hear a great wind pick up outside, and then a soft knocking on the attic window. A large straw-colored sun hat is caught on a nearby tree branch, dancing in the wind. You pull it inside and stare at it for a moment, wondering if the serendipity should chill or encourage you. You place it on the figure. The hat is almost as large as the figure itself, but the tar is stuck fast in its place, and the additional weight does not cause it to lean or slouch.

You look the figure over. The Rhema woman had said nothing about shoes or jewelry or any other clothing. She also never mentioned a mouth, though you find the figure staring back at you with button eyes and ears grotesque without one. You take your index finger and swipe it across the face, creating a slash of a mouth.

"Last thing," the old woman had said. "You need to give her a breath." You had nearly laughed at this point in the story. Now, however, you solemnly bend over the figure, inhale softly, and exhale onto its slash-mouth. Then you step back and watch it.

The tar-baby sits right there and watches back.

The longer you look at the creation, the more absurd and uglier it seems. The spheres of tar are lumpy and misshapen. The buttons are too large, and the ears are crooked. The entire package is buried in the fabric of the old dress and the oversize hat, like a child that has snuck into its mother's closet. You grunt, something between a laugh and a cough, and pain rattles in your chest.

All that work, all that labor, all those sleepless nights and lost days, and that awful smell. You have ruined your body. You have ruined your house and maybe your marriage—for this? Just to create this grotesque thing? This is your great work that will protect your neighborhood from the interlopers?

Another wave of exhaustion overtakes you, and you fall asleep right there on the floor of the attic. You wake in the same spot, stiff and groggy. The morning sun warms your face, and the air smells like fresh rain. As you turn to stretch out your back, you notice the girl curled up on the tarp wearing your mother's dress and a straw-colored hat.

She is sleeping soundly, her chest rising and falling lightly with her breath. Your first impulse is to reach out and touch her—to wake her, or to see if your fingers will sink into her dark skin like tar. But you resist. You know the power of that skin.

You think back to the man in the story. "He encouraged every gentleman he suspected of having ill intentions to kiss the tar girl's hand. The gentlemen would immediately be smitten, unable to think of anyone but the tar girl. Now incapable of directing their charms at anyone else, they were exposed for the frauds they were and chased from the neighborhood. And when the man died, the tar girl remained, the glue keeping the neighborhood that he had built intact."

As you watch the young woman sleep, you can already feel her pull. You know that this will work. Lucius Foote will not be able to resist her, but you must be careful. You cannot let her touch anyone else. You do not know how long it will take for the girl to unmask Foote as a charlatan, but you will need to keep her close so that her pull does not spread. You wrest your weary body out of the attic, away from the girl's pull.

When you return, the girl is awake. You are surprised and cautious, but you have everything under control. For a week, you bring her food and water, and you take away her waste. Everything she does, everything she is, appears deceptively human. It is hard to connect this sweet and beautiful girl who calls you Father to those nightmares, but your perpetually sore body will not let you forget. You spend this time telling her that she cannot touch anyone other than one and only one person. You must remind yourself not to touch her.

When you finally bring her out of the attic, you fall back on your usual lie: Isaac. You call her your niece, though she knows that you brought her into this world. You tell her that this is a game, and she plays along. You watch her sit on your garden wall. You watch neighbors pass by and glance at one another with reticence. At least she does not touch them.

You just miss the moment that Lucius Foote strolls down Orchard Street and touches her skin for the first time, but it happens. When you catch him walking away, you doubt whether it has worked. The aches in your shoulders and ribs and hips suddenly feel more acute, and you cough tar-stained spit into your fist. You wonder then, and many times after, if this is all worth it, if you have done something too strange to justify.

But you wipe the spit away. You are a good man. You did what you did to protect your home.

You watch Foote become more and more enamored with Baby, who seems to have plucked your mother's name out of thin air and taken it as her own. You watch Foote's attention shift from Original Hill to Baby. You watch Original Hill lose trust in Lucius Foote and turn back to you.

You forget to watch for Gina until you catch her kissing Baby on the forehead. But you are still not a bad man. You have a lot of balls to juggle here. And it is all very strange, but the ends justify the means.

All this time, you hide the fact that you have utterly lost all sense of smell, and that all food tastes like ash on your tongue. You tell no one about the clouds that now ring the edges of your vision. Your muscles never recovered from that flu, and your hands—especially your hands—seem to be deteriorating by the day into a painful stiffness. Your lungs burn always, and you do your best to suppress a cough that causes your ribs to ache. You wipe away more black spit. But you never, ever let them see you sweat. You are a good man, a healthy man.

Your only regret is that you cannot stop dreaming about the man from the story, stirring that tar and forming the figure and clawing at that crack in the bridge. He never leaves you.

Even now, when you must stand before Gina and Foote and Baby to answer for what you have done, you stand tall. You speak clearly. You do not waver as you tell them the story of the man who made a person out of tar to save his home's soul. Just as you finish, the girl asks, "So . . . Father, what am I?"

And you tell her. "Tar. You are only tar."

As soon as you say this, you hear voices. They seem to come from all around you, low but building. You feel the steps on which you stand begin to quake. Shadows flash through the windows, dark figures against the receding sunlight. As the voices grow nearer, you start to recognize some. They are your neighbors.

All of Original Hill is gathered on Orchard Street. The Thornes, the Iveses, the Woods, the Reeds, the Bushes, the Burdocks, and the Branches all begin to pound on your door and scratch at your windows. You are sure you hear stones and bricks thudding against the house. It is louder than the worst winter storms. Over the din, you can make out a few fragments of shouts. They are demanding to be let inside. They want *her*.

You look back at the girl, and in her eyes, you can see that she has defied you. You were not as careful as you thought. She has touched everyone.

You are not a sick man. You are not a bad man. You are a good man. You did what you needed to do. It was all just too strange.

A window breaks. Your wife and your rival run to bar the door, which bends at its hinges. Glass shatters beside the girl's head, and before you realize what you are doing, you grab her wrist and pull her toward you, out of the way. Then you realize she is not wearing her gloves.

You release her arm, but it is too late. All you want is to grab again. Before you can, the doors and windows crash open. Your wife and your rival run for cover. But you stand on the steps beside your creation, squeeze your eyes shut, and shout, “Get out!”

When you open your eyes a moment later, the neighbors are all still there, standing in the foyer. But the girl has vanished.

Rhema

•

You do not know this man, but you recognize his face. It is the same face on the postcards that are stuffed into your mail slot encouraging you to vote for city council this November. These are the same eyes you have watched glaze over in boredom when you enter that gray meeting room in City Hall, the same mouth that would pucker with disinterest as you stood at a podium to tell the story of Sankofa's rape. When he speaks, you recognize that same gruff drone that would ask Nia and the other Justice for Sankofa volunteers what, exactly, they expected the city to do about a place that was demolished nearly seventy years ago. You would just sit quietly, massaging your ruined hands.

In a less literal but truer sense, you recognize the sleeplessness in these once-bored eyes, the uncertainty in his voice, the wrinkles that cut deeper around his lips like a dog left to starve. He is desperate, and it is a desperation that you have seen time and again.

Usually, the white people who appear at your door are women. Often, they have already sought out other forms of so-called "alternative medicine" to cure their varying ailments—migraines, insomnia, anxiety, aches of the body, mind, and soul. You are not entirely sure why they come to you. You certainly didn't call them, but perhaps they come out of some deep intuition that drew their foremothers to your foremothers, expecting you to care for them in ways doctors will not. You are no healer, never claimed to be. You simply know forgotten things. But knowing is often enough, and they pay handsomely for it.

You invite this white man inside and offer him a cup of coffee. He begins to tell you how his body is failing him. *Political life is hard on the body,* he says. *I've been told you might be able to give me something to help.* You keep your face from cracking, though your lips threaten to sneer. You have seen for yourself how deeply politics can etch itself in flesh. You can still recall the premature gray in your father's hair, the cane your granddaddy walked with—and they were real leaders, not some old man trying to freeze time.

And what does he expect you to offer him anyway? Immortality? The fountain of youth? You are ready to turn this man away, but his slate eyes meet yours, and you see that desperation once more. It is the anguish of a dying man clinging to life, grasping in the dark for something, anything. With the right push, he can become exactly what you've been waiting for.

"What would you do to save this neighborhood's soul, Mr. Fox?"

The man straightens his spine. "Whatever it takes."

You speak his language. You agree with him on Lucky's youthful priorities, though you know that this man's are just as dubious. You even tell him that the house he now sits in predates his precious *Original*, this world that he wishes to return to but that never was. He does not see what you are telling him. Instead, he gives you promises that you know he is not planning on keeping. No matter. You guide him away from the impossible thing that he has come for and toward another almost-impossible thing.

"I would like to tell you a story, Mr. Fox," you say. "Then it will be up to you if you are willing to do what it takes to protect this place you love so much."

When the man leaves, he believes that you have handed him some dark, volatile secret. He recognizes its power, even if he dismisses it at first. He may even believe that he somehow tricked it out of you, with charm or with cleverness. He may believe that you volunteered the knowledge simply because he asked, because who are you to deny him? That is the story that he has been told since he was a boy, that he tells himself throughout each day.

He believes that you have given him something that he can use for his own devices. He cannot imagine that you are sending him off to do your work, work that you have waited nearly all your life to complete.

You sit at the table, your hands trembling with anticipation. It all felt too easy. After the years of waiting and mourning, it's all too convenient, him dropping in like this. You feel a twinge in your wrist and press your thumb into it. Well, you can't take it back now. All you can do is wait for the story you told him to take hold.

•••

This is the story that you know.

In 1938, a girl named Rhema was born in a place named Sankofa, but her path was laid out long before then. When her granddaddy arrived nearly thirty years earlier, Sankofa had been a handful of houses clustered about a commercial street on the outskirts of a city that was barreling headfirst into the electric modernity of the new century. There was an AME Church, a barbershop, a grocer, and a convenience store that sold baked goods on the weekends. The residents were largely the same modest group of Black folks who had settled there in the 1880s. No one could remember who had first thought of the name Sankofa, and many insisted that multiple members of the party had received divine revelation simultaneously. Rhema's granddaddy married one of the daughters of an original founder and invited his brothers to settle in Sankofa, too.

This is a story you know well.

Rhema's granddaddy owned a barbershop downtown, right by City Hall. It wasn't like the barbershop where the boys and men of Sankofa spent their evenings listening to the radio and running their counsel, letting their music spill out onto the sidewalk. This was a white man's barbershop, frequented by the city's politicians. Her granddaddy had quite a few regulars, and even those he groomed less frequently referred to him by name rather than "boy." He became friendly with the city's leaders, and they came to know him as a credit to his race.

In 1915, her granddaddy overheard the mayor speaking

with another city official about a large plot of land going up for sale right by Sankofa. By the end of that day, her granddaddy had called up his brothers and every business owner in the neighborhood and told them to pool as much money as they could get together. By the end of the week, Sankofa had doubled in size.

It wasn't just the land purchase that established her grandaddy as one of Sankofa's fathers. If his morning patrons at the barbershop mentioned job openings, he made sure Sankofa folks knew about them that evening. He also established an Urban League chapter to help folks keep those jobs. In 1925, he led the fundraising to build a community hall on the north side of Sankofa, a towering lodge built from oak where folks could host everything from charity luncheons to cribbage games. He brought W. E. B. Du Bois and Booker T. Washington to speak there, and years later would boast that he possessed a ledger with both men's signatures.

As more folks heard about Sankofa, more began to arrive from farther afield. Rhema's father would greet them at the Union Depot with her granddaddy's business card, so they all knew who they could contact if they needed help finding work or settling in. Her father was her granddaddy's mirror. He stood by his old man's side at the barbershop, on the Urban League, at the head of the neighborhood.

This is a story rarely told.

When her grandaddy had married Rhema's nana, he had been too new to the neighborhood to catch the wary distance most of the neighbors kept from her. Of course, they could not deny her handsome features or the soul with which she led the church choir. But outside of the psalms and spirituals, the woman was regarded as too quiet. This quiet, some whispered, held a thing that many had hoped to leave behind when Sankofa's founding families fled the South.

By the time her granddaddy caught on, they had already married and borne Rhema's father. Granddaddy alerted his son to Nana's strangeness when he was old enough, but both believed, like the rest of the neighborhood, that the woman was harmless as long as she kept what was cloaked in that quiet stowed away. The trouble was, when Rhema's mother died bringing her into the world, Nana stepped in to care for her. From the moment she laid eyes on the babe, Rhema's nana loved to speak to her.

My Baby. Baby. Baby.

Rhema was sure that she could remember Nana cooing as she was rocked in her arms. Nana's songs were peculiar spirituals, unlike the ones she sang at church, with words Rhema often did not understand. Rhema listened with bated breath to Nana's bedtime stories, the same ones Nana's mother had told her. They were impossible stories of strange happenings, of women casting damning incantations on those that scorned them and reanimating their lost loves with tar and turpentine. Hoodoo fairy tales, her granddaddy scoffed.

But Nana always shook her head at that. "They are true," she said, "truer than most."

As Rhema grew older, Nana showed her that if you

were quiet enough, the land could speak to you. Even the house, which her granddaddy had built with his brothers from wood and brick, could speak through the materials from which it had been wrought. Nothing, Nana taught her, was without language. It was through this language that Rhema learned the knowledge that Nana carried, that Nana's mother and her mother's mother had carried: how to pull wellness and good tidings from the earth, how to dispel an evil eye or expose an ill intent. She learned that, like a tree, a well-told story could take root and bear fruit as real as a shiny apple in your hand.

Rhema knew well enough not to share her knowledge with the rest of Sankofa. The neighborhood would not tolerate such a thing. But privately, she held on to Nana's lessons for dear life.

Rhema was a budding teenager when Nana passed on. By then, Sankofa had boomed far beyond the small community Nana's father had founded. Flashy cars drove down Main Street, honking at children who played in puddles. They celebrated public festivals, and there were increasing talks of getting involved in the movement gaining traction in places like Montgomery. Nana's death did not slow the work that Rhema's granddaddy and father spearheaded. They stood at the bow of the ship, barreling forward into a new future, side by side as always. It was fitting that the two perished together, in an automobile accident, leaving Rhema alone with nothing but Sankofa.

The neighborhood tried its best, but all this death surrounding the young girl was a bad omen. Many remembered Rhema's proximity to her nana and worried about what that strange, quiet woman had handed off to this quiet girl. When Rhema turned up pregnant one day, it only proved that the girl had a troublesome nature.

Folks might have come around eventually. Even those who judged her harshest for having a child outside of wedlock may have forgiven her in honor of her father and granddaddy. But at the end of Rhema's third trimester, the I-94 came through. There was hardly time for the neighbors to organize before white men arrived with sledgehammers to splinter their homes and wrecking balls that sent brick and mortar tumbling into the streets. Men, women, and children were pulled out of stores by their arms and hair, then sent scrambling by city workers laying asphalt. Even those whose houses were not demolished for the sin of being in the highway's path packed up their shiny Cadillacs and sped away from Sankofa. When Rhema's baby was born, there was no one left to help—let alone condemn her.

This is a story you never tell.

To ask how the thing happened would be an insult. It would be pointless to parse out how much of the blame lay with the restless baby, who for a week howled with anger at the world it had been forced into; or with the din of the construction that threatened to split open Rhema's head; or with the men who threw cans at those few who remained; or with the fumes that choked out rational thought and made everything taste burnt; or with the ever-present fear that somebody might come with a torch in the night to finish the purge that the highway's construction had begun. The simplicity of it was that, however she sliced it, Rhema was to blame.

Maybe if there had been more neighbors, someone might have insisted on checking in on the lonely girl with the new baby. Someone might have noticed sooner that the baby had stopped crying at night. Had it not been for Mr. Farmer and his memory of the girl's father and granddaddy, it is possible that no one would have known anything at all. If he hadn't knocked on her door, Rhema would have followed her daughter into that unknowable darkness.

But Farmer had swept up hair at her granddaddy's barbershop. And her father had handed him the keys to the house that he was now emptying into his sedan. Farmer thought of Rhema as a nice kid in a bad spot. It was a lasting respect for her ancestry that brought him to her door.

When the girl opened the door, she looked dead where she was standing. Farmer asked how she was, how long ago she'd seen a doctor, if she was alone, if she was planning on staying here or moving like the rest. Her eyes only stared through him. But as soon as he asked after the baby, something fearful flashed behind her vague expression, prompting Farmer to ask if he could come inside. Her body tensed, but Farmer easily pushed past her.

It was long past sunset and the girl's lights were all off, but even in the darkness Farmer could see that the walls were stained by smog. The smell trapped within was unbearable. He held his handkerchief over his nose and mouth, looking all about the house. Anytime he turned back to the girl, her movements were sluggish and aimless, though her eyes kept darting to the bedroom. Farmer made his way through the doorway and into the small room with a bed, a rug, and wooden chifforobe all centered around a rosy-pink bassinette.

The second he saw it, he knew it had died. Asphyxiated. Judging by the little body, it had been days. Maybe even a week. Farmer turned away from the horrific thing and faced its mother. As soon as his eyes fell on her, she devolved into a cough that rattled her little chest and doubled her over onto her knees.

"Damn it," Farmer swore. With one hand still holding the handkerchief that shielded his lungs, he grabbed her and hoisted her to her feet. He pulled the poor spasming girl through the front door, out of the house, and let her fall to her knees in the front yard. "Why didn't you just go with the rest of them?" he demanded. "Why didn't you go?" But if the girl understood him, she was too busy retching into the grass to reply.

Farmer gathered the few others in the neighborhood who had stuck it out, but when they all returned to the house, he was shocked to see that the girl had gone back inside. Farmer pounded on the door.

"Listen, girl," he shouted through the door. "It isn't right, you know. We've got to bury it."

"Lord-a-mercy," a woman muttered behind him.

"Rhema, come on now. Give it to us. To bury."

"Her!" the girl shouted, though her voice was so croaky with smoke and dust, at first Farmer did not recognize it. "And she is mine!"

"Don't be foolish, Rhema!" Farmer scolded. "What's happened is good and done. No turning it back now. All there is to do is lay it to rest."

"It isn't human, letting a thing like that happen," one of the men grunted.

Farmer spun around and shushed him just as the door

creaked open. The girl peeked out, weakly. He pulled the door open the rest of the way and led the men into the bedroom. They did not have the time to make a casket, but someone found a hatbox, which they placed the body in. When they came back out, Farmer saw that Rhema was standing separate from the other women, who were all clutching their crosses and tying their robes tighter around themselves. Farmer looked from the shivering girl to these women. He shook his head. "Shame," he muttered. "Shame."

They buried the infant in a plot beside her grandmother, grandfather, great-grandmother, and great-grandfather. Her tiny headstone bore no name. Her mother stood back and watched as the last of the Sankofa men dug the hole, placed the hatbox inside, and covered it over. The reverends and deacons had already moved on by then, so the ceremony was swift and amateur. Rhema's lips did not move to the prayer that the men and women said over the baby's grave. Afterward, all the others quickly disappeared into their cars, leaving only Farmer to offer the girl a ride home. She gazed at the fresh soil, mute as the trees around her. Farmer grabbed her arm, and she swayed for a moment before acquiescing and following him to his car.

Passing by the growing noise and stink of construction, Farmer knew that he could not let this girl back into that killing house. "Now, Rhema," he said. "How'd you like to come with me away from the city? There's a place called Briar Heights. Some of the others in the neighborhood've already gone there, and they say it's real nice. Real nice there." The girl said nothing, so he went on.

"Say everything's all new there. We'll have things there—can build something there—"

"I can't," Rhema said plainly. They were the first words she had spoken since he had led those men into her house.

"Come on now, girl. You're not well. We've got to get you somewhere where you can get better."

"My father's house. My granddaddy's house," Rhema muttered. "Leave it? For them to pave over? You can't ask me that."

"I can't leave you there. In that house—that evil house? It isn't right—"

"You can't ask me that," she said.

Then he was parked and she was stepping out of his car. She shut the door behind her before turning and looking at him through the passenger-side window with empty eyes. "Thank you kindly for taking me home," she said.

As she turned away, he begged. "Rhema. Please. Please!" But she kept her back to him. He watched her mount the stairs, enter the house, and shut the door.

The baby death and its mother's madness were the final signs that the last of Sankofa's residents needed to get out. Soon, every house on the block was in the process of abandonment, except for Rhema's. Many times, Farmer considered knocking on her door again, forcing her to come with them, for her own good. He was sure that it was what her father and granddaddy would have wanted.

But what would everyone else say? If he brought this cursed woman along with him, how could they possibly leave behind the pain and humiliation of Sankofa's demise? There were moments when the memory of that awful, choking smell that inhabited that house returned to him so suddenly, he began to cough. So, days later than he had originally intended, Farmer packed the last of his possessions into his car and made his way to the road. All he could do now was imagine some sweet-smelling thing and hope that it would cover over the toxic memory of that corrupted house.

Roses, maybe . . .

This is a story you cannot tell.

Rhema was alone. She sat on the edge of her bed for unknowable hours, neither eating nor sleeping. When she was lucid enough, she found herself muttering, *My baby, baby, baby*. In her complete deprivation and seclusion, she fed on her most buried recollections.

Much of her life had been defined by her granddaddy, Sankofa's beloved, and her father, his ardent would-be successor. But now, sitting in the center of the ruins of everything that they had built, Rhema thought of her nana. In the clarity of that dark house, she found solace in Nana's old songs and stories, which seemed to her the realest representation of this disorderly, logicless world. She found solace, and also instruction.

There was no one left to see her—let alone stop her—from stealing away in the night and exhuming the hatbox. It was hardly grave robbing, she reminded herself. She had brought this child into the world, so she ought to be the one to decide what was done with her. Under cover of darkness, she pilfered a pail from the construction site not ten feet from her door, filling it to the brim with tar. She wrestled her largest pot—the one Nana had used to boil hogs' heads for stew—and filled it with a mixture of tar and turpentine. Then, she delicately placed the body from the hatbox into the concoction. Just as Nana's stories had told her, she began to stir.

Soon, the tar began to bubble and boil, scalding the undersides of Rhema's hands. However, she did not stop, even to grab gloves or oven mitts. Her sweat dripped into the pot and her jaw ached from gritting her teeth against the heat. The smell that arose mingled with the smoky stench already eating away at the house, producing an odor that turned Rhema's stomach and burned her lungs. Still, she did not stop.

Then the tar began to thicken, and she could hardly move the wooden spoon more than an inch at a time. But she pushed and pushed, inch by inch. Like a prayer, she chanted, *My baby, baby, baby.*

Rhema had not slept or eaten in days. Her body could not stand it, though her mind willed it on. The longer that she pushed at the wooden spoon, the more the tar's fumes filled her throat. She began to cough, deep within her chest. As her body shook with each cough, she gripped the spoon tight, pushing, pushing, pushing.

But then she could not push any longer. Her hands locked up. Her body buckled and crumpled to the floor, her knuckles clutching her heaving chest. She could not unfold her fingers out of the fists still gripping the spoon.

She stayed there for days, halfway between sleeping and waking. She could not feel the floor beneath her or hear the noise from outside, as if a thick, numbing mist had embraced her. Her mind seemed taken over by fog, incapable of solidifying a clear thought or memory.

Sometimes she heard voices conversing around her, but her eyes were too heavy to see who spoke. They grew fainter each time she heard them.

When she did finally rise, she felt new and raw, like a thin film had been singed off the surface of her skin. In the moonlight, she could see that the pot and the wooden spoon were spotless, with no sign of the tar concoction. The only remnants of her attempt to revive her child were a noxious odor that had sunk deep into the walls, a lingering tickle in her lungs, and an ache in her hands. When she lifted the hatbox from the kitchen table, she felt the weight of something inside. She knew better than to open it.

Instead, she took the hatbox, walked behind the house, and crossed the highway. The road was nearly finished, and the workers had all gone for the night. The moon reflected off the smooth asphalt like a placid river. She felt like a ghost. Only months ago, she would have been walking through the walls of her neighbors' homes, trampling their gardens, upsetting their tables and chairs. Loyal dogs would have barked at her, and curious cats would have meowed. But now, the ground beneath her feet was flat and dark and silent.

She carried the hatbox across the wide expanse of the highway. She could not take it back to the graveyard, to lie with the rest of her family. Graves were for the dead, Rhema told herself. What she needed was a hiding place, somewhere she could keep the child until she could get her strength back.

Across the highway, she came to a steep slope where the construction had cut into the hillside. Plans for a bridge were underway to accommodate for the drop-off, which would have been unnecessary when Sankofa had followed the hill's natural gradation. If she had decided to climb, she would find the northern side of Sankofa and eventually the community hall toward the top of the hill. But here would do fine. The freshly churned dirt was so loose, she could easily use her hands to push it aside. She dug a shallow hole, placed the hatbox inside, and covered it over. As she worked, she whispered into the humid night air, *My baby, baby, baby.*

Her wrists were screaming by the time she rolled a rock the size of a house cat on top of the ground that now held the hatbox. She took a paring knife from her pocket and did her best to carve a cross into the stone. She kissed the protective totem and made her way back home, where she would stay and wait for decades.

This is the story you know. You know it so well that you can hide it inside another story.

There were moments before the day this white man showed up at your door when you had considered telling Rhema's story, if only to find someone to finish it. You know that you cannot do it yourself. A single night ruined your hands and your lungs for good, making a second attempt at resurrection impossible. You had considered that Nia or Lucky or others before them might help you, but they never possessed enough animal desperation for this story. Besides, you are not cruel. Even if someone else were able to bring your baby back, you know that doing so would break their body. You would not wish the chronic aches in your chest, the pain in your joints, the loss of taste and smell on any innocent person. But finally, someone despairing enough appeared at your door.

As you tell the desperate man a different fable, you tuck Rhema's story inside it without him noticing. You sew it in the lining of the subtext, in the breaths between words, in the detailed instructions on where to find the pieces and how to make the thing. You bury the bones of one story inside the tar of another.

You do not know if your hidden story will work. Even if he is willing, even if he seems strong, seven days of intense labor may not be possible for a man his age. But if he cannot resurrect her, let him try, you think. Let him ruin his home and burn away his senses. Let him break his back and shatter the bones in his hands. Let his mind turn to mud—it is already mud, after all. Let him pour all his hatred into this creation, let him fill it with his desire for a shallow and bleached world. You'll help him. You'll send him all the hatred that you've nursed in your heart for seven decades, the smallest disdain and the most personal betrayals. Let him work himself to death but let him live to see the true fruits of this labor: a beautiful Black girl, returned to the world.

For a long while, you will not hear anything from the white man. You will assume he could not complete the task. Then you will learn that the girl has come back after all, and you will rejoice. But when you meet her, she will not be what you expect. She is a woman, not a child. She is wary of you, not warm. You are so overcome by her presence that you press her hand to a hot radiator and chase her away. After she has gone to confront the man who made her with your instructions, you wonder if you have made a grave mistake.

Because, that story you hid Rhema's story inside of? That is its own story, not to be used as a vessel for another. Even if you felt you needed to hollow it out to convince that desperate white man, you certainly should not have changed the ending. Because, in the end, the tar girl does not become the glue that keeps the man's neighborhood together. In the end, the tar girl is dissatisfied touching only the gentlemen that her father tells her to. No matter how often he forbids it, no matter how thick the gloves he puts on her hands, the tar girl must touch and be touched. In the end, she touches everyone in the town. Not even her father, who knows what she is, avoids this fate.

Because one day, the tar girl's father must tell her the truth, the story of her creation. He tells her what he knows, not realizing that this is only a small part of the story. But the message is clear: She is not human; she is tar. As soon as he tells her this, he touches her too, and she vanishes.

That is how the story ends. But you have changed the telling, and therefore changed the story. You have made the story hold something new. Now as you sit in your home, the home your granddaddy built, silent but for the faint hiss of the radiator, you wonder where that girl goes to after her maker touches her. What does she do now that she knows she is not what she thought she was? Where has she been all these years? It occurs to you that the story does not even give the tar girl a name—like the baby, whose gravestone bore only a cross.

This is a story you do not know, and the best teller is likely to be the girl herself.

Tar Pit

Original Hill

•

The streets of Original Hill were empty. An early autumn cold snap had driven the residents inside. The cold, they all agreed. That was what kept them indoors.

The chill provoked the trees of Original Hill to shed their finery in anticipation of winter. Red and brown leaves settled in piles and remained undisturbed. No one's children cannonballed into them. No one's dogs yapped at the squirrels and field mice that played among the crisp dead leaves. No one raked the lawns or cleared the gutters. Instead, the leaves sat there to rot.

If a person had walked those streets north of the highway, they would have smelled the pungent and earthy aroma of mulch. They would have seen the Kikuyu grass yards smothered a yellowish brown. They would have heard the rustle and hum of living things searching for warmth and shelter. But the neighbors all agreed that it was too cold to go outside, and those outside of Original Hill seemed to have forgotten that it existed.

It was not difficult for the residents to stay indoors all autumn. Teachers refused to go into school, so children remained with their parents. Dr. Wood, who had once insisted that even her oldest patients come to her practice, now conceded to making house visits—*though it was as if all her patients were already in her house, or that she was in theirs*. Groceries were ordered right to their door. *Was this the right address?1 Orchard Street?*

Even their social lives went uninterrupted. The doors to the country club remained firmly shut, and yet its members seemed to see one another more often. Ms. Branch and Mrs. Thorne's book club was as well attended as ever. Really, none of the ladies could make any excuse, since they all slept on the kitchen floor inches from one another. Mr. Reed and Mr. Burdock maintained their game-night watch parties, though they often had to turn up the volume to drown out the wailing of infants and the howling of all the neighborhood's dogs, who had also chosen to occupy the sitting room.

Just as before, the neighbors often bumped into Lucius Foote, though instead of running into him outside of Bush's store, it was on the stairs or beside the coffeemaker—*not their model of coffeemaker; they would never buy this coffeemaker*. Foote was not nearly as talkative as he had once been, everyone agreed. He seemed changed, preoccupied and withdrawn.

Perhaps political life's begun to take its toll, Mr. Ives guessed.

That doesn't bode well for my vote come November, Mr. Reed said.

Oh, I wouldn't go that far. He's such a peach. Mrs. Bush smiled.

And he's been getting on well with Fox, Ms. Branch observed.

Eugene Fox was just as present as ever, if not more so. He strode from one room to the next, shaking every neighbor's hand and pulling them into conversation. He made sure that the temperature of the house was comfortable and necessary home repairs were documented. He seemed pleased to be crossing everyone's paths so much more frequently.

His wife, on the other hand, made strange demands like, *Get your Labrador off my sofa* and *Why did you eat all of the meat in my fridge?*

My, my, my. We're all in this together, aren't we, Mrs. Thorne huffed.

Everyone agreed with that, too. They had stayed out of her garden. What more could she ask?

There were also times when some of the younger children fell into bizarre tantrums and demanded their parents take them home. They wanted their rooms, their beds, their stuffy/dolly/blanky/ball. These youngsters would eventually be soothed with assurances that they had everything they needed here and that they would go home as soon as Mommy and Daddy got what they had come for.

They're just at that age, Mrs. Reed sighed. *It's hard for them to articulate what they want.*

Come to think of it, it could be that Gina's attitude has something to do with that niece, Mr. Burdock said.

That girl might explain Lucius's mood, too, Dr. Wood theorized.

Whatever happened to her? She has to be in the house somewhere, doesn't she?

Find her need her get her.

Grabhergrabhergrabher.

Everyone was crammed inside the house at 1 Orchard Street, looking for the girl. She had brought them all together, and then she had disappeared. With no sense of where to begin their search, the neighbors knocked and jostled against each other, seeking her out. They shredded the wallpaper and trampled the Foxes' furniture until the cushions were soft as mud. The plumbing was constantly overflowing, creating dark stains on the hardwood floors. Pools of stagnant water seeped through the first-floor ceiling. Many avoided the bathrooms if they could, and most forgot to bathe altogether. After a month, clothes were still unwashed, as Old Man Fox hadn't yet fixed the laundry machine. The neighbors whispered about Mrs. Fox allowing her home to stink of body odor. But they braved the stench and the filth, the sores from sleeping on the carpet, and the tantrums from young ones, because each of them believed the same thing: *They just needed to touch her again. Just one more time. Then they could go.*

In the meantime, they attempted to continue their lives as if nothing had changed. They took business calls and apologized for the noise. They depleted the cabinets and refrigerator as if it were a supermarket, each household insisting on serving their own dinner. They tucked their kids in whatever corner did not stink of dog urine. They acted polite as ever, even as they elbowed their neighbors for floorspace. All the while, they told themselves that it was the cold that kept them inside. The cold, they thought, and *her*.

Though the thought had occurred to each of them, none could accept the idea that the girl had left completely. The possibility that she might be somewhere in that vast, frigid outside was too overwhelming to acknowledge.

Not only that. Everyone felt the same tether to these walls. She—or something of her—was still there.

1.

The house is more crowded now and everyone avoids touching one another. I watch them eat and sleep and laugh and fight and worry and look for me. Mostly look for me.

There was a time when I wanted so desperately to stick. I thought if I did *that*—if I touched them and they touched me, and we *stuck*—I could adhere myself to the world. I wouldn't have to worry anymore about being drawn back to the place where I was before. I could only feel that I was not sticking to them; I did not imagine that they might still be sticking to me. My stickiness makes them need me violently. It scares me how they need me.

So I stay in my hiding place and observe them. They are all human, and I study them to figure out why the voices of the house insist that I am not.

I must be human. The walls came from trees, and the nails came from stone, and the dust from skin and hair. They all speak as if they are still these things. I came from Father, who is human, and so I should be human, too. But I think it is a problem of substance. The tar in me. The rug is no longer a plant because it has been transformed with not-plant elements, just like Father had to transform me with not-human elements to bring me here from the darkloudhot place.

I came from the darkloudhot place, but I am not of it. No. I will not go back. Never.

For now, I will stay in my hiding place until I understand more of how to parse my tar from my human. I watch and I listen to the people in the house, but sometimes I get distracted by the house's other voices. They used to ignore me, but now they address me. They want me to speak back.

2.

What are you, they want to know.

I tell them I am human.

No, no. What are you now.

I think I am human. I am human-shaped.

You are not human. We know what human is, the voices of the house say. But when I ask what human is, none of them can agree.

The wood-once-tree says that to be human is to cut back, to draw lines around. *What is the difference between a forest and an orchard*, the wood muses. *Whatever a human says.*

The glass-once-sand says to be human is to manipulate, to change the world into something that suits you.

The dust and the spores and the bacteria in the air insist to be human is to sort, to draw a circle and call it *Me* or *Other.*

Those once-plants say that to be human is to harvest, to grow in rows and take up and split and shuck and shell and crush and juice. Those once-animals say that to be human is to kill without hunger.

Must I do all this—cut back, manipulate, sort, harvest, kill without hunger? Then will I be human? I don't believe that Father or Lucky or Gina have done these things, and yet they are. I know it is polite to express my thanks to the house even though it has been entirely unhelpful. *Stupid house,* I don't say.

But the house just continues asking, *If you don't know what you are now, then what were you before?*

3.

Lucky still talks to me even though I do not talk back. He does not seem to mind. I never said much before anyway.

His suit is wrinkled and spotted with stains, and he has not showered or brushed his teeth in months. The neighbors are willing to ignore this while he continues working his charm and vying for their votes. Though, they have noticed that he is more distracted, prone to dropping out of a conversation mid-thought to pull up the edge of a carpet. He looks for me more fervently than anyone. Maybe it is because he is my One and Only. Maybe it is because he touched me first, or because he did not resist me. He used to say we share things that the other neighbors do not. I am not sure if he still believes he and I are so alike now that he knows I am tar.

But he has not stopped speaking to me. He mutters under his breath as he smooths his hand along the banister-once-tree or presses his stubble-rimmed lips to the curtains-once-cotton. He sequesters himself into nooks of the house where he believes no one can see him and sucks on cigarettes while busying his fingers with his lighter, though he never brings forth a flame. I watch him and remember the joys of textures against my naked fingers, the thrill of secrecy mixing with the ecstasy of the sensation. I press my body against the roughness of the wall and feel a little more human.

"Baby . . . Baby . . ." Lucky murmurs, rolling the cigarette between his teeth. He says that this house, these people, this whole neighborhood is crazy, and why don't we make a run for it, just us two?

If I could reply, I would remind him that I cannot leave this road. Maybe some of this road's tar is in me; I do not know. I would say that I see how unhappy he is trapped here. He is stuck to someone else—that friend beneath the birchbark—and must feel his pull, too. I would ask him: If I were more human, if I could release everyone from my terrible touch, would you go? Is it really my stickiness alone that keeps you here?

But I do not talk back to my One and Only. If I did, he would know where I was, and he would try to touch me. He would grab me, hold me between his teeth, and never let me go.

4.

I am the only one who sees the moments when Gina breaks. She wants to be a good hostess. She makes sure that there is food to eat and tidies up the house. But no one notices; they just eat and dirty more. In their search for me, they break the oak leaves carved out of wood-once-tree from the walls and scuff the floors and back up the drains and break the dryer, the kettle, the doors. Gina cannot keep up with it all, though she tries. I know how much it wounds her to see the people mistreat her house.

I am the only one who sees the moments when something silent shatters inside her. Even though it is deathly cold outside, she walks out to the garden without a coat or hat and stays for as long as she can bear it. She is lost to me there. From where I am, I cannot see outside, though if she stays close enough to the house, I can hear her teeth chatter. I can hear the hum of her breath.

Sometimes I snap at the house for making her so distraught. *Can't you clean yourself up? She only wants to love you, to care for you.* The adrenaline coursing through my form feels distinctly human.

But the dented floors-once-wood and dirtied rugs-once-sheep are too engrossed with themselves to care how they have been treated. *If you love her so much, then you clean up after the humans.*

I would, but I know if I come out to help Gina, she will try to touch me. Once, I stuck out a finger—just a finger—for the mirror-once-sand in Gina's vanity to catch. It was only for a second, but Gina saw it. She cut her hand bloody smashing it into the glass, moaning, "Baby, please!"

I have not stuck out another finger since.

5.

Father is still campaigning. Rubbing elbows is easier when everyone is already shoulder to shoulder. People listen to him and consult him for all kinds of reasons, probably because they are staying in his house. He tells Gina that his approval numbers are climbing steadily, so by November he should far surpass Lucky.

"That's wonderful, dear," Gina says, chasing a neighbor's dog out of her closet.

It is as if the crowded house has not changed him at all, except that he only uses his left hand now. His other hand—the hand that grabbed me, protected me—hangs from his wrist like he does not want it to exist. This makes fixing things around the house difficult, but he never asks for help.

When he is not speaking to the neighbors or repairing the house, Father rests in his study. If he sleeps, I cannot tell the difference between his slumber and his waking. I have not seen him eat either, and yet he does not get any thinner. Still, I can see that he is not well. When he is alone, his body curls like a dead beetle in the corner. He coughs up gray spit that fills up paper cups, which he tosses out the window so that no one else will see. As the rest of the neighborhood jostles and writhes in the other rooms, Father keeps perfectly still in his chair. I think moving pains him.

Sometimes, the quiet in his study is so total that I am sure he can hear me breathing. His eyes will widen, and he will whisper into the dark, "Baby?"

I almost call out to him. I almost step out of my hiding place and fall to my knees and apologize that I have ruined everything he has worked so hard for. I want to ask him why he kept the truth of my tar from me, and does he know how I can get rid of it? He made me with his human hands, so I must be human, no matter what the voices think.

But then I look to the hand that hangs ignored and unused at his side. He is my father, but he is like the others, now. He will try to touch me too, and it is my fault.

I want to tell him that I did not disobey because I

do not love him. I only wanted to be more a part of the world. Now that I have messed things up, I have to hide away. I can't think about my hiding place too much because it is too narrow for a human to fit here. I ignore that part for now.

Ignoring what is inconvenient seems to be definitively human.

6.

I have taken something.

I had realized that, even if I did succeed in becoming more human by studying the people in the house, how was I to know if anything had changed? So I asked the floorboards-once-tree in the attic to creak a bit. It took some convincing—and suffering more inquisitions over what I was and where I had come from—but eventually they agreed. As I had hoped, the neighborhood flooded up the stairs as soon as they heard the floorboards' soft groan. When the coast was clear, I stole out into the parlor and snatched the lighter from the pocket of Lucky's jacket.

I paused for a moment to wiggle my toes in the carpet. I could not remember how long it had been since my body had stretched out like this, since I had held something in my hand. But then I heard the people start to trickle back down the stairs, and I leapt back into my hiding place.

For a while, I just hold Lucky's lighter in my hand, ignoring the slow contemplation of its oil and plastic-once-oil. I wait until I hear the restlessness of the people in the house settle. I know that most are sleeping, but some are just looking for me less fervently. Then I press my thumb to the lighter. I can almost hear it in the moments before it comes. A low click, and the fire arrives.

The fire speaks high and breathy. It is bright and alive and excited. Its dreams are big, and its hunger is vast. *I could be a lantern,* it says, *or an eternal flame. I could play in tobacco or cannabis. I could lick your finger and make you drop me onto the floor or that bed. Then I could eat the floor and the bed. Then I could eat the room. Then I could eat the house. Then I could ride the wind on embers and eat every other house in sight. I could char the grass and scorch the earth. I could find my way to a forest and become a forest fire. I could be a flame or a blaze or an inferno. I could live in the last of the dying kindling only to leap up again. Let me eat. Let me eat. Let me eat.*

The fire has only just arrived, and already it wants so much. But rather than entertain any of its fancies, I press it to my finger. The pain grows slowly, and then very quickly, until I must pull my finger away. But it has done what I need. I briefly press my finger to the wall and, blinking my eyes in the flickering light of the flame, I hope to see nothing when I pull it away.

But there I see the mark, the piece of me left behind solidifying into the wood-once-tree. A black spot on the light wood.

I kill the fire in spite, though this is not the fire's fault.

I am still tar. I am not quite human yet.

7.

I sneak out quickly to snatch a muffin from the kitchen counter. When my fingers touch the sticky crystal sugars on top, I find that I am famished. I stuff two muffins into my mouth only to realize that I am also thirsty. I fill a glass with milk and down it as I hear people bumping toward the kitchen again. I am gone so quickly that I forget to put down the glass. It shatters when it hits the floor. The neighbors stare at the shards of glass, which now look more like the sand they once were.

Back in my hiding place, the food and drink give me trouble. There is no room for it inside me. I am uncomfortable for hours until I can sneak out again and excise it from my system. I decide to forgo eating if I can. Lots of things eat and drink, so maybe those are not especially human activities.

I have also noticed that some of the neighbors bleed on certain days of the month. I have never bled, am not even sure if I have blood, but I try because it seems very human. I think of the area between my thighs and concentrate until something warm oozes from me. It is too dark in this place to see if it is really blood or only tar. I wonder about my insides—if they look human the way my outside does. I remember the bones from Father's story. But there is no space for bones in my hiding place.

8.

I insist on sleeping because that is a human thing to do. When I sleep, I dream, which is very good because most humans dream. But often when I dream, I am back in the darkloudhot place. I am listening to my memory-mother say my not-name, again and again. *Baby. Baby. Baby.* Then her sound is swallowed up by the roaring and the crunching. It sounds like a cyclone tearing a house apart. Or it sounds like a hundred cyclones, each taking only a small piece of the house as they pass until there is nothing left.

I try to get a sense of what I am in this place. Do I have a body here? Is it tar or flesh or both or something else? Do I have a voice or eyes? I must have ears to hear all this pandemonium. As I begin to sense my body, I feel something pointy and leafy and smooth and wriggling. I wake up back in my hiding place in the house.

9.

There are days when the whole house falls quiet. Gina is out in the garden and Lucky stops whispering his plans for us and Father sits mutely in his study and the rest of the people follow suit. These are the worst days.

In the people's silence, I can hear the voices in the house more present around me.

What are you?

Human.

No, you aren't.

Yes, I am. Leave me alone.

Where did you come from?

I don't want to talk about it. Leave me alone.

I came from a tree that used to stand at the edge of a lake and drink up the water through the soil, until a human cut me down and took me many miles and I was divided from my tree into what I am now, and then I was taken again and eventually brought here and fitted together with pieces of other trees and rubbed down with minerals from the ground to make me shine and look healthy *but, you know, I was more* healthy *before they took an axe to my trunk.*

Well, I'm sorry about that.

It isn't very different, you know. I am still surrounded by tree and mineral and insect and fungus and bacterium and such. The conversations are just more boring.

You're right, there.

I think you were a tree. Or part of you. Have you ever been birch or pine?

Leave me alone, I say.

Then another voice pipes in, *Where did you come from?*

And I say, I have decided that is a rude question to ask.

Where did you come from?

A human.

Oh, that's funny. I also came from a human. I thought of myself as very human, then, but then I was shed off, and I became dust. *That's what they call me when they sweep me up. But* dust *is a very diverse category. I spend much of my time with things that used to be plants or other animals or minerals*—lots *of minerals here. Are you dust?*

No.

Are you sure? Because, let me tell you, for the longest time I swore I was human—skin and toenails and eyelashes. The whole shebang. But then I was swept away and all of a sudden the humans started to call me dust. *It's easy to make that mistake, to miss the transition. You know, humans have an expression: You are dust, and to dust you shall return.*

I am not dust.

Well, that's too bad, I guess. But there is something so mineral about you. Did you used to live in the ground?

No.

Are you sure? It can be very dark and hard to tell.

Then a third voice joins: *I like dead things. I like to eat them.*

Well, that's very nice for you. Never speak to me again.

I think you are a dead thing, but I cannot eat you. Why is that?

I'm going to stop talking to you, now.

And I do. But as I sit in the quiet dark, I can hear that my heart does not thump. It growls.

10.

The fire does not try to ask me what I am. It does not argue with my being human. It has always just arrived, which means it has not observed humans the way that the other voices have. The fire only thinks of itself, its endless possibilities. Even as it burns my finger, it dreams of what mischief it may one day make.

As I press my finger to the wall, I watch the flame yawn and stretch, wriggle and dance. *Can you do this?* it asks, making itself tall and thin and then squat and wide. It is the closest thing, I feel, to what I am.

I kill the fire. No, I think, I am human. But when I take my finger away, the tar mark remains.

I want to throw Lucky's lighter against the wall. Being human used to be so effortless before I knew—before Father told me what I really am. Nobody knew the difference. Except the Old Woman who burned me.

I think about the Old Woman. She grabbed my wrist and showed me the truth. Why has she not come after me if she touched my skin?

11.

I resolve to find out. On another silent night, I emerge from my hiding place and creep around the sleeping neighbors. I can hear people still wandering through the house—seeking me, needing my touch—but the voices inform me that no one is set to cross my path. I move quickly. I take Father's coat and noiselessly make my way through the door.

The moon is full, and the air is freezing. There is solid water all over the ground, little crystals teasing one another beneath my bare feet. I wrap myself in Father's coat-once-animal and tread down through the frost-once-river. My breath catches as I see my lovertrees. Even in the dark, I see they are adorned in vibrant, fiery colors, glittering with ice crystals. They have dressed up for one another.

I want to kiss each of my lovertrees, but I resist. I am not sure if tar is bad for trees. Instead, I continue down the road.

Soon, I cannot feel my feet. The freeze penetrates the coat to my arms and chest. My body is tense and hard. If I freeze in place, will the people realize that I have left the house and come for me? Or will I be left here, still as stone through the rest of autumn and winter? When spring comes, will I thaw?

My knees and ankles are beginning to stiffen. Moving my legs is becoming difficult. Then I hear a low rumble. I am not sure what to make of it until I come to the bridge that crosses the highway. The cars beneath speed past with no regard for the frozen landscape, ignorant of the silent neighborhood.

I stop just before the bridge. I must cross to get to the Old Woman. I crossed once before, but I was in Lucky's car, and it all went by so fast. I don't even remember how

I crossed back. Now, it is just me and this empty bridge and the cars gnashing beneath. The growl of the highway pulls my mind back to that terrible roar in the place before. The bridge will lead me back to the darkloudhot place, I think. That is where it is taking me, where the roar will rip away whatever humanity I have cobbled together and shred it apart, leaving me only a voice without thought. I try to banish the idea, but it sticks fast and will not be shaken off.

My body starts to tremble—whether from cold or fear or frustration, I do not know. My numb feet will not move. I want to beg them, plead with them, but it is like I am back in that dark place where thinking is impossible. If I stand here too long, I am sure to freeze, and then I will never reach the Old Woman. She showed me the truth once, I remind myself. If I want to figure out how to become more human, how to stop pieces of myself from sticking to everything, I must cross this bridge.

Still, my feet will not budge. However, I realize, my hand and my arm will. I start to reach my fingertips toward the other side of the bridge. I stretch and stretch and stretch until I realize that I am stretching too much, that my body should not accommodate this distance, that I am halfway across and yet my feet have not moved—

I am on the other side of the bridge, and the snarling traffic is behind me. It is as if time reset its pieces. If I know exactly how it happened, I don't let myself remember it.

Then it happens again, and I am standing in the Old Woman's kitchen. I do not remember entering. The Old Woman is staring at me as if I have walked through her wall to get here. Perhaps I did. I silently scold myself because it is not human to walk through walls.

She is wearing a bonnet and a nightdress. Her eyes are wild, like I have just woken her up, which I probably have. Many squares of quiet linoleum-once-tree separate us. She keeps her distance. She *is able* to keep her distance. She does not look at me with the mix of aversion and need that all others I have touched do.

Anger bursts inside me, like a thumb has pressed me down and ignited a well of oil in my stomach. "How?" I shout at the Old Woman. My voice scrapes my throat on its way out and bounces around her silent walls, shaking us both. "You touched me. How are you not stuck to me?"

She keeps looking at me, eyes misty with wonder. Finally, she says, "Oh my Baby. Baby Baby Baby."

She says, "I have been stuck to you for seventy years."

12.

Will you call me your mother? But you are not my mother. *You don't remember?* I have no mother here. Only a father. *I see. How about "Ma," then?* That's fine, Ma. *My Baby—*

Ma, were you the one that put me in the darkloud-hot place? Did you leave me there? *I don't know what you mean. I put you in a place to keep you safe, so that you would not leave while I tried to bring you back. I am sorry it took so long; I didn't mean for it to—* It was a wrong place, not the kind of place you put a person. *I had to keep you here. Safe.* But I wasn't safe. *I had to keep you here.*

You hear the voices, don't you? *I used to.* They say I am not human. Why? *I'll have to think about that. You are very special, Baby. Very special.*

I never want you to stop holding me like this. *I never have to stop.* But I have to go back to my house, now. *Why don't you stay?* I want to leave. I want to see the people I love. *Okay. But you'll come back?* Yes, Ma. *Anytime. You come back anytime.* Do you know why I cannot leave this road? *I'll have to think about that, too.*

Making my way back to Father's house, I hardly remember traversing the bridge over the highway. Even the cold feels less clawing. In fact, a pleasant warmth has spread through me by the time I arrive back at the house. I wait until the house tells me that nobody searching will cross my path, and then I slip back into my hiding place. I look at the many marks on the wall, the many proofs of my inhumanity. I feel Lucky's lighter in my pocket and consider calling up the fire. Not yet, I tell myself.

Soon.

13.

I become very good at sneaking away from the house. I leave at dawn before most of the neighborhood has risen and return after dark without anyone seeing me. I find that I hardly have to listen to the voices of the house because I can predict where the people will and will not be. Maybe to be human is to be predictable, keep a ritual. I keep my own rituals, now—Lucky's lighter, my visits to Ma.

When I am with Ma, she gives me various tasks: sweeping the floors, making the bed, playing card games with her. It is good to be out of my hiding place, to stretch my limbs and see my human shape. She prefers to cook, and when she allows me to help, she never lets me near the stove. Maybe she is afraid that I will leave a piece of myself behind on the hot range, or maybe she does not want me to hear the baiting of the flames.

The fire is the only thing that speaks in Ma's house. The light bulbs do not gossip, the doors do not debate their hinges, and nothing asks me where I came from. I can see that the walls are made of wood-once-trees and plaster-once-stone and brick-once-clay, but they are quiet. They do not seem mute or muzzled; they choose not to speak. It as if the house has spoken enough and if it said anymore, it would let loose something terrible.

Sometimes, Ma asks me to just sit with her, neither of us saying a word. "There is so much we can learn from silence," she tells me. I realize how unfamiliar silence is, especially around people. Ma sits with me without thrusting some secret or advice or direction at me. But the silence is also worrisome. In it, I can almost hear the echoes of the darkloudhot place grinding and gurgling. Ma does not recognize this place when I describe it to her. How could she have put me there when she doesn't know about it?

I tell her I do not remember anything before the darkloudhot place. Only a voice saying a name. Not my name but something like it. She asks where I got this name—Baby—and I tell her that I found it again after my father brought me here. My name was lost in the other place.

Sometimes she asks me to wear some of her clothes. Her dresses and blouses fit alright, but her pants are small on me. I do not change my form to fit them better, though I wonder if I could. She wraps my hair in scarves like the batik ones she wears. It is strange to be enveloped in all this silent fabric. Even my own dresses stop speaking in Ma's house.

Once, Ma put a warm, soft brown coat over my shoulders. It was difficult to tell what it was at first, because it did not use its voice—not even the dust on it spoke.

Ma said, "This belonged to my nana. I always wanted to give it to my little girl. It's ermine."

When I looked in Ma's mirror, I saw a lissome, sleek animal. I quickly threw the coat off and tried to give it back to Ma. "I am not an ermine," I said. "I am a human."

She looked at me for a moment, and then she laughed so hard that her whole body shook. She kept laughing as she took the coat-once-ermine from me and kissed my head.

What's the matter? Why are you laughing? *You reminded me of this old story, about a woman who put on a fox's skin to become a fox in the evenings.* A human woman? *I suppose.* Why would she want to be a fox if she was human? *That is a question the story does not answer.*

14.

The neighbors begin congregating around the doors and windows. They move the filthy nests that they call beds closer to the walls and sip their coffee while staring out at the road. At first, I thought they were seeking fresh air. The house smells awful, and it gets worse the longer the whole neighborhood lives here, though the voices of the bacteria and fungi seem delighted. Then it dawns on me that the people are pressing against the sides of the house because they sense that I have been leaving. I have to be especially cautious so that no one catches sight of me walking to Ma's house.

The fact that everyone is stuck inside Father's house has not hindered the advance of the election. With November fast approaching, I watch Father and Lucky cycle through the kitchen, the dining room, and the foyer, making grand speeches about the state of the neighborhood and shaking hands with whoever might be there. Both of them preach variations of, "We all know that the very soul of Original Hill is in jeopardy. I can make certain we stay on the right path, to ensure we all have a brighter future."

In more private moments, I hear each of them lean into neighbors' ears and promise, "I'll bring her back. Only I can."

Both are liars—not because I won't come back but because both have the power to bring me out of hiding. They only have to need me less. It is vexing being crammed in this hiding place, having to sneak around. I miss the garden. I miss my lovertrees. I miss Gina's goodnight kisses and Lucky's strokes and the game where I touched everyone. I miss how Father looked at me with a secret pride, just for us two.

These false promises are the only acknowledgment that any of these people are searching for me. Most of the time, they act like they aren't seeking me out in every corner, erupting at the slightest hint of my presence. Maybe if they admitted it, they would not stick so much. The harder they resist, the deeper they seem to sink into their need for me. Ma does not resist me, so the pull is not as urgent. She can touch me with moderation and dignity, not like the frenzy that forced all the neighbors inside Father's house.

But still, Ma is stuck, I think. I am sure that is why she asks me to stay with her. She may not even realize how much she needs my touch. And even she struggles against my strangeness. She asks questions like, "What flavor would you like for your birthday cake?" and waves me away when I tell her, "I was not born; I was made."

15.

One morning when I arrive at Ma's house, a stranger opens the door. She is pretty, and her skin is so dark that I wonder for a moment if she is like me. But she has an ugly mouth. No; her mouth is making an ugly shape.

"Can I help you?" she asks.

I tell her that I've come to see Ma. Her mouth makes an uglier shape.

"Who?"

I become incredibly impatient with this stranger's pretty face and ugly mouth. I wonder if it would be such a crime for me to just push her down. Or perhaps I could make my form very small and just go around her. I've never done this before, but I wonder if it is possible. The stranger continues to leer at me as if I am some species of tree lice when Ma calls from within, "Nia, who is it?"

"It's me, Ma!" I yell so loud that the stranger jerks her hand to her ear.

"Well, come in, then. Don't you two let the heat out."

The stranger looks at me for another minute, then

turns her body at a grotesque angle that only just allows me inside.

Ma is pouring coffee into ceramic-once-stone mugs. I take a seat at the kitchen table and wish her a good morning. The stranger rushes in behind me. "Let me, Auntie," she says, taking the pot from Ma. I can tell that Ma is annoyed, yet she smiles. She sits at the kitchen table beside me and rubs her thumb on my wrist. Her touch is silk-soft.

"Do you want some?" the stranger looks at me, irritated. I shake my head. Too hot.

The stranger snatches up the mugs and places one in front of Ma. She sits across from us. Her deep eyes dart from Ma to me. She has so many questions building up behind her teeth, but before she can release them, Ma says, "This is Baby. She's come to visit for a little bit."

The stranger's eyes hop back to me before she stretches her hand out. "Nia," she says.

I keep my hands on the table, both for her safety and because I do not like her very much. After a pleasurably awkward moment, she retracts her hand. Her attention turns to Ma.

"So, Auntie. We're going to be demonstrating on the steps of City Hall next week. Weather should be nice—cold snap'll be warming up. We'd like you to tell your story at the rally."

Ma's grip on my wrist tightens. I turn to her and see resistance in the line of her mouth, the depths of her eyes. The stranger does not seem to notice this or does not want to. She is ignoring what is inconvenient to her. So, I say, "Maybe you shouldn't, Ma."

"Excuse me?" The stranger's eyes are on me again.

I keep myself turned toward Ma. "If you don't want to—"

"And why wouldn't she want to?" the stranger asks.

But Ma nods. "I don't know if I have it in me to tell that story anymore."

"But, Auntie," the stranger protests. "Your account of what happened is crucial."

I feel my face growing hot. I don't like this stranger needing Ma. Her need feels too much like the people's in the house. If Ma's house talked, I'm sure the voices would agree with me.

Ma takes her hand off mine and begins to massage her own wrists. "There is such a thing as telling a story too much," she says.

The stranger frowns, her eyes once more passing between me and Ma. "Is something wrong, Auntie?"

Ma smiles. "Course not. I'll think about it, alright? Now, enough business talk. Why don't we play a game?" Ma quickly stands from her seat but then pitches back down as she starts to cough. The stranger leaps up and pats Ma on the back until she stops. The stranger gives me a look like, *What the hell are you here for, anyway?*

I go get Ma's Vicks and a pack of cards. When I return, Ma is right again and seated back at the table. If the stranger thinks that I am stupid or lazy, that is fine. I think she is stupid, too.

I resume my place beside Ma. The stranger keeps giving me a stink eye, but I don't bother with her because Ma is trying to teach me how to play rummy. After a few hours of stink eye, the stranger leaves and Ma and I are alone again.

I ask, What is the matter, Ma? Did that woman bother you? I can keep her away. *No, Baby, it isn't that.* Then—*I've told this story for years, now, and for the first time I've wondered if I should keep telling it.* Don't, if you don't want to. *Something has changed.* What? *You, Baby. You came back.*

16.

Not long after, I meet the stranger again on my walk home. I am thinking of my lovertrees when she drives up alongside me in a quiet little car and asks if I need a ride. I shake my head and say I am alright, but then she asks where I am headed.

If I tell her that I am going to Father's house, she might tip off the people inside, and then they will find me. So, I say, "The trees."

She asks, "What trees?"

I want to see my lovertrees, but I have not been able to since the people in the house have been watching the street more intently. The neighbors seem more aware of my comings and goings each day, though they still are not willing to leave the house. I am dying to know if either of my lovertrees has succeeded in inching any closer to the other.

I tell the stranger none of this. She nods at my silence. "Hop in," she says. "I know just the spot."

"Is it far?" I ask. I cannot stray too far from this road.

"No, it's just west of here," she says.

As soon as I slide into the seat, her quiet car speeds forward. I feel that uneasy sensation of being pulled backward, back toward the street and toward Ma's house.

While she drives, the stranger asks, "So, are you family?"

I make a little noise. It is hard for me to concentrate while being tugged between the car and the house.

She is quiet for a moment before saying, "I'm sorry you and I got off to a bad start. I'm sure you can understand, I'm protective of Auntie Riri. Let's rewind, okay? I'm Nia—"

I groan, and the stranger notices my discomfort. "You okay?" she asks. I make a small noise again. She assures me that we are almost there.

Where we stop is not far at all, but it looks unlike anywhere I have been before. A dirt path winds down a hill and comes out to a lake surrounded by trees that extend as far as the eye can see. They are big trees, too, much taller than my lovertrees, bursting with every color imaginable. The lake is vast, and I can only just see the shore on the other side. The water holds the trees' vibrant crowns in its ripples, like a hundred dancing flames.

"I come here when I need to get away," Nia says. "It's peaceful. You'd hardly even know the highway's right on the other side of those trees." I can barely hear the hard rush of it over the chattering trees all around us.

As we walk down the path, Nia tells me that she is a writer who came to the city years ago on a fellowship. She was only supposed to spend a year here but she got involved with the people and didn't want to leave. That was how she first met Ma. The place where she came from, she said, didn't have nearly as many trees. I try my best to listen to her, but it is hard not to be distracted by the chorus of foliage. They aren't interested in me the way the walls and the dust and the nails in Father's house are.

There is too much to talk about here, outside, where it is just cold enough to make me shiver but not at all terrible. I keep reminding myself that people listen to people, not trees.

When Nia asks where I came from, she does not say it the way that the voices of the house do. Her voice is pleasant on the ear and makes me want to answer. Still, I do not wish to tell her about how Father said I came to be. So, I talk about the darkloudhot place and the horrible roar. She is quiet when she listens. She looks at me the way that Lucky did when I told him about it, and I do not like it. I do not want her to be so interested, so I stop talking and look out at the lake. I tune into the cacophony of dragonflies, thrushes, cattails, water lilies, and tiny fish just beneath its surface.

Nia does not speak for a moment. Then she asks how long I plan on staying here. I tell her I can't leave. "Because of Auntie Riri?" she asks. I shrug. She is quiet again before saying, "Where are you staying?"

"Nearby," I tell her.

"Original?"

I nod. Nia smirks. "Well, if you need any help getting to know the city, let me know. You sure as hell won't stumble onto anything worthwhile there."

"Why?"

Her brows make a funny shape. "Haven't you noticed that you're sort of *unique* in that neighborhood?"

I think for a moment that she can tell that I am not human, like the voices in Father's house. How can she see it? What have I done?

I puff out my chest and simply say, "No. Not at all."

She says nothing to that.

We wander on and come to a slope of laughing grass. Its merriment tickles something in me, and I start to giggle myself. I want to go to it, to immerse myself in its unbridled joy. Without giving it another thought, I dive into the grass, running all the way up the slope and tumbling down to Nia's feet. She looks at me as if I am strange. But then she, too, runs up the slope and rolls down. Then we are both running up and tumbling down, and we are laughing and the grass is laughing and all the trees and the lake are muttering, wondering what is so funny, but we ignore them.

Finally, we are sitting in the grass, our cheeks and clothes streaked with green, breathing heavy with giggles still on our tongues. "Where'd your shoes go?" Nia asks. I look down at my feet and wriggle them into the grass. I can't remember the last time I wore shoes.

Then Nia looks up above my eyes and says, "Your wrap fell off." She looks around the slope until she spots the fabric-once-plant and jumps up to get it for me. When she brings it back, she is looking at my head. "You've got some grass in your hair. I can just—" She reaches out her hand.

I jolt away. "You can't touch me."

"Whoa, okay, okay," she says. She hands the wrap back, but I'm not sure what to do with it. Ma always puts it on. Nia is giving me a peculiar look.

"When was the last time you got your hair done? 'Cause if you're looking for a place, the woman who does me—"

"Nobody can touch me," I say.

"Nobody."

"Only Ma," I say.

"Auntie Riri does your hair?"

I shake my head. Her hands are bad. She is just able to wrap it, and even then, she has to take breaks.

"So, you do your own hair?"

"I don't know how."

Nia narrows her eyes at me. "So, you don't do it yourself, and you won't let anyone else— Do you want it to look that way?"

I shrug.

"Well, how would you like it to look?"

I nod at her hair, which falls from her head in beautiful braids. I can see that she is about to ask more questions, so I say, "If I touch anyone else's skin, it will hurt them."

Nia says nothing. The trees and the buzzing insects and the mushrooms have gone back to their own conversations, unimpressed by the thing forming in the quiet between me and Nia. After a minute, she just nods and says, "Okay."

Nia takes me back to Ma's house. Even in its voicelessness, I can tell that it is relieved to have me back, as if the whole house heaves a great sigh. Is this what humans hear, this nothing?

Ma is in bed, dreaming. Her lips are moving without sound. I touch Ma's cheek, feeling its softness and strange cold. Ma's eyelids float open, and she slowly rises.

Baby. Baby, My Baby. I thought you'd gone back.

I am so upset that I bite my own tongue. The muscle throbs inside my mouth. Why would she think that I would return to that place? Am I that bad at this human business? It seemed so easy before I knew what I was, how I came here.

Instead of replying, I follow Ma as she rises from bed and shuffles to the kitchen to put on a kettle. She calls up the fire, which heats the ore that boils the water, and she wraps her arms around me and pulls me close.

You know you can stay as long as you want.

I have to go back to my father's house, I say.

17.

The sky is dark as I approach the bridge. No matter how many times I cross it, I am wary of the thrashing cars beneath. Most times, I hurry across, back to the road that I am made from. But this time, before I reach the bridge, I turn down a street that runs parallel to the rasping highway before veering away from it. There is nothing on this street but large walls of stone and iron and dirt paths littered with plastic-once-oil. I walk forward, leaving behind the road that I am stuck to.

My thoughts wander to Lucky and Gina, the tenderness of their hands and lips, the adoration in their eyes. I think of Father, how he never had the chance to touch me like that, how desperately I wish for him to. As I try to imagine Father and Lucky and Gina, their faces become smudged and cloudy. The world around me seems to blur. My body feels less defined. My steps slow. I am growing weaker. It is harder and harder to breathe. I am alone, now. I am leaving behind those I love, who love me.

Then I hear the roar and the heat in the darkness. I

gasp as my skin seems to evaporate off the bone and my muscles stretch behind me, beyond my joints—

Time resets its pieces. I am standing back at the edge of the bridge, catching my breath and regaining my strength, with no memory of how I got back here. I run the rest of the way to Father's house, careful to dodge the eyes of the people within.

Settling back into my hiding place, I cannot stop thinking of the lake. What an awful thing it would have been not to hear the grass's laughter, or the conversations between the trees and the water. Is it really possible that Nia did not hear any of them? I swear that I saw her ears perk up as we were tumbling through the laughing grass.

My curiosity gnaws at me. I ask the voices, Why don't humans seem to hear you?

Humans do not listen, is all that the drywall-once-mud says.

But why?

It is a human thing, the floor-once-tree says.

But Ma knows about the voices. She says that she could hear them once, only there are no voices to listen to in her house. I tap into the murmuring and gossip of the walls-once-trees. They sound so much like the trees beside the lake.

I whisper in the air, Why would a house stop speaking?

The voices all hush. They mutter among themselves for a moment. There are usually so many answers to a single question, even between just a few planks of wood-once-tree. But this time, the whole house offers just one reply: *Something unspeakable happened there.*

I stop listening to the house. This answer is obvious and stupid and doesn't really address the question. Maybe that is why humans don't listen to houses. I ignore them when they start to ask again, *What were you before? Where did you come from?*

It does not matter. I am here now. I am stuck here, to this road, to these people.

18.

I am awoken from a nightmare of the darkloudhot place by the sound of Father muttering to himself. He is sitting in his office, next to a whispering corner of the house. I move my body in ways I must ignore in order to press myself closer to him to listen better.

"Baby. Come back, Baby."

I can't, Father. Not until I am less sticky and more human, I say, so quietly he'll think it is his own mind.

Still, his eyes dart around his dark study. He whispers, "I did not make you to be human."

Why did you make me?

"To bring us all together, Baby. And you've done well. You've done so well."

You are not well, Father. You are hurt, you are sick—

"I am not!" he shouts. Something in the house shifts, making a noise that quiets Father again. He waits, but when no other sound comes, he whispers, "It's Original Hill that's hurting. We used to know who we were, what our purpose was. We've lost that. But you've united us, Baby. We need you."

I don't like being needed like that.

Father does not speak for a moment. I wonder if he

has dozed off in that sleepless way he has become accustomed to. But finally, he says, “To be needed is the greatest thing a person could ever want. Don’t you know how many people wish they were as needed as you are? It means you have a purpose.”

I don’t like this purpose.

“But that is the purpose you were made for.”

I don’t want it.

“But it is you! It’s in your skin!” Father’s voice echoes throughout the study. Then he whispers, “Please, Baby. *I* need you. Come back.”

When I am more human, I tell him. He does not say anything to that.

I lean away from Father. I can hear the muttering of all the neighbors in the house. They all seem distressed, lost, needy. Nia is nothing like these people. When I told her she could not touch me, she was not indignant or questioning or angry or confused.

I have learned that there are so many different sorts of human, but she is the kind of human that I want to be.

19.

I have a Friend now.

We lie in the laughing grass once more, looking out at the lake. We sit in silence for a while, the way that Ma and I do, only here I can listen to the voices all around. My Friend has brought a bag-once-hemp with her, and she is acting strangely. I can anticipate her voice before she speaks.

Nia’s lips move slowly. “If you want, I can braid your hair. It won’t look professional, but I’ve done it plenty of times. I know you said you don't want me to touch your skin, but what if I wear these?" She pulls some plastic-once-oil gloves out of her bag.

I wish to tell her that I do not want to make her wear those, that none of this is necessary. She shouldn't touch me at all. But she is already putting them on, so I nod. At first, I am afraid for her. Will the gloves be thick enough to stop her from getting stuck to me? Will my hair remain hair, or will it melt away in her hands? It is silly. I never asked these questions before I learned what I really am.

Nia begins tugging at my hair with the comb-once-oil. "Your hair is strong," she says, "and long, too." I feel the plastic glove against my scalp and hiccup. But she does not pause or gasp. She does not seem overcome. She just keeps pulling and separating and laying and wrapping. I relax into the heat of her gloved hands.

I do not know how long we are sitting on the grass as she braids. Whenever I glance at the sun, it has taken up a different place in the sky. Something is released into the air as she tugs and twists. We breathe it in, and breathe it out, passing it from one set of lungs to the other. She pulls good-smelling oil against the strands of hair. Neither of us speaks for some time until I ask if she has ever heard the voices of the trees.

She laughs. "I'm a poet," she says. "I hear them all the time."

But she is talking about a different kind of hearing, so I tell her about my lovertrees. I tell her how I miss listening to them recite verses to one another, how I wish I knew if they had finally succeeded in knotting their roots together.

As I speak, I feel Nia's braiding slow until it stops. I turn to face her. She holds a glassy look in her eyes.

"Baby," she says. "That's beautiful." We stare into one another before I turn away again. After a moment, she continues braiding.

But she does not fully understand. I have decided that I want her to. So I tell her what the trees are saying now, about all the gossip and the drama in the park. The more that I speak, the more her tugs start to feel haphazard. Just when I worry that she may stop again, that what I am saying is too strange for her, she simply asks, "Do you really hear all these voices?"

I would nod but I do not want to ruin her work, so I shrug.

"What do they say about people?" she asks.

I have to think about this. These trees speak so little of people, and yet so much, too. "They think people draw circles around themselves," I finally say.

"Circles?"

"Underneath us, the trees are always talking, through the roots and the fungi," I explain. "They speak through the bark and the oxygen they make. The tree and the forest are indivisible. They think it strange that we are not the same."

"The trees think that."

"Most everything thinks that."

After another long quiet, Nia says, "Sometimes we draw circles around ourselves without really meaning to. I used to be a quiet little thing in a big, loud place. I got lost pretty easily in all that noise. You know what I mean?"

"Yes," I say.

"My mom used to call me her lonely girl 'cause I didn't like socializing. But people need people to live. Even the quiet ones. Even the introverts that don't like being around people so much."

"Maybe."

My Friend smirks. "Well, *I* know it. That's why I'm still here after all these years. I'm stuck to these folks, and they're stuck to me."

My mouth makes an ugly shape that my Friend does not see. She does not know what she is talking about.

Her voice grows hush, hesitant. "That's why I need Auntie to keep showing up for Sankofa."

"No."

"She's the only one who can speak to what was really lost. The community needs her."

"Please do not need her," I say.

"Baby—"

"It *hurts* to be needed," I say. "Why do you want to hurt her?"

"I *care* for her," my Friend grunts. Her braiding is more clipped, more bellicose. "I've been taking care of her for years. When I met her, she was totally alone. Between me and Lucky Foote, we've kept that house from falling down on her head."

"Lucky *needs* more than he *cares*."

"Wait." Her hands stop, and her face leans forward to look in my eyes. "You know Lucky?" She blinks, arranging pieces behind her eyes. Then something fits into place. "You're that girl. That day, I was there when you fainted downtown. I didn't recognize you—but it is you, isn't it?"

I don't say anything. I don't nod or shrug.

"You know, none of us have been able to get in touch with Lucky for months. The lady at City Hall says he's been busy campaigning. You two aren't still . . ." She leaves something floating in the air, but I do not pick it up. I do not want to think of Lucky in that house, campaigning in his tattered, smelly suit and patchy beard. I want to be out here among the voices of the world.

Nia nods, as if she understands my silence. Her hands begin to braid again. But she cannot leave it alone. "Lucky said you're Fox's niece? I guess that's why you're in Original, then. So, how did you and Auntie—"

"Ma showed me something about myself I could not ignore."

"Yeah, she has a way of doing that," Nia whispers. "And you call her Ma . . ."

"That's the name she asks me to call her," I say.

My Friend sighs, and though her hands do not stop braiding, I can tell that my name for Ma upsets her. But she leaves Father and Lucky and Ma alone for now. To cheer her up, I ask about her poetry. She talks for a while about her love of words and her frustration with their inadequacy.

"You'd think language—expansive as it is—would be an infinite playground, but it's limited," she says. I can hear the puckish shape her mouth takes when she says, "Maybe we should learn to talk in the trees' language."

I frown. "The trees don't speak a different language. Humans just can't hear it."

"Why not?"

"Human is limited, too."

Nia scoffs. "And nothing else in nature is?"

I am tired of her not understanding. "*Human* is a limit we make ourselves," I say. "It's just another circle we draw."

When the sun is low and red in the sky, my Friend finishes her braiding. She pulls out a small handheld mirror and holds it up to me. I hardly recognize the face that looks back, framed by the elegant braids descending from the knots on my crown, which is now a neat network of dark diamonds. I want to throw my arms around her neck and squeeze her tight and kiss both her cheeks. I almost do before I stop myself.

"Do you like it?" she asks.

All I can do is nod.

"You look beautiful, Baby."

I turn to her, catching and holding her gaze as she holds mine. The grass giggles beneath us and the chattering lake shimmers red, but a quiet throbs between us. Finally, my Friend says, "You're wrong, by the way. About *need* being such a bad thing. Everyone needs somebody."

"What about the people that aren't human?"

"What do you mean?"

I consider asking if she has anything that can make fire so that I can show her. She's been open to the trees and the voices and my other strangeness, but that might be too much. She might run—or worse, she might try to touch me.

So I let us live in the wordlessness. I notice her eyes

are glassy again. She did not touch me, I have to remind myself. I did not touch her skin.

So why is she still looking like that?

20.

Back at Ma's house, I cannot stop staring at myself in her mirror. "Nia did a bang-up job," Ma says, but she does not see how truly beautiful it is. My braids fall about my face, immaculate in their variety and inconsistency. Nia apologized again afterward that they did not look "professional." But I would not want them to look any differently.

I have looked in many mirrors—Ma's mirror, Gina's vanity, the windows of other houses—but this change makes me notice everything as if for the first time. How smooth my skin is, how perfectly spaced my eyes are from one another. I dab at the divot between my eyebrows, right in the center of my face, splitting it in two. I lift my dress so that I can feel the scar above my belly button and then lower, between my legs. If someone took a sharp knife and traced it from the divot on my forehead through the scar on my belly, I would become two perfect mirror halves.

Except for my hair. I marvel at the places where the little hairs rebel against the twist, where the weave becomes tighter and then looser. With the asymmetry of these braids, I am no longer my own reflection. I see the work of Nia's hands on me, in me. She has transformed me, changed my shape in ways that extend beyond the hairs on my head. As I trace the braids that fall down my face, I feel a crossing taking place within me. Something is stepping through and filling the empty parts of me.

21.

Back in my hiding place in Father's house, I cannot stop running my hands over my braids, feeling their secure and irregular ridges. I realize how fearful I have been to change. My form is my most human thing. But now that Nia has transformed me, the imperfection of my braids makes me feel only more human.

I try to get the voices to notice, but they do not care about my transformation. They still only ask where I came from. They want to fit me into some category so that they can decide where I belong. Many of them—the bacteria and microbes, in particular—say that this is what humans do, but they're doing it to me in their own way. The voices are trying to decide how they can speak to me.

But I will not limit myself. My Friend has shown me that so much more is possible if you do not.

22.

One evening, my Friend asks if I want to come with a few of her friends to the lake. I agree. When I arrive with Nia, they wave to us. "I already explained your thing about being touched," she whispers into my ear. We sit among the blue grass, closing a circle. Nia leans very close to me, making sure never to let her bare arm touch my sleeve. But she is so close, I can feel her heat.

Nia's friends only seem part-human. Their nostrils and eyebrows and earlobes are pierced by metal-once-ore. Their skin is perforated with ink-once-plant. Their hair, too. These wonderful androids sit by the darkness of the cool, humming lake. They all have personalities that fizz and pop, but they do not mind my quiet. A few of them compliment my "vintage fit," and I only need to smile in reply. They are happy to talk on and on without me. I like not being pressured to contribute. They make it easy to pass as human.

One of them pulls out a bag-once-oil and empties clumps of dried plant into a small metal-once-ore box. After grinding it, they sprinkle the plant into paper-once-tree and roll it up. Then they set the tip on fire and begin to smoke. As they pass the burning plant around the circle, I listen to the fire delight in consuming the plant, hissing as its smoke becomes part of the people. Though I am listening to the fire, sometimes I hear snippets of the circle's conversations.

"Place is really fucking nice."

"Yo, Nia. Was this park here during Sankofa?"

"And before. It's a natural lake so it's been here since the glaciers melted at the end of the Ice Age," Nia says.

"Damn."

"You can tell. This place has an old spirit. You can feel it."

I try to feel what my Friend's friend is talking about, but all I can sense is the air is filled with the plant's smoke. Nia takes the burning bundle and puts it to her lips. Her mouth closes around it, and her chest expands as she inhales the smoke. The fire is unconcerned with her. When she exhales, her body shudders out of shape for a moment, as if she melts into the night a little. She gives to it me and asks if I want some.

The fire does not care whether we eat its smoke or not. It has noticed the trees and is trying to find a way to leap off the bundle and onto a bigger meal. It wants to know how dry the grass is, if the wind is just right to carry an ember. I take the fire and I put it in my lips.

Nia reacts—I have done this wrong. I am smoking the wrong end. But my lips hardly burn. Instead, my whole body warms at once. My cheeks grow hot like embarrassment, but I am not ashamed. I close my eyes and lean into the sensation, trying to see how hot I can get. The air in my chest crackles. The warmth feels good. But when I open my eyes, everyone in the circle is looking at me.

I spit the fire out of my mouth and cough on the smoke. The fire grumbles, as my saliva has put some of it out. No one says a word; they only gawk at me, but they are not afraid. Worse. They are all leaning toward me, their eyes glassy and wide with wonder. Their expressions remind me of the neighbors' before they were stuck in the house.

"How'd you do that?" one of them finally says. He looks at Nia. "Did you see that? I swear to God, it looked like her cheeks turned orange."

"Like hot coals," another one mutters.

"Yeah! Yeah! How'd you do that?"

"You guys are so fucking high." Nia laughs.

"I swear— Do it again."

I am leaning out toward the edge of the circle. Nia picks up the smoldering bundle. "Alright, guys," she grunts. "Quit ragging on Baby."

"I wasn't—"

"Who's got a light?"

"Man, this must be some gnarly shit."

"Yeah. Yeah."

They leave questions floating in the air, but when I do not pick any up, everyone returns to their conversations. Still, I feel that the space between Nia and me is holding something new.

When we leave the circle to walk back to her car, she is quiet. The lake is buzzing with nighttime gossip, and the trees offer debriefs from the day's events. But my Friend says nothing for a long time. Finally, she stops in the grass and turns to me.

"I believe that there are a lot of things in this world that people can't explain. I believe that even the things that people think of when we say *things that can't be explained*—like God or dark matter—are just the tip of what really can't be explained. But I also think a lot of it boils down to people not being open to a kind of knowledge that challenges or contradicts whatever the truths we accept might be. I think that kind of challenge scares a lot of people." Nia gazes up at the treetops, swaying in the night wind. "And the more time we spend together, Baby, the more I get the sense that you're something that can't be explained—at least, not in a simple or straightforward way. But because of who I am and where I come from and who my people are—namely, the kind of people that were *inexplicable* for a very long time—I just want you to know that the challenge doesn't scare me. Okay?"

I look into Nia's earnest eyes, teeming with moonlight. I want to reach out to her. I want her to close her lips around me like I did around the fire. I want once more to be the fire, and also to be something else, something subtler and longer lasting. I want to be with her and in her shape and form.

And I realize that this is it. This is what it is to be human, this yearning. I know that the most human thing to do would be to reach out and press our bodies together.

But I cannot. If I reach out, then she will be changed. Everything else will pale to her need for my touch. The line between what she is and what she could be is so clear, I could step on it. I could step over it. I can imagine the touch of her skin, or I could confirm it.

But I do not touch her. I do not change her. I choose this. It is the first line I draw.

23.

When I return to Father's house that night, the neighbors are acting unusual. Most have gathered in the foyer, cramming themselves together to make room but still spilling into the parlor and kitchen. The children and the dogs and cats are playing at the edges of the crowd while the adults look to the top of the stairs where Lucky—my One and Only—and Father are standing. Both smile wide with their yellowy teeth. Father gestures with his left hand.

"I hope I'll see all of you bright and early at the ballots tomorrow. I know there's been some trouble coordinating with the city, so I want to thank everyone who's volunteered to run the polling places. It is our civic duty as Americans to elect our representatives, and I'm sure I speak for my colleague Mr. Foote as well when I say that I am looking forward to a fair and just demonstration of the democratic process."

Lucky nods emphatically as he steps forward. "Well said, Mr. Fox. And thanks to you and Gina for graciously opening your home as a polling location. Folks, there has been a lot of talk about the soul of Original Hill in both our campaigns. Though my opponent and I may have different ideas on that, I think I speak for both of us when I say that I see it here today. Seeing this commitment to our community and to our*selves* as Original's people, it just warms my heart. It reminds me that we can triumph over anything as long as we stick together."

Everyone in the foyer applauds. Then they spend the rest of the night searching for me.

The next day, I watch from my hiding place as the neighbors set up polling stations in each of the rooms. They hang old shower curtains and sheets and name them polling booths. They gather wicker baskets and reassemble cardboard boxes from the recycling, naming them ballot boxes. Some of them sit at the dining room table or the kitchen counter or the living room couch and ask others for their ID or if they are sure that they are registered at this location. They form queues and move about the house in a much more organized fashion than the erratic scrounging I am used to.

None of the voices of the house find this odd—or, maybe to them, the behavior is just as bizarre as what they typically ignore. But I am transfixed by the way the neighborhood transforms the transformed—the once-plant-once-bedsheet-now-polling booth, the once-tree-once-paper-now-vote. Everything is something before, and everything becomes something new.

At eight o'clock in the evening exactly, the polls close

and new people arrive to collect the ballots. They hesitate before entering the house, their eyes darting to the scratched-up walls and mounds of filth all across the floor. Many hold their hands over their noses at the putrid smell of living. I press myself as deep as I can into my hiding place, watching as they avert their eyes from the grimy faces of the neighbors who hand them the once-paper-now-votes.

Once they have left with the ballots, the neighbors seem suspended in anticipation. Lucky leans on the stairs in the foyer. Father sits in his study with Gina, his right hand hanging limp at his side. At nine thirty, a man calls to announce that Lucky has won reelection to the city council seat.

At ten o'clock, Father walks into the kitchen, grabs the cleaver, and chops off his own right hand.

24.

The election has not made anyone happier or less stuck. Even after winning, Lucky only seems to hunt for me more urgently. He forgoes food and rest. No one in the house sleeps anymore. They are all too busy seeking my skin.

Father has not left his study since the night of the election. Dr. Wood was able to stitch him up quickly after he cut off his hand, so he did not lose too much blood. He refused to be taken to the hospital, even though it was the only way his hand could be reattached. While Dr. Wood berated Father for acting so foolishly and Gina wiped his blood off the kitchen table, Father said nothing. He has not spoken to anyone since. Aside from Gina, who cares for his wound-once-hand and brings him food that he hardly touches, nobody visits him.

I am afraid for him. I know why he did it, but I don't think it worked. He is still stuck to me just like everyone else.

It is peculiar to see the people in the house so unhappy when I want to celebrate. I hold a human yearning, now. Not just a craving or a curiosity—a need, stronger than the hunger-like thing I used to hold. But I will not let my need eclipse my Friend's being. I will never touch her, even if I know that nothing else will satisfy me. If I can make my need into yearning, then so can the people in the house. They can all become unstuck and stop seeking me. If the neighbors can transform the house into a polling place with just a few minor adjustments—really, by simply saying it is so—then they can do this, too. They just need to be shown the possibility.

But most of all, I want to step out of my hiding place and show them all my Friend's handiwork, how she has changed me. I understand, now. To be human is to decide that one is human, form and substance be damned. I was wrong about the things you know being unchangeable. You change things by knowing them. You name them anew.

I click open Lucky's lighter and hold it to my finger. The fire sputters to life and starts dreaming aloud. I hold it to my thumb as it scorches. The pain is excruciating, but I am too afraid to pull the lighter away.

I think about Nia and Ma, how much they have shown me about what a human can be and do. She can be quiet. She can hear the poetry in the voices all around, or at least want to. She can change. She can connect without touching. She can still want to touch anyway. She can yearn. She can do all these things and still be human, I decide. I whisper, "I am human." Then I pull the flame away and press my thumb against the wood-once-tree and envision myself as free from this road, and the neighborhood as free from me.

But when I take it away, a thick black spot remains stuck to the wood.

I burn my thumb again and press it to the wood. Once more, I leave a bit of myself behind.

I do it again. And again. And again.

I polka-dot the wood with my dark marks, until I notice that my thumb has lost an entire inch.

It's not fair! Wet tears, thick and hot, streak my cheeks. My vision blurs to black. Am I crying water or tar?

This thought only makes me madder. I never would have asked these questions before—before Father told my story, before I learned I am only tar. I am tired of spending so much time watching and testing and wondering and being wrong about what human is! I do not want to live in impossible corners anymore. I do not want to be forced into categories by the neighbors or the voices of the house or even Lucky and Gina and Father. I want to stretch my body and show the world my beautiful transformation. I want to know how much more I can change.

The voice of the fire comes to me. I realize that I have not killed it yet. It dares me to press my thumb against the wall again. It whispers, *Better yet, press your whole hand.*

I do.

Now, it says, *see if you can make it grow.*

From my palm, I watch the dark tar crawl up the naked wood-once-tree, making thin, intricate lines through the crevices of the wood's grain.

No, no, the fire clucks. *Here, let me show you.*

So I press the fire against the wood and it, too, begins to crawl toward the ceiling. It flattens, splits, and spreads. I try to mimic its choreography until my entire arm is a bubbling, hissing mass. The fire laughs and whoops. It hugs my tar-once-arm and for a moment we are the same, all desire and wonder.

Then I begin to hear the wood-once-trees screaming. The fire has spread across half the wall and is eating away at it. It talks about devouring the entire house. It has become too greedy. With some effort, I flatten my tar-once-arm and smother the fire. It takes a few tries, patting down the resistant embers, but eventually, the fire is dead. The surviving wood- and wallpaper-once-trees mourn their loss and commiserate in their misfortune. The rest of the voices gossip or complain about the smoke. My aching tar snaps back into shape. I have absorbed all the tar prints that I left on the wall, and I notice that my thumb has regained its inch.

Then, I see the damage the fire has done. It has eaten a hole through the wall, just large enough to stick my head through. When I do, I see Gina staring at me from the edge of her bed.

"Baby?" she whispers, and for a moment I think things will be alright.

"Gina! Why do I smell smoke?" Father comes barging into the room. Lucky is not far behind. Both their eyes fall on the hole and refocus on my face. Father frowns. "How the hell did she—"

But before he can finish, Lucky dives at the hole and starts clawing at it. The fire has weakened the wood so much that it crumples away like sheets of paper. I press myself back against the wall behind me, but there is hardly any room here. Suddenly, Lucky's eyes widen. He stops tearing at the wall and stumbles back.

"What the hell?" he gasps.

The fractured glass of Gina's vanity mirror reflects back at me what Lucky sees, what they all see. My hiding place inside the walls is too small for a human body, so I have stretched mine flat to fit. I have been ignoring this because it is not human. Now, I see the dark, wide mass clinging to the back of the wall with a perfectly imperfect girl's face and beautiful braids. It is so very, very not human. My eyes land on Father, who gapes at me like I am some vile, rotting thing.

Then, his face makes another shape—a greedy, needy shape. I want them to run away from me, call me a monster and go. But they don't; they won't. Instead, Father takes a step closer, and then another. Gina rises from the bed. More neighbors are entering the bedroom, now, drawn in by the commotion. They all crave my touch.

The wood-once-tree in the wall is scared of me because I let the fire burn it. Still, I beg it to tell me how to get out. The house allows me to seep through the floorboards, away from the people. The last I see of Gina's bedroom is Father leaping at the hole in the wall.

I sieve throughout the crevices of the house. It's very not-human of me, but I have to get away. Once I'm outside in the cool night air, I resolidify. I can hear the neighborhood in uproar inside. They'll soon figure out I've escaped and chase after me. I have to leave, and I can't be followed.

I think about the fire, the wisps at its edges that dissipate into invisible waves of heat. The dark road in front of me blends seamlessly into the dark of the night.

It starts with my fingers and toes, the tips of my eyelashes and the hairs on the back of my neck, and then it is the meat of my cheeks and thighs, and then it is my rib cage and tailbone and spine and heart and lungs and eyeballs, and then it is my thoughts and voice and emotions. I lean into the darkness, becoming the road and the night, moving with careful deliberation.

I ease toward my lovertrees, who whisper about me to one another. I wiggle myself into the cracks and crevices of the concrete that separates them, and I break it. I crush it until it is gravel-once-sidewalk, and now there is nothing to stop them from twisting their roots together. Nothing but time. My beautiful lovertrees. I kiss each one, then I continue down the road.

If anyone sees me, I am beyond nightmare. I have become something so unhuman, so other, that I cannot be held within any person's understanding. The night is so cold it almost freezes me, but I am warmed by the heat of my purpose. It feels good.

Then I come to the bridge over the highway. My body tenses at the sound of the cars crashing beneath. This is the road I am bound to, but I am tired of being afraid of it. I take a deep breath, and I melt into the asphalt.

It feels familiar here. It is dark, it is loud, and it is hot.

I panic for a moment, but I do not feel the confusion and obscurity, the incessant roar that characterized the place that I came from. I feel as if I am on the edge of something vast and imperceptible. So I wrap myself tighter around the bridge, easing my form into all the potholes and fissures, just as I did in the sidewalk. Now that I am in it, I feel how the bridge has been decaying. It reminds me of that dead rabbit in the road long ago, and I have become one of the voices eating away at it. I was horrified then, but those voices were only making the corpse a part of the world again. Resetting the pieces.

Grasping the bridge, I think of my Friend, whose touch I still yearn for, who made me draw a line to protect her. Must I leave her behind? It is hard for me to say. Everything is so new yet familiar in this shape.

I sense the highway beneath me, extending for miles in either direction. My recognition grows stronger. But the roar of my nightmares does not terrify me, does not chase away my thoughts and memories like before. I have changed since I last was here.

What did you come from? What were you before?

I am the darkloudhot place. And more.

With one swift gesture, I break the rotten corpse. The bridge splinters to meet the highway.

Sankofa

Nia

•

The morning after the Orchard Street Bridge collapsed, Nia went to visit Auntie Riri. She had to take a series of congested side streets from her apartment to avoid the highway, which had been shut down to clear away the debris. Apparently, an enormous fire had broken out on the bridge and folks as far as downtown had seen the smoke—a huge black column reaching into the dark night sky. Fortunately, no one had been caught under the bridge as it crumbled. It seemed like the city had no idea how the fire had started.

Arriving at Auntie Riri's place, Nia had a clear view of where the bridge had been. Nothing there now but open sky where she was used to seeing a slab of concrete. On the road beneath, enormous trucks were hauling away ragged chunks of asphalt. She inhaled the brisk morning air and smelled ozone. She wondered if rain might be coming.

Inside, Nia found Auntie Riri brewing a pot of coffee,

paying no mind to the workers clearing off the I-94. The scent of coffee was so strong, Nia's hand flew to her nose. "What's that you're making, Auntie?"

Auntie Riri frowned. "Just the same old coffee, baby. You want some?"

Nia nodded, taking a seat at the kitchen table. "I came to check on you since I heard about the bridge," she said. The elder only nodded as she brought two mugs to the table. The strong, earthy scent of coffee nearly knocked Nia back. She cleared her throat and glanced at the doorway for a sign of anyone else in the house. "You all alone here?"

Auntie Riri nodded, both hands cupping her mug. She was staring down into the liquid with a faraway look unfamiliar to Nia.

"You alright, Auntie?" Nia asked.

"She's left," Auntie Riri finally said.

"Oh? She go somewhere with her uncle?"

Auntie Riri didn't seem to hear her question. "I thought she was my pain, baby."

Nia hummed. "Well, recently, she's been both our pain." Though Nia could not imagine thinking of Baby that way. Peculiar, maybe, but a pain?

"I expected my own pain to knock on my door," Auntie Riri sighed. "Of course, I hoped for joy and forgiveness, but I knew better than to anticipate all that. I thought she'd be different—have a girl's hurt. Not a woman's. Certainly not a whole . . ." The silver morning sun flashed in her eyes. "She wasn't my pain—at least, not mine alone."

Auntie Riri seemed to focus on Nia for the first time since she had arrived. "I had a little girl, you know."

Nia frowned. "What do you mean?" Nia had cared for this woman for years, now. She knew everything about her—her childhood in Sankofa, her medical history, the finances she needed help organizing. She knew her favorite hat to wear to City Hall and the brand of hose she preferred. But the older woman wiped her stray tears and told Nia a story that she had never heard before.

"I didn't ever name her," Auntie Riri said. "The highway took that from me. I only called her 'My baby.' But she has a name. She has a name."

She took Nia's hand in hers, and her grip was stronger than it had ever been. Suddenly it clicked why the coffee smelled so strong. That noxious, smoky odor, the one Nia could never get used to, the one that Auntie Riri had frequently dismissed Nia's worry over, the one that layered itself over every other smell in this house, was gone.

The kitchen was quieter, too. Even the men working outside didn't compare to the constant growl of cars down the highway. The house was at peace. As she held Auntie Riri's hand, Nia began to understand that Baby hadn't just left. She was gone, and she would not be coming back. She sat with Auntie Riri for a good long time, in the quiet and the fresh air.

When Nia returned to her apartment that evening, she splayed herself across the secondhand couch, staring up at the ceiling. She was supposed to meet a poet friend later at an open mic, but she couldn't seem to stand. All she could think about was Baby.

She had spent many nights in bed thinking of that afternoon by the lake when she had braided Baby's hair. Of course, Baby was beautiful—an irritatingly otherworldly kind of gorgeous. She spoke in riddles and poetry, described the world like no other person Nia knew. Of course, Nia had been attracted to her the moment they met. She lost count of the number of times she had felt an intense urge to invite Baby's lips against her own.

She had sworn that something had been growing between them. That last night together, after they left her friends at the lake, Nia remembered the look in Baby's eyes, their intensity. Had her little speech been too much? Had she scared Baby away with her fearlessness? She hadn't thought so. She didn't think so, now.

But Baby was gone, and it probably didn't have a thing to do with Nia, no matter how she felt. Alone in her apartment, she allowed her heart to break just a little bit—only fracture, really. She was a big girl. She had long ago sworn off crying over girls she wanted to touch and couldn't.

Nia considered writing about Baby, but it seemed too daunting. How could she capture even a fragment of Baby? How could something as limited as language describe all her mystery—her insistence against the touch of her skin, the way that the wind through the grass sounded like laughter around her, how she appeared to glow like an ember that night she smoked. Not to mention the fact that she was somehow related to Old Man Fox and had been dating Lucky Foote? The truth was, Nia had no clue who this woman really was, and now she never would. Recalling what Auntie Riri had told her, Nia realized that she didn't even know her real name.

Yet, she was sure that it wasn't a coincidence, the disappearance of the bridge, the smoky stench, and her friend all at once. Nia couldn't imagine how, but she was certain that girl had been the cause of it all. Nia sighed deeply, once more detecting ozone in the air. A storm was definitely on its way.

With the election over and Lucky's second term secured, Nia went down to City Hall to arrange the meeting he had promised months ago. She assumed it would be difficult to schedule a time, especially considering the bridge collapse, but she was shocked to find numerous city officials grumbling about Lucky being MIA. He wasn't just avoiding her and the other activists; he wasn't showing up at all.

A few weeks later, another Justice for Sankofa organizer confirmed that Lucky had left Original Hill. Apparently, Fox had somehow gotten him deposed through some bullshit politicking. Allegedly, Lucky was now living in Briar Heights. Nia nearly choked when she heard this. *Lucky Foote in Briar Heights?*

Later, a fellow poet who worked on the city's arts council told Nia of a rumor that it was actually Lucky himself who had orchestrated his own ousting.

"Why would he do that?" Nia asked.

"Something about thinking he couldn't leave the place on his own. He thought he had to be thrown out, so he got Fox to send him back to Briar Heights. Did you know that's where he's from?"

"Imagine *Lucky Foote* in Briar Heights," Nia snorted. "It must be hell for him."

"I bet that's how he convinced Fox to do it. Fox hated him."

Nia nodded. Somebody like Fox wouldn't be able to see Briar Heights as anything other than a fate worse than death. She would have sworn that Lucky felt the same way. And yet, this seemed like exactly the sort of trick Lucky Foote would pull.

When Nia got back home, she decided to look the man up. She expected to find a glossy headshot with that beaming, Mister Hollywood smile advertising some new political scheme to "clean up the hood" or something. But all she could find was an address to an apartment in Briar Heights that Foote shared with a "B. Orson."

With Lucky out of the way, Old Man Fox theoretically would have taken his place, but word spread that he had suffered what most people described as a "health scare" after the bridge debacle and had also left the neighborhood. Fox's wife stayed behind for a while, and Nia heard bizarre stories of her hosting lavish parties in his absence. From the way people talked, Mrs. Fox seemed to have flung open her doors and invited everyone into the house, with parties lasting for weeks at a time. After a few months, the historic house was so run-down, people were hesitant to go inside for fear that it might collapse on top of them. Then, Mrs. Fox abandoned the neighborhood too.

The man from the city's commission on historic places who met with Justice for Sankofa sighed when Nia brought up the house at 1 Orchard Street. "That really *is* a beautiful building, with the proper care."

As autumn slid seamlessly into winter, all plans for rebuilding the Orchard Street Bridge stagnated while the city struggled to fill Lucky's council seat. The delay wouldn't last forever, but Nia and the other organizers used the time to discuss how they could shift this period of instability into an opportunity. Some nights, as she left her comrades' apartments, Nia would step into the street and hear the sound of bare feet padding across asphalt. She would turn toward the sound and swear she saw the shadow of a skirt whip around the corner. But when Nia reached that corner, no one was ever there.

Shortly after the city council drama was settled and the highway was reopened, the post office troubles began: They had begun to receive an inordinate number of letters addressed to Sankofa. Nia fielded a slew of angry phone calls from city officials who assumed this was some form of protest, though she assured them that Justice for Sankofa had nothing to do with it. This became clear when the postmaster began to receive complaints from the neighborhood's residents that their mail was not being delivered. They had each independently begun to list their addresses as being in Sankofa. FedEx, UPS, and USPS all had to make awkward adjustments.

This confusion spread beyond the postal system. Residents of the neighborhood began to receive notices that their licenses, vehicle registrations, passports, insurance policies, sweepstakes entries, and credit card and loan applications were all being rejected because of an incorrect address. Parents received calls from their children's schools requesting that they provide their *correct* contact information. Voter registration was totally upended. The DMV was flooded for weeks having to reissue documentation that confirmed the neighborhood was called Sankofa. Even the mayor had to issue a statement assuring that this was nothing more than a bureaucratic headache.

No one could quite figure out how it was that an entire neighborhood had lost its name. While a few of the residents quietly suspected that the name had not been lost but *replaced*, nobody could remember any other name for that land aside from Sankofa.

Whether spurred by the fire on the bridge, the unceremonious loss of their city councilmember, the degradation of the house on Orchard Street, or the confusion over the neighborhood's name, many residents chose to leave Sankofa behind. Those who stayed were curious to see what would happen next, and they were open to any combustible event that might punctuate the strange evolution their neighborhood was experiencing.

The renaming of Sankofa was a miraculous beginning, but it had to be earned. Nia knew that this gift couldn't be taken for granted. As the organizers continued holding meetings with the new city councilmember over recognition of the neighborhood's racist history, they finally began to feel some give. Deep discussions were held, olive branches extended, proposals considered. Funds could be redistributed, events could be hosted, even some new affordable housing would be built. They were moving forward, and it felt productive.

In some ways, these opening doors made Nia's work more challenging. Now, they had to seriously consider the best way to heal the wound that the highway had caused. Auntie Riri's testimony was a start, but she was just one former resident. There was so much more history to be exhumed, so many more individuals to be reconnected, and endless voices to bring into the conversation. If they were really going to honor the neighborhood's spirit, Nia had to have some idea of what Sankofa's soul looked like.

It was a warm summer day as Nia made her way down the steps of City Hall. The autumn when the bridge and the smoky smell and the girl had all vanished was getting farther in Nia's rearview. An unobstructed sun kissed the back of her neck as she hopped into her car. She was planning on having another look at the house at 1 Orchard Street, which had fallen under the city's jurisdiction after being abandoned by the previous owners. She was hoping to convince the city to renovate it into a community space.

But rather than taking the exit to Sankofa, Nia drove farther west, to the edge of the neighborhood. She stopped at the park, stepped out of the car, and looked out at the lake. From here, she could see the grass where they had once made a circle. She closed her eyes and listened to the birds and the crickets and the water lapping at the shore. She had come here before, to see if she could really hear the voices of the trees. She hadn't, yet. But she would keep trying. Nia kicked her shoes off, allowing the blades of grass to tickle her toes.

She began to wonder about this park. When had these dirt paths been cut? And these lawns seeded with non-indigenous grasses? Had it been after the I-94's construction, or before? Some answers Nia could seek out, and some only the trees knew. But she was certain that this place indeed had an old spirit. It felt so close, she could almost touch it.

Then, not quite knowing why, Nia opened her eyes and turned back to the street. Maybe she heard a voice or felt something like the breeze against her back. The hot sun was hitting the asphalt, causing the air to ripple in long waves all the way down the quiet street. The heatwaves created the shape of a girl—a slight woman, really—walking down the road. Her long braids swung beneath the brim of a sun hat, and she wore no shoes. Nia shielded her eyes with her palm, but then the mirage shifted, and the woman was gone.

Nia would see her, now and again, like this. She hadn't dared to ask Auntie Riri about it, but there were moments when Nia caught the elder gazing out of her kitchen window following something down the street just out of Nia's view. Nia had no doubt that her friend also appeared to Lucky in Briar Heights, and to the Foxes wherever they had gone. She imagined them glimpsing the flash of a smooth, dark leg, the wink of mother-of-pearl-button eyes, a sigh in the trees of a wild wood. They may even see her in the form of a girl, sitting on the side of the road, listening to the voices of the world. They might notice her lips moving and wonder what she is saying. And what would they do then? Run from her? Or reach out for her, despite knowing better?

But Nia would not reach for her. Every time she caught a giggle in the breeze or the scent of rain coming, she would whisper her thanks. She would revel in the moment for as long as it lasted, letting it salve her loneliness. But she would never linger there. She would not need it.

Instead, Nia would try to hear the voices of which her friend had spoken. If she was lucky, she might even catch her friend's voice whispering her own name into the air.

Sankofa.

Acknowledgments

This book would not have been possible without the advice, affirmation, and love of so many.

Thank you to the Rutgers University–Newark MFA Program for providing the time and space to explore this work. Particular thanks to Alice Elliott Dark, Naomi Jackson, Akil Kumarasamy, Simeon Marsalis, Evie Shockley, and Rigoberto González for your guidance and to Melissa Hartland for wrangling the cats. My deepest gratitude to John Keene, whose wisdom and encouragement allowed me to complete this novel. Thanks to everyone in the RU–N MFA class of 2024 and my fellow workshop participants for your thoughtful reading and community.

I had the great fortune of finishing this novel with the support of the Tin House Residency, and I am grateful to Lance Cleland, Yimei Shao, and my fellow resident Mico Astrid for those wonderful conversations.

Thank you to my fellow soft pencils, Leyla Brittan, Aislinn Brophy, Michael Kennedy-Yoon, Tara Tai, and Alyn Wallace, who read parts of this novel in its earliest stages.

I am enormously grateful to Alicia Kroell and the entire team at Catapult for taking a chance on this novel. Heartfelt thanks to Alyssa Jennette at Stonesong for believing in my many stories.

I would be remiss not to acknowledge the Black feminist, womanist, and post-humanist writers and thinkers whose literature inspired this novel. Thank you Sylvia Wynter, Hortense Spillers, Octavia Butler, Nalo Hopkinson, June Jordan, Audre Lorde, Helen Oyeyemi, Kara Walker, and the Combahee River Collective. My eternal gratitude to Toni Morrison, who opened the door for me to play in the language and the history. Thank you to the historians, artists, and activists who fought and continue fighting to preserve the legacy of Rondo in St. Paul, Minnesota—one of the roads from whose tar I am made. Thank you to all people working to exhume histories of Black communities buried beneath highways and city planning initiatives, endeavoring to prevent these histories from being repeated.

My family applauded me at my highest highs and bolstered me at my lowest lows. Thank you, Mom, for reading everything I write. Thank you, Dad, for your boundless love. Thank you, Grandma, for encouraging me to be curious about our family's stories.

Lastly, thank you, Jordan. These folks made this book possible, but you make living possible.

© Jordan Villegas-Verrone

P.C. VERRONE's work has appeared in *FIYAH*, *PodCastle*, *Nightmare*, and numerous anthologies. He has been a Tin House resident, a Playwrights' Center fellow, and a We Need Diverse Books Black Creatives Fund Revisions Workshop winner. He graduated from Harvard University and holds an MFA in creative writing from Rutgers University–Newark. He lives in Dallas, Texas, with his husband, a historian.